THE ROGUE PRINCE

LORDS OF THE VAR: A QURILIXEN WORLD NOVEL

MICHELLE M. PILLOW

MICHELLE M. PILLOW® - MICHELLEPILLOW.COM

The Rogue Prince (*Lords of the Var*®) © copyright 2005 – 2018 by Michelle M. Pillow

Fourth Print Edition July 2018

Third Print Edition October 1, 2017

Second Print Edition June 2011

First Print Edition April 2007

First Electronic Printing September 2005

Cover art © Copyright 2015

Published by The Raven Books LLC

ISBN: 978-1-62501-213-5

ABOUT THE ROGUE PRINCE

Cat-shifter Prince Reid is always looking for a good time, and no woman is safe when he turns on the charm. When the opportunity arises to go on an ambassador's trip, he jumps at the chance—especially when that trip includes exotic destinations and available women. What more could a rogue prince want? But he never thought he'd find a woman who could bring him to his knees with just one look. He will do anything to protect her and make her his...forever.

Jasmine St. Claire appears to have it all, but looks can be deceiving. Escaping her gilded cage by joining a foreign transport, she didn't plan on leaving one man's rule for another. Yet it would seem the charming Var prince has decided he wants to claim her for his very own.

ABOUT THE LORDS OF THE VAR SERIES

The cat-shifter princes were raised to not believe in love, especially love for one woman, and they will do everything in their power to live up to their father's expectations. Oh, how the mighty will fall.

Lords of the Var® series is a continuation of the best-selling romance series, Dragon Lords, and is part of the Qurilixen World. They can be read as stand-alones, but the author recommends reading books in order of release.

For details please visit www.michellepillow.com

WELCOME TO QURILIXEN

QURILIXEN WORLD NOVELS

Dragon Lords Series
Barbarian Prince
Perfect Prince
Dark Prince
Warrior Prince
His Highness The Duke
The Stubborn Lord
The Reluctant Lord
The Impatient Lord
The Dragon's Queen

***Lords of the Var*® Series**
The Savage King

The Playful Prince
The Bound Prince
The Rogue Prince
The Pirate Prince

Captured by a Dragon-Shifter Series
Determined Prince
Rebellious Prince
Stranded with the Cajun
Hunted by the Dragon
Mischievous Prince
Headstrong Prince

Space Lords Series
His Frost Maiden
His Fire Maiden
His Metal Maiden
His Earth Maiden
His Woodland Maiden

Dynasty Lords Series

Seduction of the Phoenix
Temptation of the Butterfly

To learn more about the Qurilixen World series of books and to stay up to date on the latest book list visit www.MichellePillow.com

AUTHOR UPDATES

To stay informed about when a new book in the series installments is released, sign up for updates:

michellepillow.com/author-updates

To Brent one of the coolest people I know.

NOTE FROM THE AUTHOR

Dragon Lords fans know the cat-shifting Var as being the villains of the story, but every conflict has two sides. With King Attor dead, it is up to the Var princes to pick up the pieces. Though these stories can be read as a standalone series, they do begin where the *Dragon Lords* left off, most significantly after *Dragon Lords 4: Warrior Prince*. There is also a prequel story, *Dragon Lords 9: The Dragon's Queen* that tells the story of how Attor became the cat-shifter king and how the Var-Draig war really started.

Lords of the Var® are interconnected to many Qurilixen World series installments, including: *Dragon Lords, Captured by a Dragon-Shifter* (the dragon-shifters and cat-shifters in modern day times), *Space Lords, Zhang Dynasty* and more.

To find out more about the books, including

reading orders, visit my website, www.MichellePillow.com.

As an added bonus in the *Lords of the Var*® series, see cameo appearances from some of your favorite *Dragon Lords* prince and princesses.

To stay informed about when a new book in the series installments is released, join my newsletter mailing list at: michellepillow.com/newslettersignup

KING ATTOR OF THE VAR

"Women are like fruit on a tree, to be tasted, enjoyed, and then discarded for the next piece. Hold one too long and it will be sure to rot in your hand."
- King Attor of the Var

PRINCE REID, Var Commander of the Outlands, grinned before even opening his eyes. Oh, yeah. Life in space was good—*really good*. Bless his twin brother, Jarek, for knowing all the right places to stop. And bless their pilot, Rick, for having the foresight to book the Galaxy Playmates' mansion in advance.

He was in one of the playmate's bedrooms. The whole place was decked with pink silk and gauze. It was soft and feminine, just like his company on the bed. Grinning, Reid ran his left hand beneath the covers to touch the woman at his side. His fingers skimmed her naked breast causing her to sigh in her sleep. She was brunette and gorgeous, with a dancer's body, if not a little genetically altered. Then, turning to his other side, he suppressed a groan to see the blonde. She was smaller, petite, and just as beautiful as her friend. She'd taken more convincing to join the party, but if anything, Reid knew how to charm the women. Besides, being Var made it easy to sense a woman's longing, and she'd been more than willing. Feeling a stir by his leg, he sat up. He didn't need to look under the covers to know a fiery redhead curled between his knees fast asleep.

With a skill born from years of practice, he artfully untangled his limbs and got out of bed without waking anyone up. Jarek wanted to get going early this morning. He couldn't blame his brother. Duty called, and they were already overdue.

They were supposed to be on an ambassadors' mission to Nozando. But, hey, 'duty' happened to call to the Galaxy Playmates' mansion. Rick couldn't get a refund on his money and who were they to say no to duty?

Normally his youngest brother, Prince Quinn, would take care of such ambassador trips. But Quinn's wife was having a baby, and he didn't want to leave the Var palace. Reid frowned, pausing as he got dressed. His brothers, Falke, and Kirill, were also having children. He was happy for them, of course. He liked children well enough, and they seemed to like him. He'd be proud to hold his nephews in his arms and help raise them, as was the Var way.

The children weren't why he frowned. Reid frowned because his brothers were having children with life mates. Each was married and would be mated to one woman for the rest of their long lives. For the Var, who lived hundreds of years, it was a long time indeed. If their mates died, his brothers would be forever alone.

Life mates were a privilege best reserved for the lower classes—tradesmen, farmers, even hunters and lower ranked soldiers, all men who could ill afford to keep many mates on a planet barren of women to begin with. His home planet of Quril-ixen suffered from blue radiation that made female children damn near impossible to conceive.

Yet, being surrounded by mostly males, hadn't stopped Prince Reid from finding the pleasures of the female sex at an early age. Thank the stars for these ambassador missions and for his father's harem of women. His father, King Attor, had only slept with half of the women, leaving the other half as fair game to his sons when he died. Reid unabashedly took advantage.

"*Mmm*, prince." The brunette on the bed moaned, distracting him from his thoughts. She tossed but didn't wake up. Reid watched her flop her arm around where his heat would still have been. He knew they'd all probably sleep in. He'd demanded a lot out of all three of them the night before. Poor women had to try and keep up with his stamina. They'd done an alright job, and he couldn't blame them for not fulfilling him completely. He was a Var, a cat-shifter, and his carnal appetites were difficult to slake.

Reid studied his dark complexion in a mirror, as he pulled the cross laces at his waist. Running a brush through his long, dark locks, he straightened out his waist length hair. He knew women considered him handsome and so what if he knew it as well? He was in top physical shape and knew how to carry himself.

"*Mmm*, prince," the feminine words were followed by a soft giggle. This time he didn't turn around.

Reid wore the clothes of his people, mainly because they showed off the muscles of his outer thighs through the side cross laces. The shirt was more of what Jarek called a tank, with laces on the side of the ribs beneath the arms. He'd been listening to his twin brother, trying to pick up on Jarek's worldly ways. Though he did find being the 'sheltered' barbarian drove the women wild. They all wanted to train and tame him. He let them pretend, but the truth was Prince Reid would never be tamed.

Looking at the three very satisfied women, he knew he'd never be happy with one woman. There was no way one woman could satisfy his unrestrained needs. He'd cripple the poor thing in less than a week if she were to try.

No, Reid couldn't understand why three of his brothers chose to bind themselves. To his thinking, life mating wasn't wise with the Var kind. Once life mated, it couldn't be undone. The Var lived a long time and passed that long life on to their life mates, aided by the same mystical power that guided them, and the radiation from the blue sun. But a lot could happen in the hundreds of years they lived. If a life mate died, the widower would be condemned to centuries of heartache. Many Var had died from such a fate.

That's why Reid and his twin brother Jarek planned on never falling in love. What was the point? With so many beautiful women out there to sample, who wanted to choose just one and risk centuries of unhappiness? Sure, they might take half mates eventually. A man did need to have sons. But, never a life mate.

He looked at the women on the bed. The blonde sighed, tossing in her sleep. Her hand fell on the brunette's chest. He grinned.

It was like their father always said, *"Women are like fruit on a tree, to be tasted, enjoyed, and then discarded for the next piece. Hold one too long and it will be sure to rot in your hand.*"

Reid didn't relish the idea of rotted fruit. He liked his refreshments new, ripe, and so very juicy. With that in mind, he glanced at the brunette's larger breasts and grinned. No, he'd never fall in love. He didn't want to. Taking the memory of the Playmates with him, he left the seductive bedroom.

"About time," Jarek teased, pushing up from the wall when Reid came out of the room. Though he looked like Reid physically, Jarek was dressed the same as his crew—tight black pants and a looser shirt. His long, dark hair was pulled back from his face showing off a black tattoo climbing up his neck. "I was about to send in reinforcements. I was worried you wouldn't be able to handle so many."

Reid laughed. "You should be scared that I'd bring a couple of half mates onto the ship with me."

"Don't even joke about that," Jarek rolled his eyes. "I already caught Rick trying to smuggle two of the girls onboard. If not for their protesting, he might have been successful."

The Var princes were born of different women, all but Reid and his twin, Jarek. Kirill, the oldest, was the new king and the first to fall for a woman. It hadn't surprised Reid much that Kirill had found a life mate. Ulyssa, the new Var queen, was a good woman. She used to work for the Human Intelligence Agency and made a good match for the Var leader. She was smart, cunning, and knew how to use a weapon. To her credit, she loved Kirill very much.

Still, only one woman? Reid didn't understand it.

The second to fall, Prince Quinn was the Var ambassador. He had mated to an ESC scientist who'd come to Qurilixen to rid it of bio-weaponry. Doctor Tori Elliot was highly intelligent, if not a little overly serious, also a good choice for the royal family. Reid's father had brought the weapons to the planet to kill their long-time enemy, the Draig, a race of dragon-shifters. Though now it seemed King Attor's hatred for the Draig was unwarranted for Kirill had managed to make peace.

The biggest shock of all three was when the stoic commander of the Var armies, Prince Falke, life mated to the space captain who'd kidnapped him. Reid had been positive that Falke would never succumb to one woman. But Samantha had captured his brother's heart somehow, making the big bad warrior feel love. Now Sam was highly intelligent, but she was no ex-undercover agent like Ulyssa and no overachiever scientist like Tori. She was, on the other hand, a bit of a hardheaded smartass and Prince Reid could more than appreciate that quality in her. In fact, to Falke's irritation, he gladly encouraged it.

"Are you sure we have to go to Nozando?" Reid asked, falling into stride by his brother. It wasn't far to the docks and, being early morning, they were alone in the lavish hallways.

"Duty calls and, unfortunately, it calls away from here," Jarek said. Of the twins, he was the quieter one.

"I say you should've let Rick take his stowaways."

"There is always nef," Jarek teased, "if you feel yourself too distracted to do your duty for our kingdom."

Their father, King Attor, was killed not so long ago in battle. He had been a good king, one who worked hard for his people, but he encouraged men to drink nef, a drink that calmed the Var sexually and gave them restraint and control in the bedroom. Reid never drank the stuff himself.

"Ugh," Reid grimaced. "Our father was a good man, rest him, but I never agreed with his views on complete sexual detachment. Why should we tame our natures? We are Var. We should be proud of our prowess."

Long ago things had been different for the Var people. It was a wild time, a time when the Var let emotions rule their head and their hearts. They acted rashly and on pure instinct. Reid liked his ancestors' way of thinking. Life was too short to hold back from sexual pleasures, from any worldly pleasures. No the only use he found for a mate was to keep his house clean and to cook. He could well hire a servant for that which would cause less of a headache.

There was no way Reid would drink nef to calm his appetites.

The old king had been a hard man, but Reid respected his father and his ideals. King Attor had urged the Var men to prove their worth and dependability with emotionless detachment. He taught by example that proving great prowess in the bedroom showed prowess in the field of battle until strength in one meant strength in the other.

If this was true, Reid knew he had more than enough prowess to make up for all three of his brothers who had settled down. He thought of his conquests with a sense of male pride and vanity. In fact, he should be damn near immortal.

"Besides," Reid said as they waited for the metal door leading to the space docks to open, "you're one to talk about duty to the kingdom. While I have been down fighting a war, you have been up here, flying around space at your leisure."

It was an old argument, to which neither one of them took offense.

"Ah, not again. I have four brothers who do not need me to help run the kingdom." Jarek dismissed Reid easily. "It was decided that I would go out into the universe and learn its ways. That is what I have done. I didn't hear any complaints when I sent back the new mainframe parts for the palace's central computer."

"Speaking of which, Kirill still wants you to change the settings," Reid said. "Siren lasered Tori in the ass and locked me in the weapons chamber because I called her a rusted piece of cyber trash."

Jarek laughed. Siren was what the computer mainframe called itself, ever since Jarek programmed the finicky female personality into the Var palace.

"You think that's funny?" Reid arched a brow.

"No, what's funny is that I don't remember the security codes to go in and fix her." Jarek grinned.

"Are you guys coming or what?" Rick yelled from the ship. "If you plan on standing there talking, I'll just go and find myself another playmate to—"

"We're coming!" Jarek yelled, waving his hand to urge Rick back inside. To Reid, he said, "Come on, let's go get this over with."

2

FOUR DAYS LATER...

JASMINE ST. Claire watched her husband as he gave his speech. It was the same one he'd given in palaces, at dinner tables in rich people's homes, to himself in the bedroom mirror. It was the speech she'd written for him, down to the last word. But she knew that, looking at her face frozen in a graciously supporting smile, no one would believe it if she were to tell them. To the world, she was a vacuum, an empty attachment that came with Doctor Chadwick St. Claire.

Jasmine widened her smile on cue, as her husband told the joke she'd written for him. As always it got a big laugh. This was her life—marriage to the very rich, very prominent doctor. She'd been young and naïve when she'd said her vows. Chad had swept her off her feet, wining and dining her over a few short months after he'd visited her father's home. Reality hit during the honeymoon and marriage that the good doctor wasn't what she'd envisioned in her dreams. She had no one to blame for it but herself.

She'd made her rich bed, and now she was smothered in its silks. No one ever told her what would happen after the fairy tale ended. There was a reason for that. Happily ever afters didn't last.

Jasmine took a deep breath, keeping her face blank. The jacket to her gown was hot, but she knew she couldn't take it off. Chad paused for effect, as she'd marked in his speech to do, and then continued to speak the words that flowed eloquently out of his mouth.

The mountainous planet of Nozando hosted a giant medical conference every couple of years. The conference was funded by the MAPH, Medical Alliance for Planetary Health. The Alliance had their hands into everything in the medical field, such as drug supplies, health insurance, scientific medical study, and advancements. Chad hated to miss a single one of these conferences, as it was his opportunity to get noticed by the big boys. Everybody who was anybody in the medical field attended or sent representatives.

This was Chad's first year speaking and he'd been particularly nervous about it. Jasmine had paid for that nervousness in more ways than one. But it wasn't anything she wasn't used to. Such were the consequences of being married to Chad.

The conferences were in their third day with only two more left. She'd sat through the numerous speeches, but had been excused from attending the parties afterward. Jasmine wasn't fooled. She knew strippers entertained the men at the parties, both on stage and in the bedroom. Like always, she turned a blind eye to Chad's indiscretions. She had her reasons for doing so.

Jasmine was seated at a round dining table, decorated with a giant centerpiece of flowers, and littered with the fashionably square wine glasses of the others. She didn't talk to any of them. She didn't really talk to anyone unless Chad introduced her to a prominent doctor. It was easier that way. As the crowd applauded her husband, she dutifully stood and clapped in support of him. He nodded his thanks several times before climbing down the side steps of the stage.

Chad was a handsome man, so refined and graceful. Just looking at him, he appeared to be a gentleman. In her husband's case, looks were not necessarily deceiving, for he was every inch the gentleman. He was dressed like the other doctors, in a dark, form-fitting suit jacket that reached to his knees and buttoned all the way down the front.

Underneath, the pants were a full jumpsuit, acting as both trousers and undershirt.

Though a slender man, his very presence demanded attention. He embodied everything for which those with money and affluence strove. He was attractive, clean cut, and though not exactly chiseled with muscles, he was toned and considered very easy on the eyes. He had black hair, sprinkled only lightly with gray at the temples, and light blue eyes. He was a charismatic man, pleasant to be around. If he wanted you to like him, you most probably would. He used his charisma and grace to his fullest advantage. That charm is what had made Jasmine love him, and when his charm went away, so had her love.

Jasmine lifted her gloved hand to his cheek as he leaned over to kiss the side of her face. It was a very chaste kiss, one she was used to. The affection was all for show. The audience clapped louder. Obviously the show had worked. The picture of the happy couple was complete.

"Perfect," she whispered into his ear.

Jasmine pulled back, and Chad graciously helped her back into her seat. To say her husband didn't love her wasn't fair. Perhaps he loved too much, put her too high upon a pedestal, expecting her to stay there. Who was she to judge how Chad felt? He said he loved her every single day. But, then again, she always repeated it back to him.

Chad reached across the table and grabbed her hand, squeezing. It was odd that he would do so, and she glanced at him. His eyes bore steadily into hers, and she leaned forward.

"Doctor Ellington is here," Chad said. "Smile more."

Jasmine widened her smile though for the life of her she couldn't remember who Doctor Ellington was. Chad let go of her hand, and they both turned their attention to the podium. An elderly doctor in dark blue took the stage.

"At this time, we would like to pay our respects in honoring a great man and distinguished scientist, Doctor Simon Martens. Doctor Martens recently passed away while eradicating biological weaponry from a primitive planet," the speaker said. A holographic image of an elderly gentleman appeared next to him on the stage. It was a photograph of the late Doctor Martens. He had been a round, balding figure with kind eyes. "But it is his work documenting and classifying alien insect species that has paved the way for great leaps in modern medicine…"

Jasmine listened with half an ear, not thinking about anything. She kept her eyes forward, not caring to look around. She took a cue from the crowd, slowly nodding her head at something the speaker said. It took all her concentration just to keep the look of lifelessness off her face.

Jasmine stared at the smile on Doctor Martens face—non-threatening, happy, kind. There was a man who'd known contentment in his life. She wished she could trade places with him, give her life for his.

3

REID GLANCED over at Jarek and shook his head. Nozando was a beautiful planet, full of lush foliage over mountainous terrain. It was one of the prettier places he'd visited while on ambassador trips, not counting the Galaxy Playmates' mansion, of course. Not, that he'd been too many places on ambassador trips.

Reid nearly groaned remembering the mansion. If he didn't have a duty to his people, he'd consider living there on the floating island paradise, surrounded by half-naked women, the most beautiful humanoid women the universe had to offer. Surely the owner would give him a job. He could be a bed trainer.

Reid and Jarek stood in the back of the confer-ence hall, their arms crossed as they waited to speak. Already he could tell the gathered crowd was uptight. These were not his type of people. All of the men wore suit jackets, and the ladies donned formal gowns, varying in style, all with subtle coloring. He scanned the large room for someone pretty to look at. There were some nice looking women. Most of them were older, which wasn't necessarily a turn-off, but they all had sour looks on their faces.

Having just arrived an hour before, they'd been lucky enough to miss the long day of speeches. As he thought about it, Reid knew the decision to go to the Galaxy Playmates' mansion had been a good one. Now all he had to do was go on stage, make his little diplomatic speech, and they could leave. Maybe if they all put their money together, they could rent the mansion again. The idea did have merit. Reid wondered how much they'd need. He'd have to talk to Rick about it.

Rick, and the rest of the crew waited in a separate area while they negotiated the refueling of Jarek's ship, *The Conqueror*. They also acquired the usual supplies.

Reid was impressed. When the Medical Alliance threw a party, they really threw a party. They even gave out free medical supplies to all the ships and had something called a 'door prize'. Reid wasn't sure what the tradition was, but the winner would receive a top-of-the-line medical booth.

Doctor Garrett, the conference coordinator, went to the podium. Reid didn't care for the man. It wasn't anything in particular about him. He was just too full of himself.

Shifting uncomfortably in the jacket Jarek had given him, Reid tugged at the constrictive sleeves. Apparently, his usual attire wasn't appropriate, though he did wear his cross laced pants and tank underneath the jacket.

"At this time," Doctor Garrett began, "we would like to pay our respects in honoring a great man and distinguished scientist, Doctor Simon Martens..."

Reid felt a pang of regret, as he saw the likeness of Doctor Martens flash on the stage. The scientist had been a great man. Simon had come to Reid's home planet of Qurilixen with Quinn's wife, Tori. He was attacked and killed by one of the Var house nobles while trying to help rid their planet of biological weapons, the same weapons Reid's father had brought there.

"Doctor Martens recently passed away while eradicating biological weaponry from a primitive planet," Doctor Garrett continued.

Reid frowned and leaned to Jarek. Through the side of his mouth, he asked, "Who is he calling primitive? Sacred cats, let's get out of here already. These people are strange."

Jarek grinned but said nothing. Reid knew his brother agreed with him.

Doctor Garrett briefly listed the highlights of Doctor Martens' long, impressive career, before stating, "Please join me in welcoming, Doctor Marten's daughter, Stella Martens. Miss Martens will be accepting a gift from the Var of Qurilixen on her father's behalf."

Again there was applause, as a short, over-weight woman walked up to the stage. She wore a silvery-blue dress that fell in one piece to the floor. Except for the fact that she had hair, she looked just like her father.

"And here to pay their respects to this great man are Ambassadors Reid and Jarek of the planet Qurilixen," Doctor Garrett finished.

"Ambassadors?" Reid asked, wondering why Doctor Garrett hadn't used their royal title.

"It'll get us off the planet faster. This is a room of doctors and scientists. If they hear the word prince, they'll try to get us to donate money for their projects. Trust me, it's not pretty."

Reid grinned. "Good point, Ambassador Jarek."

A polite clapping ensued, and the two Var brothers stepped up to the stage, keeping in stride with each other. As the front light fell over them, the clapping faltered before lifting once more. Reid was used to the reaction of shock from women and didn't care. Both he and Jarek together often made the ladies more than excited. But, when he saw some of the men look at them in snobbish disgust, it was all he could do not to start a fight. It would be fun to crash up the party, and he could use the exercise. However, it was out of respect for Doctor Martens that he held back.

Climbing up to the podium, Reid smiled at the crowd, feeling suddenly mischievous. If they wanted to act as if he were a barbarian, he'd be the barbarian. Reid glanced at Jarek. Jarek saw his look and suppressed a grin.

4

JASMINE CLAPPED without bothering to turn around until she heard the applause falter. Glancing over her shoulder, she froze. Two identical, very large men stepped forward into the spot light. Her mouth went dry. They didn't look like the typical ambassadors she saw at these events. They both had long, dark hair, black as midnight. It reached all the way to their waists. The one on the right kept his pulled back neatly, showing peeks of a black tattoo marking on his neck, whereas the one on the left allowed his to fall freely about his shoulders.

Their height was all the more intimidating because of their massive girth. Even clothed, she could see their strong arms were joined to broad shoulders and thick chests. Both men looked exactly the same from the build to the color of their dark brown-black eyes, but for some reason Jasmine found herself staring at the one with his hair down. There was something about him, an arrogant confidence, a wildness, a nonchalant devil-may-care attitude.

Her breath came rapidly, and she couldn't move. Time seemed to slow. She willed him to look at her so she could see him fully. A smile curled his lips, and his eyes stayed forward. He didn't see her in the crowd.

Feeling a hand on her elbow, she gasped and turned. Chad stared at her, his eyes narrowed in what she could easily interpret as anger. Jasmine's heart skipped a beat, and she shivered, just then realizing she'd stopped clapping, her gloved hands pressed tightly together as she stared too long at the Var ambassadors.

"I don't feel well," Jasmine said, leaning forward so only he could hear her. She glanced away from his face, before lying, "I think I might have forgotten to take my pill today with all the excitement about your speech."

Chad didn't move. The grip on her arm tightened, but looking at his face, it was impossible to see that anything was wrong.

"May I be excused?" she asked, already knowing the answer.

"You may go after the presentation. I don't imagine these two savages will speak for long," Chad said, whispering into her ear.

Jasmine nodded.

"I am Ambassador Reid."

Jasmine turned her attention to the stage, trying to tell herself that the savage man didn't give her chills with his low voice. Reid was the one with his hair down. Ambassador Jarek, who had the tattoo, stood silently at his side.

It was a strange reaction in her chest, one she'd never had. Maybe she really had forgotten to take her heart pill. It would be the first time in nearly four years of marriage. Jasmine didn't feel right at all. She was beginning to sweat, and her heart raced violently in her chest. A tremor worked up her body.

"We would like to thank Doctor Martens for his service to our planet by presenting this knife," Reid paused, pulling his jacket back to unsheathe a decorative knife from his waist. Jasmine was stunned to see a portion of his taut flesh along his side, inadequately hidden by cross laces.

Several of the onlookers gasped as Reid wielded the weapon in his hand. With a light throw, he tossed the hilt up and caught the blade. The Var man's back turned to her as he offered the knife to Stella Martens. Stella paled and drew back slightly at his motion. Jasmine couldn't see what the Var man did or said to her, but Stella blushed and nodded, instantly relaxing. Reid lifted the knife up, offering it. The woman hesitated before taking it from him, her blush deepening.

Reid turned back to the podium. Jasmine expected a speech, but instead, the man simply said, "Thank you."

Reid nodded at Jarek and both men walked back down the way they'd come. There was a long silence before someone slowly clapped. Soon others followed suit until the hesitant sound followed the two men from the room.

"Short and sweet," a doctor at their table said, laughing.

"What do you expect of primitives?" a woman answered.

Jasmine watched a second longer as Reid disappeared through the back door. She glanced at Chad. He was studying her carefully. She managed a weak smile for him. He didn't return it as he again looked at the podium.

5

"Nice speech," Jarek said, chuckling, as they left the conference. The sound of hesitant applause was behind them.

"What?" Reid grinned. Both brothers made their way down the long corridor toward their ship. The accommodations coordinator had offered to give them a room, but they had declined. Reid was glad for it. He was already tired of this crowd. "It got us out of there, didn't it? Besides, all I had to say about Doctor Martens I said to his daughter. I don't need to impress these men. She's the one we came to see."

"Agreed." Jarek nodded. "Let's see what the guys are up to."

"Yeah, I'm ready to go," Reid answered. They passed a servant carrying a tray of drinks. The slender man hurried past them, eyeing the twins as if they would attack him. "These people are stuffy prudes."

"Agreed." Jarek chuckled, again nodding.

Finding *The Conqueror* on the docking strip where they'd left it, the brothers looked around. They heard a shout of laughter from the other end of the docks. Jarek groaned, motioning as he said, "This way. I'm betting they didn't even get all of our supplies loaded."

They found the crew lounging before a holographic viewer watching a play. A woman bent over, her tiny skirt lifting to show ruffled underwear as she picked something up off the ground. The men laughed harder. Reid and Jarek exchanged a confused look.

"Oh, man!" Rick nearly jumped up in his chair as he clapped his hands in exaggerated merriment. Reid liked Rick a lot. He had a love for the women and an easy-going nature that went well with the mischievous glint that was constantly in his brown eyes.

Sitting next to Rick was Evan Cormier. Evan was a good man to have on a ship, a hard worker, and a hell of a smart guy. The man was part telepath, a fact he didn't share with too many. He had short black hair, with glints of silver along his temples, and according to the Galaxy Playmates, he had a sex appeal because he was able to 'read' what a woman wanted and give it to her. It had been more information than any of them had wanted to hear at the time.

Lucien and his brother Viktor sat on Rick's other side. The two constantly bickered but were really quite close. They were half human, half Dere, and had a milky white complexion that contrasted the strangest red-brown and red-green of their eyes. Lucien was a communications genius, and Viktor was one hell of a mechanic. The man could rig anything, as he'd proved his first few days aboard their ship when he rigged all the private view screens to play human porn around the clock. Now, with the press of a button, deep space didn't seem so lonely. None of the all-male crew had complained.

All four men were originally part of Sam's crew. But, when Sam married Prince Falke, they'd gladly come along with Reid and Jarek. Dev was missing, but Reid guessed he was still aboard the ship. Dev was half Belvon, a demonic looking race with red skin. Aside from the intense coloring, he appeared humanoid, only larger. He was the ship's muscles and a bit of a loner.

Dev was all about maintaining order. Rick was all about breaking it. It often led to humorous fights. Sometimes when the crew was bored, they'd provoke them into an argument for the sake of entertainment.

The only men who had flown with Jarek before he took over Sam's crew were Jackson, a dark blond security officer who kept to himself, and Lochlann. Reid guessed, if anything, Jackson was training with Dev in the virtual reality room. The two fighters spent a lot of time in the VR.

Lochlann sat next to Evan. Reid couldn't help being a little uneasy around the man. Lochlann was born on Qurilixen, like the Var princes, except he was a Draig, a dragon-shifter. It had been strange for Reid to find out that Jarek had been out flying in deep space with a Draig, even while their people had been fighting. Technically, the Var and Draig were no longer at war, but it didn't ease the natural distrust between the two races.

"We ready to take off?" Jarek asked. The men moaned.

"Already?" Rick whined. "We just landed. We still haven't checked out the merchandise."

The men laughed.

"Didn't you get enough?" Lochlann teased, his voice soft and low.

"I swear you tried to conquer the whole mansion," Lucien added.

"Almost," Rick mumbled. "I had to get my

money's worth. But I've never been with a...what kind of creatures are here again?"

"You're not missing a thing," Reid answered. "All snobby old women."

"Ah, but they're rich," Viktor said, raising a finger.

"Yuck." Lucien shook his head. "Not worth it. I can take the age, but not the snob."

"I don't know," Rick answered, his voice laughing. "We are broke."

"Excuse me." Reid heard the soft, feminine sound in the corner of his mind, but it didn't register. All the men ignored it.

"Whose fault is that?" Evan said, leaning over to punch his arm. "You're the one who spent all our scavenger hunt prize money."

"I didn't hear you complaining when Ruby was giving you a lap dance," Rick said, affecting a pout. "Or when Garnet was doing her famous naked massage."

"Oh, yeah," Viktor said. "That was nice. Not very relaxing, but nice."

"Did you see the giant...?" Rick began, getting excited and motioning his hands as if to make breasts.

"Excuse me," the feminine voice said louder. She sounded irritated. All eyes turned around. "I'm sorry. I don't mean to interrupt your—you."

Reid's breath caught in his throat. The woman who spoke was no old lady though she definitely looked like a rich doctor's wife. She was beautiful, not genetically enhanced stripper beautiful, but natural woman beautiful. Looking at her, he much preferred the natural.

She wore a light cream colored gown of silk. The V neck dipped from her slender throat to show a modest amount of cleavage. A gem necklace hung in the V. The silk clung seductively to her body, not tightly, just hugging enough so that it showed teasing brushes of her curves when she moved. Over the cream dress, she wore a long jacket overdress of light blue. The two sides clasped just beneath her breasts with a sapphire jewel. Both parts of the gown went all the way to the floor.

Reid was disappointed. He wanted to see her legs. He'd bet she had great legs, really long. Licking his lips, he could already imagine pushing them apart, not that it took much to get his active imagination going.

Dark brown hair swept up from her face, crowning her head in a thick braid before trailing freely down over her shoulder. Even partially up, the thick waves hit just below her perfect breasts. Her solid, dark brown eyes looked like Lithorian chocolate, and he'd bet her lush lips would taste just as sweet. To his carnal pleasure, her tongue brushed over them nervously.

Her eyes roamed over the crew. That's when he noticed he wasn't the only one staring at her. He glanced at the men. Evan looked polite, but he always looked polite. However, his brow was slightly furrowed in thought. Lucien, Viktor, and Rick all had inviting smiles on their faces. Reid had the insane urge to slap them off.

He frowned. That wasn't like him. The woman was beautiful, why wouldn't they stare at her? Sacred cats, he wanted to stare at her. Why the hell was he looking at the crew? As he turned back, he caught Jarek's eyes. His brother smiled slightly, and Reid knew by the look that he was amused. Jarek was laughing at him.

"I," the woman began. She licked her mouth again, and Reid felt his body lurch. "My name is, ah, Mrs. Doctor St. Claire. If I could, I'd like to speak with Ambassador Reid."

Reid let a smile curl on his lips as she finally turned her eyes to look at him. Her hands gripped tightly in front of her waist, her knuckles white. He smiled. How sweet. She was nervous meeting him. It was no wonder, either. He'd seen the men to whom she was exposed. She probably wasn't used to getting attention from a real man.

"I am Ambassador Reid," Reid said, throwing

his voice with sexual confidence. The tone had melted women easily in the past. To his amazement, she stayed upright, not giggling or swooning. In fact, she wasn't even smiling.

"I know, I saw your speech," she answered.

She glanced over his body. Reid grinned. Oh, yeah, Mrs. Doctor St. Claire was definitely checking him out.

"Ah, honey," Rick said. "What do you want with Reid? I'm sure I can help you. I'm the brains of this operation."

"Don't listen to Rick," Lucien immediately put forth. "He's just a pilot. I'm the one with communication skills. Talk to me."

"Oh, don't—" Viktor began.

"Enough," Jarek ordered, holding up his hand. He shook his head, grinning. "Why don't you guys go and make sure all of our supplies are on board the ship so we can take off? Reid, why don't you help the lady out?"

Reid grinned and nodded at his brother. Oh, he'd help her out all right. He'd help her out of that dress and then he'd help her to straddle his waist as he…

"Thank you," Mrs. Doctor St. Claire said to Jarek, bowing her head slightly. Jarek smiled. She didn't return the look. Her face stayed blank.

Jarek placed a hand on his brother's shoulder,

patting it lightly as he began to follow the grumbling crew. When they were alone, Reid motioned toward a chair. "It's not fancy, but would you like a seat?"

"No, no thank you, ambassador," she said.

"Call me Reid."

"Ah, all right, Reid," the woman said. "Reid."

Reid grinned. He shrugged out of his jacket, knowing he'd give her a better specimen to look at if he took the stuffy thing off. "Do you mind? It's hot in here."

"Oh, no, no," she said. "Actually, ambassador—"

"Reid." Reid threw his jacket over the chair, amused by how she kept her eyes turned to the side.

"Reid," she said as if the word caused her pain.

"And you are?" he prompted.

"Mrs. Doctor St. Claire," she said, her brow furrowing slightly.

"That's a mouthful, *fea*,' Reid answered, again dipping his voice to see if she'd shiver. She didn't. "You got something smaller?"

"Oh, Jasmine. You may call me Jasmine."

"Jasmine," Reid rolled the name slowly on his tongue. "It's almost as lovely as you are."

The woman actually frowned. It wasn't the response Reid usually got as a result of his charm.

He stiffened, watching her closely. What exactly was going on here? For a woman who'd come to invite him to bed, she didn't seem all that inviting.

JASMINE EYED the strange ambassador before her. He was even more handsome up close. Dark stubble shadowed the man's chiseled jaw, matching the long black hair that spilled down over his broad shoulders to his waist. He was perfectly built. When he moved, it was with a liquid, streamlined grace. There was something slow and seductive in the way he carried himself—like a hunter crouched, ready to attack, stalking his prey. Too bad she was immune to such things, to him. Her appreciation of his form was like what she'd feel for a beautiful painting, or a sculpture. He was lovely to look at. That was all.

Black leather bands with silver studs gripped tightly to his biceps, tautly secured on both of his arms. His shirt appeared to be one piece of material, with two narrow straps over the shoulders. The shirt material was held together by black cross lacing beneath his arms, leaving his sides and waist exposed. She could see muscles hidden there. It was as she suspected. This man was strong. He'd be perfect. Now, she only had to convince him to help her.

"I have need of your services, ambassador," Jasmine bit her lip and hurriedly corrected, "Reid."

He smiled. It was a roguish look. She wondered if he could help himself. Her heart beat wildly in her chest, and she had a feeling it wasn't good for her to be this worked up. First, she felt the flutter in the conference hall, and now her heart was racing. Maybe it was time to ask Chad about upping her dosage. She'd been on the same level of medication for four years, ever since he'd diagnosed her heart problem.

His voice low, silky, he inquired, "Do you?"

"Yes," Jasmine said. "I've actually won the door prize, which is fantastic in itself since I've never won anything and have instructed the servants to load it onto your vessel. I don't know if you're aware, but it's a brand new medical booth. Top of the line. They just came out with it."

"You're just giving us a medical booth?" Reid asked. His brow rose skeptically on his handsome face.

Jasmine swallowed, nervously. It was odd standing alone with a man who wasn't Chad. She began to sweat, doing her best to meet his magnetic eyes.

"Why don't you take your jacket off and sit

down?" he asked, motioning to a chair. "You look flushed."

"Thank you." Jasmine nodded. She didn't feel well at all. Being anxious didn't help. Without thinking, she undid the clasp and slid her overdress off. The cooler air helped somewhat.

"Sacred cats," Reid whispered. "What happened to your arm? Were you combat sparring?"

Jasmine glanced down to the fading bruise. It covered a good portion of her shoulder. She'd forgotten all about it. Sliding her jacket back on to hide it, she latched the overdress.

"Why don't you try out the medical booth and get it fixed," Reid asked. "Come on. We have an older model on board and it should take care of that. We get banged up sparring all the time and the settings are pre-programmed for healing such things."

"No, thank you," she said. "It's nothing."

"It looks old. It shouldn't take long." Reid eyed her arm as if he could see it through her dress. She shivered at his obvious concern. It made her uncomfortable.

"No, really, I'm fine. I'll take care of it later." Jasmine took a step back, trying to calm her shaky voice.

"You should take more care when practicing

hand to hand combat." Reid said, studying her. His voice dipped with sexual innuendos, as he added, "Though, if you like, I'll show you a few moves. I should like to see what you can do."

"What?" Jasmine asked. Was this man crazy? Was he truly offering to fight her? She glanced over his broad, muscular frame. There was no way a small thing like her could take him down.

"Although, I think there is a reason most women do not fight." He stepped closer. "You're softer and not built for it. Women were meant to be protected." His eyes flickered over her body. "Taken care of." His gaze again met hers and he whispered with meaning, "Pleasured."

Jasmine took a deep breath, choosing to ignore his ungentlemanly comments. "I had the lights off and hit a wall. The reason I came was... It's not important." She made a weak noise and tried to get the conversation back on topic. "Ambassador, I'm giving you the new booth because I wish to commission your services."

A smile again lit his handsome face, making his dark eyes sparkle. When she looked at him, she sometimes swore his eyes were dark brown and at other times they appeared almost black. Whatever the color, they were gorgeous.

"Ambassador again is it? You like men in power?"

"Ah," she shook her head. This man was impossible.

Reid tilted his head to the side and leaned toward her. If she didn't know better, she'd think he was trying to kiss her.

"I need a ride," Jasmine stated, pulling back. "On your ship. Off this planet."

She suppressed a moan of self-disgust. That wasn't the most elegant phrasing, but she'd already spent too long in the docks. Chad would be wondering where she'd gone. And when Chad began to wonder, things got bad, really bad.

"Sorry, *fae*, but we aren't a shuttle service. Why don't you ask one of these rich doctors? I'm sure they'll have accommodations more to your liking. Besides, wouldn't you be more comfortable with other women on board the ship?"

Jasmine felt as if her heart dropped, which really wasn't a good thing in her case. She swallowed nervously, trying not to shake. She couldn't ask anyone else. There was no one else. Anyone else would tell Chad. She was desperate. Who knew how many more years would pass before an opportunity like this came up? Dabbing her sleeve on her forehead, she said, "I can't ask anyone else. I want to commission you. Please, if the medical booth isn't payment enough, I do have——"

"Listen, Jasmine." Reid lifted his hand, moving

as if to touch her arm. She artfully shifted her weight, staying out of his reach. His hand fell to the side. "Can we be blunt here?"

Jasmine nodded, feeling a sense of relief. She preferred blunt. It was so much easier, not always possible, but easier.

"I know you're getting around to asking me to bed you." Reid winked audaciously.

Jasmine's relief left her until all she felt was the raw sting of apprehension, which in turn became utter and complete dismay. Could this primitive be that arrogant?

"I'm fine with that. In fact, if you like, I'll arrange for some privacy on the ship for us. I can be very discreet. But that's all I can offer, *fea*. I'm not taking you with me. I'm flattered that you like me so much you'd want to come away with me for an exotic flight of pure, rapturous pleasure, but I'm not the commitment type. So, what do you say? Want to go and have sex real quick and…?"

Jasmine felt the blood drain from her face at his words. He was serious. From between her clenched teeth, she hotly declared, "I do *not* want to have sex with you!"

"Really, *fea*, it's fine. Don't be embarrassed." Reid reached toward her. She took a step back. "I'm not rejecting you."

Lifting her chin proudly, she asked, "Will you

give me the ride or not, ambassador? I can pay you well and won't be a burden. You won't even know I'm on board."

"No," Reid said. "We don't have time to take care of a woman in space. We have many important things to do. We're very busy men."

"Have it your way," Jasmine said, turning on her heel. She left without another word. She'd already wasted a lot of time on the docks. Chad would be sure to notice her prolonged absence. She could only hope he wouldn't be mad or jealous.

REID WATCHED the lovely Jasmine stomp off and shook his head. Sacred cats! She was beautiful, even with the bruise. For the life of him, he couldn't understand why a woman as beautiful as Jasmine would want to fight. With her looks, she could easily find a man to defend her honor for her. Though, Queen Ulyssa often sparred with Falke. She was skilled with a sword and also pretty to look at.

Reid shook his head in regret. Too bad this Jasmine was so painfully shy. It was obvious she'd come to him because she wanted to sleep with him. Why else ask for him and not Jarek? Jarek was the captain and would be the one to grant passage.

However, after seeing how the men looked at her and knowing firsthand how lonely deep space nights could be, how endless, he knew it was for her own good to find a different crew. Perhaps one equipped for female passengers. Jarek would no doubt have given her the same answer.

Grabbing his jacket, he slung it over his shoulder. It was really too bad she was so shy. His body was aroused, his shaft hard and ready for action. He glanced down at his erection. He was rather big in that area. Women often were apprehensive of his size and she was a mere slip of a thing. Maybe that's what had scared her off. It would make sense.

Walking back to the ship, Reid thought of Jasmine's beautiful face. He frowned in disappointment. It was too bad. That was one memory he'd like to have made.

6

JASMINE'S HAND shook as she lifted it up to the door scanner. The light shone over her hand, reading her palm. Why was she so shaky? This wasn't like her. All she could think about was Reid's face, his roguish smile. But that was all she thought of him. She couldn't feel anything else. It was impossible.

Maybe her heart actually was getting worse. The door slid up, and she stepped inside. Maybe she should take another pill.

"Where have you been, darling?" Chad said as soon as the door slid shut. His voice was calm, pleasant, but there was a hard edge to his words that Jasmine knew well. "I've been worried sick about you."

Jasmine swallowed. The room was dim, and it took a moment for her eyes to adjust to the darker light. The corridor outside their room had been bright.

The suite was nice, rich. They always stayed in such places. As far as the material side was concerned, she had a great life. The front room had thick red carpet and a matching red couch. She found Chad sitting on it, a martini in his hand, almost empty.

"I won the door prize," Jasmine said. She walked over to the food simulator built into the wall. "Doctor Lowenstein stopped me and asked where I wanted it delivered. I had to give them directions."

"You won?" Chad asked. "The medical booth, was it?"

"Yes," Jasmine said. She pushed a button on the food simulator and said, "Earth Martini, dry, two olives, one onion."

The machine dinged, and Jasmine opened the door. She took the drink out and turned to Chad. His eyes were narrowed in on her. Only from years of practice was she able to keep her face expressionless. She met his eyes.

"And where is this medical booth?" he asked. "If you won it, where did they put it? I'd like to see."

"I..." Jasmine hesitated. Chad looked a little drunk, but she didn't point that out, as she took a step toward him. "I donated it. I said that is what you'd want me to do since you're normally so generous. I thought it would look good for you if we did that. It's not like we needed it or anything."

Jasmine knew she lied. Chad wasn't generous, unless it suited his purpose. She bit her lip, handing the martini forward. He finished off the drink he had and placed the empty glass on the low cherry wood coffee table.

"Did you," Chad said. It wasn't a question.

"Yes," Jasmine tried to force a smile, but it was difficult. Chad didn't seem to notice. "Many of the doctors were there. They were very impressed by your generosity. One even said that a generous, giving spirit was the mark of a true doctor."

Chad reached for the drink. Jasmine started to pull back, but his hand darted out to grab her by the wrist. He jerked her forward, standing as he did so. Squeezing her in his grip, he took a slow drink of his martini. When he'd finished the entire thing, he set the glass down by the other empty one.

"And just who did you donate it to?" he asked.

"The—the savage men who Doctor Martens— *ah-aah*…" Chad squeezed tighter, and her words died with a yelp.

"You like him," Chad accused. "Is that where you were, Jasmine? With the savage man?"

She gasped, shaking her head frantically. "No,

no, of course not! Why would you think I liked him
—*them*?"

"Him?" Chad repeated, pulling her arm so she
was forced closer. Her wrist hurt from the strain,
but she didn't complain.

"Chad, please, no," she said. "You know I can't
do anything like that. It's impossible. Besides,
they're—they're *savages*! They're primitive. Don't
look at me like that. You know I can't do—"

"Ah, but nobody else knows your damning
secret, wife," he said, his tone low. "Do you think I
was the only one who noticed you staring at them?
What do you think the other doctors thought? Your
tongue was practically hanging out of your head
like a whore in heat."

"No," Jasmine answered. "No, Chad, darling,
you know that's not true. I was appalled by them.
They're frightening primitives. I must have
forgotten my pill, what with the excitement of your
speech today. I know how important it was for you.
You did an exceptional job by the way. Everyone at
our table said so."

Chad pulled her closer to his chest, and she felt
the entire length of his body against her. She shivered. "I counted your pills. They are as they should
be. You've taken your pill today."

"Oh," Jasmine said, looking at his jaw. "Then
maybe you need to check my dosage? I haven't

been feeling well. Maybe it's all the excitement, or maybe I'm coming down with something. I did feel a little dizzy earlier."

"You look beautiful today," Chad said.

Jasmine tensed. His tone had lowered. She knew what that meant. Her voice a whisper, she managed, "Don't you have to go and meet with the doctors? I wouldn't want you to miss out on anything. You—"

"I think it's time I reminded you of who your husband is," Chad said. He leaned over and tenderly kissed her temple. She flinched. "It's been awhile."

"I haven't forgotten." Jasmine tried to keep the begging out of her voice. "You don't have to do this. I know who my husband is."

"*Shh*, honey," he soothed. "Now, go and undress and turn out the lights. I'll be in the bedroom in a second."

———

Jasmine hated herself even as she undressed. Sex was an unfortunate part of marriage, a part she had no interest in. Luckily, for her, it was something they didn't do too often. It was the same reason she let him go to other women. She much preferred it that way.

In a strange way, she felt sorry for him. He'd married a frigid woman. That couldn't be an easy thing for a man to face.

When they were first married, she'd tried to connect to him. In fact, she'd felt the stirrings of attraction to him, but then they went on their honeymoon, the attraction never blossomed. In fact, it was as if she were dead inside. He touched her, and she felt nothing. Any man touched her, and she felt nothing, not that she'd let other men touch her. Jasmine couldn't blame her husband for his anger that first honeymoon night.

Jasmine thought of Ambassador Reid. She felt nothing physical for him, no real longing. Her heartbeat picked up. She pressed her hand to her chest. It was a strange sensation, and it was beginning to scare her.

Hearing voices in the front room, she crawled out of the bed and slid on a robe. It was almost with a sense of relief that she heard someone with Chad. Hopefully, he'd be distracted from her and would forget all about wanting to connect with her. Going to the door, she sat down and listened.

"Doctor Ellington, please, do come in," Chad's voice said. "I'm honored…"

Jasmine lay on the floor in front of the door, wincing as she put some weight on her sore wrist. Chad had squeezed it really tight, and she could tell it was going to bruise. Luckily, she had brought her long sleeved dresses and a pair of white gloves. They'd cover it without a problem.

Looking through the narrow space between the floor and the bottom edge of the door, she couldn't see anything but the legs of the furniture. She heard a muffled greeting. There was some conversation back and forth. She turned her ear to the crack of space. The food simulator dinged once, then once again. Chad was fixing drinks. She heard a creaking sound that made her assume that the men were taking a seat on the couch. When they again spoke, their voices were clearer.

"We at the Medical Alliance were very impressed by your speech today, Doctor St. Claire. We like your ideas," Doctor Ellington said.

"Oh, please, do call me Chad," her husband said, affecting a fake laugh that Jasmine hated.

"Chad, I'm going to come straight to the point. We've had our eye on you for quite some time, ever since you worked with Doc Francis in Zigar," Doctor Ellington said. "I'm sure you have some assumptions about what we do, but you don't know the half of it."

Chad was silent. Jasmine frowned. Doctor Francis? Doctor Francis? She was pretty sure she'd never met him.

"How's your wife?" Doctor Ellington asked.

"My wife?" Chad repeated. "She's sleeping. Why do you ask?"

"Family is very important to us at the Alliance. If you were to be brought in, we'd want to make sure you had a good solid family life. A man is only as good as the order in his home."

"You have nothing to worry about with Jasmine. I have her well in hand," Chad said. Jasmine frowned. The way he said it, it was so cold, heartless. "She's a good wife."

"Can she bear children?" Doctor Ellington asked. "Surprisingly, we don't have much in the way of her medical records. Either she's very healthy, or she never uses a medical unit when she's sick. I notice from your file you don't have any children."

"Actually, my wife is surprisingly healthy, not a thing wrong with her," Chad said. "In fact, I can't remember her ever having need of a medical booth since we've been married."

Jasmine frowned. All right, she could see him not wanting anyone to know his wife was frigid, but to say she was healthy? It was a boldfaced lie. She was far from healthy. Her heart started beating strangely again.

"And we were just talking about having a baby tonight," Chad added.

A cold, icy grip squeezed over her heart, nearly choking her at his words. A baby? With Chad? No. She couldn't bring another life into this marriage. She… No. No. If she had any doubts as to what she was going to do, Chad's words gave her the final bit of strength she needed. Ambassador Reid might have said no, but she was going with him whether he liked it or not. Thank goodness she'd heard his plans about leaving tonight, or she'd miss her only chance.

"With Doc Aleksander gone," Doctor Ellington said, "we've been left with a big opening that needs to be filled. I'm not offering you the position—yet. But, well, let's just see, shall we? Congratulations on the baby. I think it's a wise decision, for your career with us."

Doc Aleksander? Jasmine froze. Doc Aleksander was a Medical Mafia boss. The galactic news had just reported that his spaceship crashed. *Doc.* Doctor Ellington had said *Doc* Francis. He must have been another mob boss. Chad was working with the Medical Mafia, and now he was joining them full force? Suddenly, many things in her married life made sense. In the past, she hadn't understood Chad's decisions, but now it was clear. He wanted to join the Medical Mafia.

"Come on, let's go to the party. We can discuss this later," Doctor Ellington said.

"Let me just check on my wife," Chad answered.

Hearing footfall, Jasmine jumped up and ran for the bed, not bothering to strip from her robe. She pulled the covers up just as the bedroom door opened. Closing her eyes, she pretended to sleep.

"Jasmine, honey?" Chad said. The door closed, and she felt more than heard him crossing over to her. "Jasmine?"

She didn't answer, focusing on keeping her breath even.

"Jasmine?" he said, a little louder.

She mumbled softly as if sleeping.

"Hm," Chad said. After a brief pause, she heard the bedroom door open and close.

Jasmine waited, not moving as several seconds passed. The door opened and closed a second time, and she knew this time Chad had really left. He'd tested her like that before, seeing if she actually slept. She waited until she heard their muffled voices leaving before opening her eyes.

Sitting up in the bed, she looked around the dim bedroom. The time had come. She needed to abandon her marriage.

"Goodbye, Chadwick," she whispered.

7

REID STRETCHED his hands over his head and yawned. His personal quarters aboard *The Conqueror* were nice. Rectangular in design and constructed mostly of metal, it had a comfortable bed and plenty of space to move around and relax. There was a dresser built into a wall. A small decontaminator, which used lasers to cleanse the skin, was built adjoining the room. Reid much preferred the use of water baths, but the decontaminator was fast and efficient.

They'd taken off the night before, and he was happy to get away from the planet of Nozando. For some reason, Jasmine St. Claire was in his dreams. She wasn't doing anything special, at least nothing he'd have done with her if she had been in his home back on Qurilixen. In fact, she'd been sitting on his couch, talking to him. What was stranger was that he'd been talking back, without trying to seduce her into his bed, or his couch, his floor, his balcony, his...

Reid groaned at the thought. He'd never invited a woman into his home, other than one of the farmers' wives who'd come to clean for him. He couldn't remember the dream conversation, but he remembered that he'd been interested in what Jasmine had to say.

Reid frowned and thought of her lush lips. He'd much prefer to have a sex dream about them, not a talk dream. The Galaxy Playmates had probably drained him of his sexual appetites more than he thought. Feeling a familiar pull between his thighs, he glanced down his naked body. His shaft was full and very painfully erect.

No. That wasn't it.

"Computer," Reid mumbled, his voice sleepy. He didn't feel like taking care of his own problem. A cyber girl would be agreeable this morning, especially if he could get one that looked like Jasmine. "Is the VR free?"

"No, sir," the computer's monotone answered. "The virtual reality room is currently being used by crew members Dev and Jackson in battle simulation."

"Already?" Reid grimaced. "What time is it?"

"Eleven, sir," the computer answered, the voice emotionless.

"Hmm." Reid knew that, in space travel, calculated time was all but useless. Outside was almost always dark, unless they were flying too close to a sun. They merely kept track of the hours so they could have a sense of normalcy. Jarek and the others were used to it. As Reid was the least experienced crewman, he was still adjusting.

"Would you like me to inform you when they are finished?"

"No, thank you, computer." Reid scratched his stomach. "Computer, give me a personal viewing screen above my bed."

A nearly transparent screen flashed before him. It was completely blue, sending a soft glow over the metal room.

"Computer, play preset channel," Reid ordered. He grinned slightly as Viktor's Earth porn flashed before him. The Var prince could appreciate the thoroughness of primitive Earth's self-documentation. It was such a great idea to train men and women in how to enjoy sex with visual tutorials. Every time he turned the shows on, the strange background music made him want to laugh. However, it didn't stop him from watching and enjoying. Humans were very inventive, and some of their positionings even gave him new ideas.

The on-screen woman's moans were soft and panting as her partner pumped into her from behind. Reid ran his hand down his stomach, intent on beginning his morning ritual of self- pleasuring. Really, there was no better way to start a day.

The memory of Jasmine's face drifted through his mind. Not being one to waste such a good fantasy, especially when it served to turn him on more, he closed his eyes and focused on remembering her lips and solid dark eyes. The womanly moans filled his head as he imagined it was her mouth on his shaft as he fisted himself, the sound of her voice panting, "Oh, oh, yeah, give it to me. Give it all to me, stud!"

The fantasy was so pleasurable, so much better than anything he'd had in a long time that he began to squirm. His knees lifted up, his heels pressing into the mattress as he really got into it. A low moan sounded, and he was surprised to find it was his voice that produced it, not the viewing screen. He squeezed harder, imagining Jasmine biting down on him, sucking, licking. His stomach tensed, the pleasure built until it was almost painful. Then, with a gasp of pure astonishment, he exploded, heavily spilling his seed all over his stomach.

Reid lay still for several minutes afterward, his body numb from the intense release. The on-screen woman kept going, moaning for more. The fact that her voice sounded nothing like Jasmine annoyed him, and he called to the computer to turn the porn off.

"Sacred cats," Reid whispered, a little awestruck by how good his climax had felt. Just fantasizing about Jasmine was better than a lot of the sex he'd experienced in the past. He wondered what it was about her, besides her obvious beauty. Maybe it was the fact that she'd wanted him but had backed out. That had to be it. It was because he hadn't had time to seduce her before leaving Nozando that made him want her so badly. She was the one night stand that got away.

Reid sighed. It had been a very long time since a woman had played hard to get with him. The natural hunter in him missed the chase, the thrill of overcoming the prey, the glorious feeling of conquest. Usually with just a few charming phrases and a couple of smiles the women were wet and ready for him.

Jasmine St. Claire was just a delectable itch he'd not been able to scratch. If he ever ran into her again, and that was a big *if*, he'd make sure to give everything he had to get her out of his system. If he ever saw her, he'd charm her out of her dress, into his bed, and right out the door. Then he'd just chalk her up to another pleasant memory.

Not, Reid again assured himself, that he expected ever to see her again.

8

JASMINE'S WHOLE BODY ACHED. It didn't help matters that her wrist was sore from Chad's hold to begin with, or that she was now cramped into a cargo hold with her one piece of luggage, unable to move around or stretch. A metal seam in the container was along her spine, poking her. She'd been curled in the cargo hold all night and was still too scared to crawl out of it. The ship could have motion detectors in it, and she didn't want to risk setting them off, at least not yet.

Jasmine wanted to make sure she was far away from her husband before she made her presence known. She'd sneaked on board the Var ship while a couple of the crewmen fussed over the price of fuel. They'd left their loading plank down, and it had been a lot easier than she thought to get by them.

Jasmine had no idea where the Var ambassadors were going, or what would happen to her when they got there. It didn't matter. She was on her way to being completely free. And, come what may, she was never going to be prisoner to a man again.

9

"WHERE'S THE WOMAN?" Rick asked as Reid came into the dining hall.

Reid stopped in the entryway frowning, looking around. Rick sat with a steamy pile of scrambled eggs in front of him, complete with thick strips of meat and a fluffy pastry he didn't recognize. Next to Rick, Lucien and Viktor were arguing over a communicator. The piece of equipment was obviously broken, and Reid got the quick impression that Viktor had taken it apart, and Lucien wasn't too happy about it.

The room was small, set up with a long metal table and a food simulator. Going to the wall, Reid stated, "Sloken."

The unit beeped and Reid took out a dark green liquid, perfect for a morning pick me up.

Evan had tried to convince him to drink something called coffee instead, but the brown stuff he procured had smelled horribly bitter. Reid thought it was a prank until Evan shrugged and drank the coffee for himself.

"Yeah, we didn't think you'd be out of your quarters for about a week," Viktor added with a knowing grin. Only problem was, Reid had no idea what the man thought he knew. Viktor glanced up from his project, only to reach over and slap Lucien's hand when he reached for it.

"She still in your room?" Rick asked. "I have to confess, I was really jealous."

"What are you babbling about?" Reid grumbled, looking at the men. He frowned. Were they referring to his morning pleasuring session? That was the only thing that had happened in his room.

"Well, the woman," Lucien said. "She did stay with you, didn't she?"

"Who? What woman?" Reid asked, sipping the sloken. "What are you talking about?"

"Um, Doctor Miss. St..." Rick tried.

"Mrs. Doctor St. Claire," Viktor corrected.

"That's it," Rick exclaimed, pointing a fork at Viktor before stabbing one of the strips of meat. "You're one lucky man, prince. She's a fine piece of ass."

"Don't call women a piece of ass," Lucien said. "You're the ass, fly boy."

"Jasmine?" Reid asked.

"There. Something you can pronounce, space cadet," Viktor told Rick. The pilot made a face but kept eating.

"Jasmine wasn't in my room last night," Reid said. His stomach tightened. Why did they think Jasmine was with him? His hand gripped the cup of sloken. He tried to remain calm.

"Well, we just thought… She did get on board yesterday before we left," Lucien said, looking at Rick for confirmation.

Rick nodded. "Yep. She sure did. Had a bag with her, too. Not fair, if you ask me. I try to take a few playmates on board, and I get yelled at. But, I suppose that's the privilege of being royalty." Though he pouted, Rick's tone indicated he was teasing.

"That's because you were *kidnaping* the play-mates," Lucien clarified.

"You talked to her?" Reid demanded, wondering why he suddenly felt excited or why his heart leaped in his chest at the mere thought of her being on the ship.

"Well, no, not really," Rick said. "We pretended not to notice her. Poor woman looked embarrassed and, well, we sort of left the loading plank down so she could sneak on board. We just assumed she was going to your room to…well, you know."

"Do you think…?" Lucien began.

"That she found Jarek instead?" Viktor finished. Lucien tried to grab a metal coil. Viktor slapped his hand back.

"Ow," Lucien grumbled.

Reid's heart stopped beating. His hand tightened on the mug, crushing it. Hot liquid poured over his hand. He jumped up to grab a towel. "Sacred cats!"

The three men watched him, laughing.

"Smooth," Rick said, continuing to shovel large forkfuls of eggs into his mouth.

"I think somebody's jealous," Viktor added, his voice soft and teasing.

"Where's Jarek?" Reid demanded.

"You can't blame the poor woman," Rick said. "You two do look alike."

"Where is Jarek?" Reid repeated, his tone darkening with a growl. He felt the beast within him arise with his irritated words. If he weren't careful, he'd start to shift in his impatience.

"Yeah, she probably thought you didn't want her, so she went after your brother," Lucien said.

"Where is he?" Reid asked, his voice rising. He was breathing hard, and he felt anger inside him. It was irrational, but he couldn't stop it. He didn't know Jasmine, had no claim on her besides a night of dreams and a morning fantasy, but that didn't stop him from shaking.

Rick motioned to the door with his fork. "Cockpit."

Reid stormed out of the dining hall.

The three men looked at each other for a brief second before jumping up. They ran after Reid, eager to watch the show.

———

"JAREK," Reid stated, stepping into the cockpit. His brother was seated in the pilot seat, typing coordinates into the controls. Reid had managed to get himself under control during the short walk over, well aware that Rick, Lucien, and Viktor could be teasing him about Jasmine even being on board the ship. "Is Jasmine St. Claire on this ship?"

"St. Claire? You mean that woman who wanted a ride? Not that I know of," Jarek answered. He stood, flipped a switch, and sat back down. "Not unless you changed your mind and smuggled her on board. Please tell me you didn't smuggle her on board. Reid, we don't have time for this—"

"No, I didn't," Reid said flatly. He turned to Rick. "You say you saw her come on board?"

"Uh, yeah." It was Rick's turn to look confused.

He turned to Lucien. "Didn't she? I mean, we were getting fuel, but she was heading right for the docking plank."

"I'm pretty sure," Lucien answered. "I mean, we were looking the other way, but she was there one second, gone the next."

"Do you think…?" Lucien began.

"Lochlann or Jackson?" Viktor finished.

"No, I've spoken to both this morning," Jarek answered. "They would've said something to me. I'm sure of it."

Rick, Lucien, and Viktor exchanged funny looks. Lucien's voice was disbelieving, as he said, "Surely not…I mean, she wouldn't have gone to…to…?"

"Dev?" Viktor finished, just as perplexed.

Reid took a deep breath. Dev had been in the VR room earlier, but that didn't mean anything. Looking around the cockpit, he demanded, "Computer, where's Dev?"

10

JASMINE COULDN'T TAKE it anymore. Her legs were asleep, she wasn't sure if she still had feet, and her wrist throbbed uncontrollably. Almost nervous, she pushed open the cargo door. She waited for an alarm to sound. Nothing. Lightly, she waved her hand, seeing if she triggered anything. Nothing again. The cargo hold was silent.

Finally determining it was safe, she sat up. She glanced around the long metal room filled with shipping crates and gasped. A red demonic looking creature sat in a chair. He had it tipped back on two legs, as his crossed ankles rested on a nearby crate. He was facing her, leisurely tapping his long fingers on his trim stomach as if waiting for her to show herself. As she stared, he glanced up from his hands. His eyes were black, matching the color of his hair. He had human features, except for the intense coloring of his skin.

Jasmine's mouth opened. Nothing came out. Not only was the creature red. He was huge, nothing but muscles.

"I wondered when you'd decide to come out," the red demon creature said. His black brow arched slightly on his face. "I don't think it would be comfortable to sleep in there, but who am I to judge?"

"Ah," Jasmine managed, pretty proud of herself for getting that much out.

"You can call me Devil, if that helps," the creature said.

"I—I wouldn't," Jasmine instantly said. "That would be terribly rude of me to do so."

"How do you mean?" he asked, tilting his head to the side to better study her.

"Well, just to call you a devil because you're… well, because you're red."

"Or because it's my name," he put forth easily.

"Your name is Devil?" Jasmine shook her head. This couldn't be right. Did she get on the wrong ship? Who was this guy and why was he acting like her presence was no big deal?

"My name is *Salebinaben Johobik en Dehauberkelsain en Thoraxian en Yyrtolzx Devekin*," he answered, his words so fast she couldn't even try to repeat them. "Or you could call me Devil, Dev for short."

"Nice to meet you, Dev," Jasmine said. "I'm Mrs. Doctor—actually, Jasmine. I'm just Jasmine."

Not feeling any immediate danger, Jasmine sighed. Just Jasmine. She liked the sound of that. Just Jasmine. Not, Chadwick's wife. Not, Mrs. Doctor St. Claire. Just Jasmine.

Jasmine.

"I'm sure Captain Jarek would've allowed you a bed, had you just asked him," Dev said, placing his large black boots on the floor. He wore all black. It actually looked stunning next to his red skin.

"Jarek the Var ambassador?" she repeated. "So I am on the right ship?"

"If it is his ship you were meant to be on," Dev said.

"You say this is Captain Jarek's ship, not Ambassador Reid's?" Jasmine wanted to get out of the cargo hold, but her legs were still cramped.

"Reid is Captain Jarek's brother," he answered, standing.

Jasmine knew that. She just assumed since Reid spoke that he was the one in charge. The Var ambassador hadn't said anything to make her think differently.

"Why don't you come out of there?" Dev asked. "It can't be all that comfortable."

She took a deep breath. He was really tall and obviously strong. However, she read a quiet kindness in his eyes, and she wasn't frightened of him. If anything, her marriage had taught her how to read a person's eyes.

"I can't move," Jasmine admitted. "I've been still for so long, and my legs hurt."

Dev crossed over to her and reached to take her hand. "Allow me to help you."

Jasmine pulled her hand back so he couldn't take it. Dev frowned as she cringed away from his touch. She held up her wrist to show her bruise. "I smashed it in a door."

Dev barely glanced at it, before stating, "A door with five fingers?"

"How could you possibly know…? I mean, you barely looked at it."

"Put your arms around my neck and I'll lift you out of there."

Jasmine obeyed, wrapping her arms around the man's thick neck. He scooped his arm beneath her knees. His skin was hot, and she realized how cold her metal bed had been. Just then, the door leading to the main part of the ship lifted.

Jasmine's wide eyes turned to the entryway. Reid was there. Or was it his brother? She couldn't see his neck with the way the light fell. His face was shadowed, and she couldn't make out whether he had a tattoo or not.

She saw just enough to know he wore the same style of clothes he'd worn the day before, black pants with the sides of his thighs and butt exposed, and a tightly fitted dark blue shirt with more cross laces beneath his arms. The pants hung low without the aid of a belt, and she saw the toned, flat ridges of his strong abs. Her heart picked up, and she glanced at her bag, wanting to get her pill for the day. She'd brought plenty to last her until she could find a new supplier.

Something about the arrogant way the Var ambassador stood told her that it was Reid. She'd actually thought about him during the long night when she couldn't sleep. He was so big that if she had the money, she'd want to hire him as a bodyguard. Maybe she could hire Dev instead? The big, red, demon looking giant seemed a whole lot safer.

REID GLANCED into the cargo hold, doing his best to control his sudden temper. His eyes easily adjusted to the dim light, as his pupils dilated to those of his cat form. Dev was in front of him holding Jasmine in his arms. Tensing, he tried to calm his raging emotions. His first reaction was to possessively rip her away from Dev's embrace.

He narrowed his eyes. All he could see was Jasmine. She looked so much different than before. No longer in an expensive gown and jewels, she wore a pair of black slacks and a tight crimson shirt that hugged to her perfectly proportioned breasts, breasts that were not too large and not too small. Her long hair was tied at the nape of her neck, completely bound back. She still looked beautiful, would undoubtedly look beautiful no matter what she was wearing. Reid became aroused, the potent force of his desire flaming his blood.

"What's going on here?" Reid eyed Dev with jealousy. Dev was bigger than him and a trained fighter, but he didn't care. Reid had trained for over half a century in combat. He balled his hands into a fist, ready to challenge the man if he didn't hand Jasmine over.

"We have a stowaway," Dev answered easily, obviously unconcerned with Reid's anger. "She needs medical attention."

Everything but concern drained from him as he stepped forward. His eyes roamed over her form. He was about to grab her when her pale face stopped him. She was eyeing him strangely. It was then that he realized what he was doing. He had no right to be possessive of her. She was a stranger and beyond that, just a woman. He was attracted to her, but he wanted no claim on her. The fact that he'd been about to fight Dev for touching her amazed and horrified him. He hardened himself, forcing a calmness to his insides.

"What are you doing here, Jasmine?" he asked, his voice purposefully hard. "I thought I told you no."

"Ah," Jasmine squirmed against Dev who instantly set her down. "Ambassador Reid. It is my hope you'll reconsider your decision now that I'm here."

"We'll turn around and take you back." Reid didn't like the effect she was having on his senses. He was aroused, sure, but he also wanted to possess her. He didn't like the feeling one bit. Such things would take him down a path he was unwilling to travel.

"Please, Ambassador, I'm not asking for much, just safe passage. You can keep the new medical booth and I...I'll sleep in here with the rest of the cargo if you don't have any other place for me. I can also pay you." Jasmine turned and grabbed her bag. Hugging it to her chest, she said, "I have jewels."

"Are you insane or merely careless? To come on a ship with strange men carrying jewels? What's to stop us from robbing you blind, ravishing your body and throwing you out into deep space?" Reid's chest heaved with deepened breaths.

She made a soft noise. He was instantly sorry but didn't take the words back. Harsh or not, they were true. Only an imbecile would put herself into the position Jasmine was in. She didn't know him or the crew.

"Honor," she said after a long pause. Her eyes dipped down to the floor. "Your honor will stop you from doing those things. You do have honor, don't you, ambassador? Or is your kind too primitive for such a concept?"

Reid's gut tightened.

"The answer is no. We won't be responsible for your safety. We're very busy men." Reid scowled. At that, Dev actually snorted with repressed laughter.

"I'm not asking you to take responsibility for me. I can take care of myself. All I ask is for safe passage to whatever your next port happens to be. I can find my way from there." Jasmine hugged the bag tighter. Reid's eyes narrowed as he saw her wrist. She moved her fingers to cover the bruise.

"Why?" he suddenly asked, the question not occurring to him before that moment. He'd assumed she'd wanted to come because of her attraction to him. Maybe he'd been wrong. There had to be more to Jasmine than he was seeing.

"I just need a ride," she said, lifting her head. "Actually, ambassador, I believe I'm talking to the wrong person. I need to speak with Captain Jarek. This is his vessel and... Dev, would you be so kind as to escort me to the captain?"

"Yes, my—" Dev began.

"No," Reid interrupted coldly. "I've already spoken on it."

"Sorry, sir, but it's the law of the sky. When in flight, the captain's in charge, unless there is a higher ranking nobleman," Jasmine stated. She didn't smile, but she looked irritatingly triumphant. Reid noticed that the woman never really smiled. It was a shame. She had the mouth for it. "I'm afraid that ambassadors are not higher ranking."

"Reid," Jarek's voice bellowed over the intercom. "Get up here to the cockpit now. We've got trouble. We're about to get boarded!"

Jasmine paled. Reid wondered at the expression. He reached for her, careful to drag her by her good arm as he ran toward the cockpit. He didn't want her out of his sight.

"Hey," Jasmine protested as she jogged behind him. "You have to be the rudest brute I've ever met. Let go of me this instant."

"Sorry, your royal highness," Reid spat, growling the mock title at her. "But, you said you wanted to meet with the captain. Here's your chance."

Bars of artificial light glowed intermediately to light the long steel corridor. Reid sped past them so fast that they were only flashes of color. He barely heard Jasmine's feet tripping on the metal floor behind him.

"Let go," She cried, the irritation evident in her voice.

Reid came to a sudden stop at the cockpit, moving to thrust her ahead of him. Jarek glanced at her and lifted a brow in question. Reid merely explained, "Found our stowaway."

"A ship hails us. They claim to be Federation Military," Jarek said.

"Tell them we do not recognize Federation law," Reid answered. Rick, in the pilot's seat, chuckled and said nothing.

Evan, who was acting as copilot, said, "They're waiting for our answer. We need to tell them something. If we don't let them board, they've threatened to quarantine the ship."

"What do you mean you're not part of the Federation? Everyone's part of the Federation treaties except for a few primitive planets and…" Jasmine's words cut off as they all looked at her, only to finish weakly, "outlaws."

"She's a real treasure," Jarek said sarcastically

to Reid. Rick laughed harder.

Reid shrugged at the comment. "What are they looking for?"

Jarek, Rick, and Evan slowly turned to look at Jasmine. Her face paled. She eyed the four men in turn, stopping to stare at Reid. Tears entered her eyes. She began to shake. It was the most emotion he'd yet seen from her.

"No, please," she whispered. "You can't."

"What did you do?" Reid demanded. "Why are you running?"

"Reid," Evan said quietly. Reid turned to him. Evan's brow was furrowed in concentration. He stared at Jasmine for a few seconds, before saying, "I think we should help her."

"Argh," Reid growled. He met Jarek's expression. His brother nodded in silent understanding. Turning to grab Jasmine, he pulled her arm, "Come on. Hurry."

JASMINE WATCHED the men in terror. When Reid again grabbed her, she flinched. Her eyes flew to Jarek, pleading with him not to give her up. He didn't seem to care, none of them did. Reid pulled her back down the long corridor.

"Please," Jasmine whispered. "I'll do anything.

Just don't tell them I'm here. Don't let them find me."

"Why?" Reid demanded. He stopped, turning to face her.

"I can't go back," she answered. Lowering her tone, she said, "I'll do anything."

"Sleep with me," Reid stated, his words a challenge.

Jasmine gasped, but quickly nodded. "Done."

"Anyway I want," Reid said. He took an aggressive step toward her. She watched as his eyes flickered with yellow. This man wasn't all human. She should've realized it sooner.

Jasmine bit her lip, making a small noise as she hit the metal wall. Not as readily as before, she nodded again. She fought her fear, saying, "Fine."

"I could see your interest when we first met," Reid said, his words low. "I only ask for what we both want. But, I enjoy your game."

Reid's hand lifted and she flinched. He frowned. To her surprise, his touch was soft, gentle. He stroked her cheek, before skimming the backs of his fingers over her hair. He seemed to hesitate, his dark eyes locking on hers. Her heart fluttered and she drew deeper breaths. Her eyes dropped to his lips, curious about the texture of them.

She expected cold dispassion when he kissed her, anticipated stiff lips, a quick peck. Instead, his kiss was soft, warm, tender. He didn't rush, didn't demand, as his fingers lightly stroked her cheek. She didn't know what to do so she just stood still, her lips parted as she let him move. Her heart skipped around in her chest, but other than that, his kiss did nothing to her but warm her lips in a very pleasant way.

He pulled back, looking deeply into her eyes. She wanted to feel joy, wanted to give him some sort of emotion to answer his fierce look of desire. She couldn't, not even to pretend. She knew her face was blank when she looked at him, with only the slight pooling of tears in her eyes giving away any hint that she felt at all.

"What will your brother do?" she asked, breaking the silence when he did not.

"He'll let them board," Reid answered.

"They'll find me," Jasmine said. "They'll scan the whole ship until they do."

"No, they'll find us, *fea*" Reid answered. This time when he took her hand, he didn't pull, just led her down the hall.

"I don't understand."

"Reid, you have five minutes," Jarek's voice boomed overhead. "Quit fooling around and get moving!"

"We'll be ready," Reid answered. He glanced at Jasmine. "We need to hurry."

11

"COME IN," Reid said, glancing down at Jasmine. She appeared nervous, and he couldn't blame her. If the Federation were after her, she should be worried. When she didn't enter quickly enough, he ordered gruffly, "Hurry. We don't have a lot of time."

"What's the plan?" she asked, still not moving. She glanced both ways down the corridor, and he knew she contemplated running. They were in deep space. There was nowhere for her to go.

"I'm going to hide you," Reid said. He reached for her, pulling her forward.

"Oh."

"With my body," he added, running his hand over the scanner to shut the door.

"Oh," she began, only to finish with a loud,

"What? You mean for us to...to...? Now? How can you think of that now? I haven't even prepared. I mean...shouldn't I bathe first?"

"Not one for spontaneous, eh?" Reid shot her a devilish grin, unable to help himself. She really was flustered to be alone with him. He'd only made that crazy deal to see what she'd say, to see if he could stir the sweet fragrance from between her thighs to tempt him. She smelled good, but he only got a hint of longing from their kiss, not the torrent that he'd expected. The hunter in him stirred, more than willing to work harder to capture his prey.

Her taste was still on his lips. She'd not kissed him back but just allowed him to sample her. He was fine with that as well, as long as she was willing. He'd never force an unwilling woman to his bed, not that he'd ever encountered an unwilling, single woman.

When he studied her, his eyes met her wide brown ones. Letting a smile curl the corner of his mouth, he pulled the cross laces at his sides and tugged his shirt over his head. Jasmine's breath caught, and when the shirt passed over his vision, she was no longer looking at him.

"Five minutes doesn't give us much time," she said softly, biting her lip. She slowly reached for her crimson shirt, toying with the hem.

"We'll manage," Reid said, watching her with

interest, as he moved his hands to his waist. He kicked off his boots, sliding them under the bed along with his shirt.

"All right then." Her voice sounded small. She still didn't look at him as she pulled off her shirt.

Reid stopped, staring at her. She wore a lacy white bra, the two cups holding her amazing breasts. For a moment, he forgot what he'd been doing. His fingers itched with his desire to touch her. Her waist was narrow, her stomach flat. He licked his lips. Oh, yeah, he could definitely work with this. Then, he saw the bruise that was still on her arm, another along her ribs, and the now matching bruise on her wrist.

"More walls?" he asked, frowning.

She looked away.

Intent on touching her, Reid let go of his pants. They had loosened enough that the material slid off his hips to the floor. He kicked them under the bed. Jasmine gasped, her gaze automatically flying to his hard member. Her cheeks colored, and she made a weak sound in the back of her throat. Reid sensed the fear in her and wondered at it. The fragrance of it brought him back to the present.

When she continued to stare, her shirt off, her body unmoving, he said, "Not that I mind you getting naked, *fea*, but we don't have time for much else."

Jasmine's face drained of color. "What? I just said that. You said five minutes was plenty of—"

"You meant five minutes for that?" Reid asked, disbelieving. He leaned over and grabbed the blankets, messing up the bed. Then, taking the long pillows, he laid them along the edge. "*Fea*, I'll require at least five hours for that—*minimum*."

Jasmine swayed on her feet. Reid shot forward, catching her before she fell over. Blinking rapidly, she looked up at him. "Five hours? Truly?"

"Excite you, *fea*?" he asked.

"My name's Jasmine, not *fea*," she whispered, looking at his lips.

Reid's head tipped back, and he sniffed. "You need to lie down on the bed now, *fea*."

"No, my name is Jasmin—"

Reid grabbed her and lightly tossed her on the bed, before lifting her shirt and throwing it at her. "Whatever you do, don't start screaming. I detect them on the ship. Just get under the covers and hold still. I promise I won't hurt you. Do you believe me?"

Jasmine nodded though the gesture hardly appeared convincing.

JASMINE WATCHED Reid from her place on the bed. He was completely nude, a fact she couldn't help but stare at. His body was solid muscle, even surprisingly so after the peeks of flesh his clothing had revealed. And when she saw his male pride, standing very tall and erect from the bed of hair between his thighs, it was all she could do to keep from running out of the room and turning herself into the Federation.

Five hours at the mercy of that? However would she survive it?

Jasmine closed her eyes. She'd get through it. She'd find a way. Opening her eyes, she tried to speak. Her lips parted, and she was about to answer when his body trembled violently.

Reid's eyes were the first to change, filling with a pale green. Next his dark flesh morphed, as it molded and grew orange, white, and black fur. Jasmine couldn't move. Reid dropped to his knees and within seconds a large tiger was before her— bigger than any she'd ever seen.

"Reid?" she asked, her voice small. "What…are you?"

A light roar sounded in the back of his throat and he jumped up next to her. Her whole body bounced as the bed shifted with his weight. His teeth were sharp, pointed fangs, connected to a very powerful mouth. Jasmine flinched, unable to help it as he neared her. She pulled back, hitting against the wall in fear.

What have I gotten myself into? This can't be happening.

Reid lowered his head to her, and she slowly lifted her shaky hand to touch him. His fur was soft and warm. She relaxed when he didn't bite her. Suddenly, his head whipped up and turned toward the door. Jasmine heard footsteps approaching. She pulled the covers over her body. Reid turned, lifted a paw to her shoulder, and pushed her down. He lounged next to her, blocking her from view of the door with his size.

Jasmine burrowed between the covers and Reid's body, feeling his warmth along her chest. She'd thought he'd wanted sex before the men came, and now cursed the fact that she'd taken her shirt off. Unconscious of the action, she curled her fingers along his side.

REID FELT Jasmine along his back, stroking him, petting him. Having her hands on his body was torment, but he didn't move to make her stop. The door to his quarters slid up. Two men in black Federation uniforms tried to come inside. Reid growled in the back of his throat, drawing their attention. Their eyes widened, and they instantly stepped back.

He watched, amused as they whispered amongst themselves. He easily heard them fighting over who would go in. Reid roared, this time louder.

"Anyone in there?" one of the men yelled at last. Reid roared again, this time loud and long as he bared his deadly teeth. Lowering his head, he stiffened and drew his paws close to his body as if ready to stand, daring them to take a step inside. He stayed down, just in case any part of Jasmine was exposed. Besides, she had a tight grip on his fur and didn't seem to want to let go.

"Shut it," a second man ordered. "No one's in with that thing unless he ate them. I only have the one life form reading."

"Yeah," the first man laughed. "I don't want to be next on the menu."

The door slid shut. Reid felt Jasmine relax, but she didn't let go of him. He turned his head to her. She was completely buried under the covers.

Watching over her, he stayed shifted, just in case the men came back. He rested his head on his paws. After half an hour had passed and she still hadn't moved, Reid hooked the blanket with his back claw and pulled it down. Jasmine was fast asleep.

12

"ALL CLEAR?" Reid asked, coming into the commons. The lounge area was equipped with a viewing screen, gaming tables, couches, and chairs. The men spent a lot of time there when they didn't want to be alone in their quarters. Lucien, Viktor, and Jackson played cards, taking shots of liquor as they hit a losing hand. Lochlann and Jarek talked quietly in the corner. His brother looked up at him as he walked in.

"Where is she?" Jarek asked.

"Sleeping in my bed," Reid answered. The men gave him knowing looks, and he held up his hands. "No, not yet. Even I am not brute enough to seduce a sleeping woman."

"Great, I'll tell Rick he still has a chance," Viktor teased.

Reid frowned, not joining in the laughter. "You do that and tell him I'll break his legs if he touches her. She's mine."

Jarek looked him in the eye but said nothing.

"I mean, she's under my protection," Reid amended softly.

"She did appear tired," Evan put forth, looking up from his hand-held. Reid guessed the man was reading another book.

"I would be too if I'd slept in a metal crate all night," Viktor said, tossing down a card.

"You said we should help her." Reid looked at Evan, coming forward to take a chair next to him. "Why?"

"She's scared," Evan said simply.

Lochlann and Jarek leaned forward, resting their elbows on their knees. Reid eyed the Draig warily but kept his mouth shut. Lochlann was Jarek's friend, and Reid wouldn't start a fight with the dragon-shifter unless provoked. The others quieted but didn't stop their game.

"Did you read her then?" Reid asked.

"Yes." Evan laid his hand-held down. "But, anyone can see she's terrified just by looking at her. And I saw the bruise on her wrist."

"Yeah," Jarek nodded. He studied his fist thoughtfully. "It was a hand. Probably a man's by the size of the markings."

"Definitely a humanoid," Jackson agreed, nodding. He stared at his cards, not giving any emotion away.

"There are more on her ribs and arm." Reid looked down, frowning. The urge to protect her was strong within him, but he assured himself that it meant nothing. It was his decision to hide her from the Federation, which made her his responsibility. He was honor-bound to protect her. That was all. That is why his stomach knotted with concern. "She told me she ran into something."

"Yeah, like a fist," Lucien said softly. His jaw tightened.

"You need to figure out what she's doing here." Jarek smiled at his brother. "That is, if not solely to be with you."

Jarek's tone said he highly doubted that was the reason. Reid shot him a wry look. "You doubt my charm with the ladies? Why wouldn't they travel the galaxy in search of me?"

The men laughed.

"Try talking to her, minus the innuendos," Evan said. Reid opened his mouth, and Evan held up a hand to stop him. "No, don't ask it. I will not tell you what I felt in her. That's her business."

"You stay out of my thoughts," Reid said. He smiled to lessen the harshness of his warning.

Evan shrugged, unconcerned. "Then stop thinking so loud."

"What I want to know, Evan, is do you think she's a threat to our ship?" Jarek asked. Reid knew his brother was worried.

"No," Evan said easily. "Not unless the Federation discovers we have her."

"Ah, I'm not worried about the Federation," Jarek exchanged a look with Lochlann and laughed.

"Yeah," Lochlann added, sharing a private joke with his captain. "We've dealt with them plenty."

"You saw her bruise. Think about it. Where do you think she got those?" Evan looked directly at Reid.

"A man," Reid deduced easily. "They were too large to be a woman's fingers. We've determined that already."

"And why is she here?" Evan continued.

"She's hiding." Reid took a deep breath, as realization dawned. "She's hiding from a man. A man powerful enough to send the Federation Military after her."

"Ah." Evan glanced back at his book.

"We were at a medical conference. A rich, powerful doctor, perhaps?" Jarek suggested.

Reid took a deep breath. He'd been so preoccupied with his desire for her that he hadn't stopped to think about anything else. He'd just assumed she'd felt the passion as he did. She was like a magnet, drawing him to her.

"A lover who beat her?" Lochlann added.

Reid met Lochlann's eyes, not liking his words. The very idea that someone could derive pleasure from hurting a woman was unthinkable to him. Seeing his brother studying him, he forced his tone to lighten, "So, if her last lover was too aggressive I'll have to be less so if I wish to seduce her."

Evan grimaced. "Or if you want to help her."

Reid kept his face blank, taking care to cover his thoughts. He glanced at Evan, willing the telepath to feel his displeasure at the intrusion.

"Don't worry, Prince Reid. I won't tell your secret," Evan said, grinning.

"What secret?" Jarek asked.

"He's only joking," Reid dismissed. Jarek nodded but said nothing.

"All of you, keep your ears open. Find out what you can, Reid," Jarek said. "The Federation was looking for her, but they didn't say for what. Your cover was brilliant, by the way. I had transport papers on file for a tiger, you know, just in case they ever found me in such a way. I have no problem harboring a criminal. I just want to know about it beforehand."

"She won't talk." Evan grinned at Reid, a

mischievous glint in his eye. "She's closed. You'll have to be tactful."

"Are you saying you doubt my charm?" Reid asked, returning the look with one of his own.

Jarek laughed. Standing, he slapped Reid's shoulder. "I think he's saying you lack tact, brother."

"Who me?" Reid winked. "Nonsense."

JASMINE AWOKE WITH A START, sitting up. She took a deep breath, trembling weakly as she climbed out of the bed. Looking around, she was disorientated as she tried to remember where she was. Then it hit her. She wasn't with Chad. A smile tried to cross her face, but then she froze.

"Ambassador," she whispered, looking around with a renewed nervousness. Reid was gone. Realizing she was still without her shirt, she found it behind her and slipped it over her head. Strangely, it smelled like Reid. Her heart fluttered in her chest.

"My pills," she said to herself though the sound of her voice wasn't as comforting as she'd hoped. Pressing her hand against her chest as if that would slow her heart rate, she took another deep breath.

She didn't have time to take her medicine that morning before being dragged from the cargo. "Computer, is the Federation still here?"

"No, ma'am," the computer answered, its tone even.

Jasmine relaxed. That was something at least. Suddenly, her muscles tensed as a thought struck her. Reid had kept his word. That meant he'd expect her to keep hers.

"Five hours," she said softly. Tears filled her eyes. Chad had only ever taken twenty minutes if that. She could live through twenty minutes, but five hours? "Please let him be joking or bragging, I don't care which."

Still shaking, she went to the door and ran her hand over the wall scanner. The door slid up, letting her out. The corridor was empty, and she quickly made her way down the hall looking for the cargo hold. Her pills would be in there.

Worse than her fear of five hours in bed with the confident Reid was the embarrassing knowledge that she'd have to tell him she was frigid, that she wasn't really a woman. Sure, she had the right parts. She looked like a woman, talked like a woman, acted like a woman. But a woman was defined by what she felt inside. Jasmine didn't feel like a woman should feel. She was dead inside.

Chad had been brutally honest about that. She

couldn't blame him. He wasn't a good man, but maybe if she could've responded to him, made him feel desired as a husband should feel, then maybe he wouldn't have turned to a life of crime. Maybe her marriage would've been different.

Jasmine knew it was too late for any of that. Regret wasn't anything new to her, nor was the guilt. Chad's and her life together should've ended before it began.

14

"HEY, stowaway, welcome. I for one am very delighted to have such a pretty lady onboard."

Jasmine nodded slightly at the man, Rick, as she stepped into the crowded lounge area. Aside from the two Var ambassadors and Dev, he was the only name she'd learned. She remembered it from the men's banter back on Nozando. Rick winked at her, kicking his boots up onto a gaming table. A pale man shoved them off. Rick laughed, taking it in stride.

"Welcome aboard, stowaway." Jasmine turned to the kind voice, recognizing the man. "I'm Evan."

"Hello," she said, her voice soft. "Jasmine."

Evan pointed around the room, introducing the men. "At the gaming table is Viktor, his brother

Lucien, Rick who you've had the displeasure of meeting—"

"Hey," Rick growled, before chuckling. "Don't hate me because you're jealous of me."

"Uh-huh," Evan said, rolling his eyes. "The blond is Jackson. That's Lochlann. I understand you met Dev already."

"Hello," Jasmine repeated. The men eyed her curiously as if they expected her to say more. She nervously swallowed and didn't move.

"Care to join the game?" Lucien asked, motioning to the cards already on the table. "We'll start over."

"Hey, you only say that cause you have a bad hand," Viktor protested.

"No, thank you," Jasmine answered before Lucien could argue.

"Are you hungry?" Evan asked.

Jasmine turned to him. He had kind eyes. Slowly, she nodded her head. She didn't know what possessed her to wander into the lounge area. She'd just heard the laughter and was curious. Now that she was here, she didn't know what to say. It had been a long time—four years to be exact—since she'd actually had an unsupervised conversation. She had no idea what to talk about or how to even break the ice. She was used to just sitting amongst people like a figurine, letting the men talk.

"Come on, I'll show you the dining hall." Evan led the way from the lounge.

The laughter automatically picked up as soon as she stepped out. Jasmine bit her lip and tried not to be jealous of it. She'd never belong to a group of friends like that.

"We can stop by the medical booth if you'd like," Evan offered, nodding down at her wrist.

"No, thank you," Jasmine said.

"It's not a problem. That bruise looks like it hurts."

Jasmine covered it with her hand. She was so used to hiding her bruises that she didn't know what to say. "No, it's fine. I can't use medical booths. I have an allergy to the laser."

"Really?" Evan said in obvious surprise. "I've never heard of that."

"It's rare," she answered. She didn't want to talk about it. "Where's the ship heading?"

She watched Evan closely while pretending not to. He blinked at the abrupt turn of conversation, only to grin. Chuckling softly, he said, "We don't really have a set plan as far as I know. I believe the idea is to aimlessly make our way back to Quril-ixen, stopping wherever we feel like along the way."

"Have you been there?" she asked. "Qurilixen?"

"Yeah, it's not bad. I actually kind of like it,"

Evan said. "The scenery is beautiful, large trees bigger in diameter than this ship, open skies. Though, it doesn't become dark except for once a year. The constant light was something to get used to. We stayed at the Var palace when we were there. Our old captain married Reid's brother, Prince Falke."

"Oh," Jasmine said before gasping. "Wait. Did you say prince?"

Evan nodded, leading her at a leisurely pace down the corridor. "You didn't know? Reid and Jarek are Var princes. Their older brother is the king."

"I thought they were ambassadors."

"That too." Evan smiled. He stopped, motioning inside an open door. "Ah, here's the dining hall. Forgive the mess. Viktor took apart the cleaning droid to see how it worked and hasn't put it back together yet."

Jasmine nodded. Without being asked, she began clearing the dirty dishes from the long table, moving them to a water basin.

Evan frowned. "I didn't mean for you…"

Jasmine stopped, confused. "I'm used to it."

"I mean, Viktor is going to fix it." Evan ran his hands through his hair. "Aren't you…I mean, weren't you rich? Why didn't you have a droid?"

Jasmine didn't answer. She didn't want to talk

about her past. If these men, though they seemed honest and trustworthy, knew she'd married a potential member of the Medical Mafia, they might not want to let her tag along. The Federation Military was one thing, the Medical Mafia another completely. She didn't even want to think about how Chad had convinced the Federation to come after her. It seemed her husband had many connections she didn't know about. "I don't mind."

"Listen," Evan said, as she kept working. "I didn't mean to upset you."

"I'm not upset," Jasmine said, surprised. She could tell by the look in his eyes that he didn't believe her. How could he possibly see through her façade in just a short time? Her face was blank, a mask she'd spent years developing.

"Food simulator is right there. Help yourself anytime, I know they won't mind." Evan turned to go. Stopping, he said, "You know you're safe here. They may act like brutes, but everyone on this ship is a good man."

Jasmine didn't answer. Evan left. She turned to pick up more plates.

"What was that all about?"

Jasmine dropped the plate, and it shattered on the floor. She quickly turned to the door. Lowering her eyes, she curtseyed low and held the position as she said, "My prince."

When a long moment passed and he didn't answer, she chanced a look up. He had a bemused expression on his handsome face. A brow arched over one eye.

"I'm sorry about before. I didn't know. At the banquet, they announced you as an ambassador." Jasmine curtseyed lower. Reid still didn't answer. "Prince Reid? Is something...?"

"I was just standing here admiring the view. I can see down your shirt." Reid grinned, finally walking into the kitchen.

Jasmine gasped, looking down, horrified. Her shirt was tight. There was no way he'd seen down it.

Reid chuckled. "And though I don't mind being called yours, don't call me prince. On the ship, it's Reid. We like to keep a low profile."

"Security reasons?" she asked, choosing to ignore his crude joke.

"No." He hopped up to sit on the counter by the food simulator and winked. "Too many people trying to kiss up for charity."

Jasmine gasped and made a face. Under her breath, she grumbled, "How noble of you."

Reid tossed back his head and laughed harder. It was a full, rich sound. Jasmine froze. Had she said that out loud?

To the food simulator, Reid said, "Sloken." The

machine dinged, and he opened to door to take out a steaming cup of green liquid. To Jasmine, he asked, "Want some?"

"I don't drink," she answered.

"Anything?" Leaning back, he sipped his beverage.

"Liquor."

"Sloken isn't alcohol."

"No thank you just the same," she said, bending over to pick up the shattered plate.

"Suit yourself, *fea*." Reid took another drink, watching her over the rim of the cup as she dumped the pieces into a trash bin.

"The name's Jasmine," she answered, clearing more plates.

"Well, *Jasmine*," he stressed her name, "you're just a bundle of joy aren't you?"

"Where would you like me to sleep?" She changed the subject as she put the last of the plates in the sink before turning to him.

"All the rooms are full, so you'll have to bunk with me." Reid set the cup down and hopped off the counter. He moved with confidence and that scared her.

Jasmine stiffened. Surely he was joking. "Why you? I can just as easily sleep in the cargo hold."

As he neared, she didn't move. She found she wanted him to come to her. She wanted him to touch her. More than anything, she wanted to feel something when he did. His hand cupped the side of her face, warm and gentle. Her heart rate picked up, but she barely noted it as she looked deep into his dark eyes. The intensity in them took her by surprise. No man had ever looked at her like that. Slowly, he lowered his mouth to hers. She prayed for a spark to ignite, anything that would thaw her insides. When his lips barely touched, he said, "Because that's what we both want."

Jasmine closed her eyes and turned her face away. There was no great rush of emotion, no great outpouring of wild desire, no matter how much she wished it. Her heart might be beating faster, but other than that, she was dead inside. "No, that's what you want."

REID STUDIED the woman before him for a moment, not sure he'd heard her correctly. That smooth move had worked on many women. The low, seductive voice. The gentle caress of his hand. The slow glide of his lips.

He didn't move, waiting for her to turn back to him in uncontrolled passion. Most women would have his clothes off in two seconds, begging him to take them against the countertop. He probably would've done it too.

Reid waited. Jasmine didn't move. He waited longer. She took a deep breath, sighing. He waited. She took another breath. She looked bored.

Sacred cats! Why in the galaxy wasn't she kissing him right now? He wanted her so badly, was on the verge of attacking her because of it. Her smell engulfed him. The energy between them was potent, sparking like fireworks, snapping the air. How could she not react upon it?

Reid, not one to be dissuaded from his purpose, leaned forward to nuzzle her throat. She might hide her expression, but her pulse would give her away. He kissed her neck, letting his mouth rest over her heartbeat. To his pleasure, he felt it racing beneath his lips.

"When you said five hours, did that include this?" she asked, her voice soft.

Reid chuckled. That was more like what he was used to. Pulling back, he looked at her face. It was blank. He frowned. She looked unmoved. Losing some of his cool, he said, "Five hours in my bed."

"Then please unhand me." Jasmine pulled back. "I'll pay what I owe, but not a second more. The next time you touch me, I start subtracting minutes."

Reid instantly let her go, feeling as if she'd

slapped him. She wasn't interested? He would never force a woman to be in his company. He closed his eyes and inhaled, smelling her. Her longing was faint, but it was there, stronger than before. He listened. Her heart raced, and her breathing had deepened. The attraction between them practically crackled around the room. There was no way what he felt could be one-sided. It was too strong, too potent. He looked at her face. It was an unreadable mask. For the first time in his sixty-one years, Reid doubted himself. It was a new feeling, and he didn't like it.

"You can't sleep in cargo. That's Dev's room," he said quietly. He couldn't look at her. Remembering what they'd concluded about her previous lover, he said, "I'm not a monster. I'm not going to force myself on you, Jasmine. If you truly don't want me, I'll back off. I'm sorry if I misread you."

She didn't move. Reid finally looked at her, meeting her eyes.

"Reid," she began but didn't finish.

He picked up his sloken and strode out of the dining hall. Once away, hidden around a corner, he stopped and took a deep breath. What had just happened? Was it possible she wasn't attracted to him? Did he only want her because she didn't want him? Is that why he felt the burning need to go back, just to be near her? Is that why he thought about her all day? Reid was the first to admit he loved a challenge, but was she just playing hard to get or did she really not want him?

"She doesn't want me," he whispered, torn between bewilderment and agony. His body tensed, aching to hold her, touch her, smell her. The first woman in his life that he felt he just had to have, and she didn't want him. "She doesn't want me."

Anger and frustration built within him. Storming down the corridor, he found Dev and Jackson combat training in the VR. They glanced at him as he stepped into the middle of a battle with a group of Grugs. The hairy beasts howled, slashing at the man with sharpened claws. Dev stepped over, letting Reid in on the action. They fought, barely saying a word for hours. Afterward, Reid slowly made his way back to his room.

Though the workout tired him, it did nothing for the sexual frustration knotted in the pit of his stomach. He hung his head.

Jasmine wasn't attracted to him.

15

JASMINE WATCHED Reid stretch his arms as he stepped out of the decontaminator. He was completely naked. Her whole body shook, but she forced herself to remain seated on the bed. Her heart beat had been a little too elevated since their meeting in the dining hall, so she'd taken another pill. Two pills in one day wasn't really a good idea, but she'd been desperate.

Seeing his naked form, she quickly turned her eyes away to stare at her feet. Reid was a brilliant specimen of male beauty, like a statue carved from Old Earth marble. She loved looking at holographs of ancient Old Earth art. To imagine those people had carved the stone with only a chisel and hammer was amazing, or that they painted a beautiful masterpiece by hand, believing in their work so much that they spent months perfecting it, sometimes years. When Old Earthlings migrated to New Earth, they'd left most of the art behind.

"Why are you looking at me like that?" he asked.

"I was thinking of Old Earth art and how…" She made a weak gesture, not about to tell him she thought he looked like a naked statue come to life.

He arched a brow.

Jasmine took a deep breath. This was a mistake. On the verge of standing, she found her legs shook too badly to support her. She stayed on the bed, gripping the mattress at her sides.

"You act as though I'm going to attack you," Reid said, his voice dull. "I already told you I'm not going to force myself on you."

Jasmine bit her lip. She couldn't look at him. "It's pleasant enough when you kiss me."

A soft sound of surprise escaped him at her admission. Jasmine had no idea what made her say the words aloud. She wanted to explain to him that it wasn't him, it was her. If a man like Reid touched her and she couldn't feel, then she knew she was truly frigid.

"You could've fooled me," Reid said. She felt more than heard him moving. The heat from his body seemed to wash over her. Or was it that she was so focused on him she imagined it? He pushed back her hair, brushing his fingers lightly over her cheek. No. It was him. He was close. Softly, he asked, "Would you like me to kiss you, *fea?*"

Jasmine slowly nodded. She finally looked at him, first his bare feet, his strong thighs, his chiseled hips, and waist. His shaft was erect, standing tall in a soft bed of hair. Not a measure of fat marred his frame. She forced her gaze upward, over his muscled chest, so defined and smooth, to where his eyes bore down on her. "Yes."

Reid gave her a slow smile and sunk to his knees before her. The hand on her cheek slid over her neck, pulling her lightly forward. At first his kiss was gentle, as he brushed his lips lightly along her mouth. Watching his face, his closed eyes, she wanted to touch him but held back. For some strange reason she couldn't explain, she trusted him.

He traced her mouth with his tongue before delving inside. Jasmine couldn't help but move her lips slightly as she tasted him. A weak sound left her, and she realized it came from the back of her throat. Slowly, she reached behind her and lifted a small container. When he pulled back from his kiss, a kiss she barely returned, she held it up and said, "You'll need this."

A confused frown crossed over his face as he looked at the label. "Lubricant?"

Jasmine nodded, pretty sure she'd never been so mortified in her life. Her body tensed, and she wished the ship would just break apart so she could drift away into deep space. Dying a horrible death would surely be less painful than this moment.

Reid didn't take the container, but instead looked into her eyes. This time when he kissed her he deepened it, moving as if to conquer her. A hand brushed over her thigh, gliding lightly up to the side of her breast. Pleasant warmth stung her nipple as he drew his thumb over it. Her hips jerked. She was dizzy, lightheaded, but she couldn't make him stop. When she was breathless, he pulled back and smiled against her lips. "We don't need that stuff."

"Yes, you do," she whispered. "I'm…"

He licked playfully at her mouth, running the tip of his tongue along the seam. "What?"

"I'm colder than the polar ice caps of Sintaz." Jasmine tried to pull back. Oh, gawd! Had she really admitted it out loud? Like that? "Sorry, bad expression."

"What are you talking about? Who told you that?" Reid refused to let her go. His hands kneaded along her sides. He made a soft, seductive noise as he brushed his temple along her jaw, nuzzling her.

"Well, my husband," Jasmine said.

Reid stiffened. His hands gripped her arms slightly, not hurting but no longer caressing.

"I overheard him one night when he had a mistress over." Jasmine pulled away. He let her go. She'd lived with her condition for so long that it no longer made her cry to think about it. Actually, nothing made her cry anymore. Perhaps she had turned into an emotionless vacuum.

REID STARED at the woman in disbelief. She was married? Mated to another man? His body was so hard for her, she was finally willing, or so it appeared, and now he discovered he couldn't touch her. For a long moment, he couldn't move. The idea of not being able to make love to her hurt too badly.

"Reid?" she asked, her voice soft, passionless.

Recoiling from her, he stood. His body had been stretched from his exercise, but the tension was slowly easing its way back into his muscles. When he looked at her, he didn't see remorse for what was happening. It was as if she didn't care. She looked at him, her eyes shaded from all emotion. That wasn't anything new. Her face was always expressionless when she looked at him. "You're married?"

"Well, yes, but…" Jasmine was slower coming to her feet.

"But?" Reid demanded, not believing her audacity. What kind of man did she think he was? Sure, he might joke about married women, but in truth he'd never taken another man's wife to his bed. For the Var, life mating was sacred and lasted for all eternity. Even half mating, though not as binding, was a strong connection that was not lightly breached. If he were to knowingly take a married woman, the blow to his honor would be devastating, not to mention that he'd never forgive himself.

"I told you my name when we met," she said. "Mrs. Doctor St. Claire. I didn't hide it."

"You did not say you were married," he stated.

"That's what the title means."

"We don't use such titles," Reid said. "I would have remembered you saying you were married."

"I'm not really, technically anymore," she tried to explain.

"How can you not be? You have said vows? You have pledged yourself? You've said the words? You've been bound?" Reid couldn't believe it. An ache was in his chest. She was taken, claimed. He wanted her more than he'd ever wanted anyone, and she couldn't be any further away from him. "Is your husband dead?"

Jasmine shook her head in denial. "Marriage is prison. I divorced him. I quit like a bad job."

"This...divorce? Is it binding? Legal? Recognized by your people?" A hope tried to awaken where his heart had gone dead. He wished Quinn was with them. Quinn, being the true Var ambassador knew the most about other cultures. Reid tried to remind himself that other humanoid cultures were different. Mating didn't mean as much to others as it did to his people, and could be undone. He was tense as he waited for the answer. He hoped she would say something he could work with.

"No, I just left."

"You just gave up?" Why was he torturing himself? He should just tell her to go. In fact, he should throw her from his room and demand she go.

"I stayed for four years trying," Jasmine said. She walked to the door and ran her hand over the scanner. "I don't call that giving up, Reid. I call that overkill."

Jasmine left without a backward glance. He was glad for it because he wouldn't have been able to force her to leave him. How could she be married?

Reid looked at his arousal. It still ached, but he ignored it. Breathing hard, he sat on the bed.

Jasmine was taken. There was nothing he could

MICHELLE M. PILLOW

do about it. He couldn't touch her. To do so would be to dishonor not only himself but his family, his people. There was nothing to be done about it. He could never have her.

The knowledge only seemed to make him want her more. She was a mystery. Regrettably, she wasn't his mystery to solve.

16

JASMINE MADE her way down the corridor away from Reid's room. The look of repulsion on his face had been clear. He no longer wanted her. Shouldn't she be happy? Isn't that what she wanted? Then why did it feel like she'd just been kicked in the gut? Why was her body suddenly all achy and hot?

"I need another pill," she whispered, pressing a hand to her chest. "Something's definitely wrong with me."

Looking back toward Reid's room, she tensed. She couldn't go in there, not right now. Reid was still in there. Unfortunately, so was her medicine.

Her whole body shaking, she decided to suffer through the little heart episode. It would be too dangerous to take another pill so soon anyway.

Slowly, she continued down the corridor. The ship was big. There had to be somewhere she could hide until the peculiar feeling in her chest subsided.

"Jasmine."

Jasmine froze. Reid's soft voice was so hard, angry. Turning slowly, she looked back. There was so much passion in him, so much feeling. When he smiled, he really smiled. When he laughed, it was a real laugh, not fake, not forced. And, like now, when he was angry, the rage poured out of him until it was unmistakable. She wished she could feel things half the way he did. He was so honest with himself.

Frowning, he leaned out of his quarter's door. Jasmine did not make a move to go to him. If his naked shoulder was any indication, he hadn't put on clothes. "What?"

"Come back here. Everyone will be going to bed soon, and I already said I'd share my room with you. I keep my word. There is nowhere else for you to go on the ship." Reid studied her a moment longer before disappearing into his room.

Jasmine stared at the door for a long moment before going back. Unsure, she glanced inside. Reid was on the floor, wrapped in a blanket. He glanced at her, but said nothing. He didn't have to. His dark eyes spoke volumes.

"You're sure?" she asked. "I don't want to put you out."

He chuckled though the sound had little humor. "Take the bed, Jasmine. Sleep."

Reid closed his eyes, and she knew that he was dismissing her. She should've been grateful that he no longer wanted her, but she wasn't. It's not like she wanted to suffer through a man's carnal attentions, counting the seconds until he was done.

Slowly, she moved to the bed. Lying down, she looked at his strong back. The long waves of his hair spread out behind him, looking like strands of dark silk against the gray pillow. He was turned away from her, and she couldn't see his handsome face.

"Lights," Reid called. The lights shut off, leaving them in darkness. Jasmine tensed, waiting for him to stalk her and strangely disappointed when he didn't.

Jasmine tucked her hands under her head. "Reid?"

"What, Jasmine." He didn't sound pleased. In fact, he didn't sound anything. Normally he sounded so full of life. His dead tone actually hurt.

"Thank you for not turning me over to the Federation. You might have saved my life." Jasmine bit her lip. It wasn't all she wanted to say to him. Part of her was so scared. She'd not felt such a thing in a long time. In fact, it was as if she'd been lifeless inside, for four years to be exact, since her wedding to Chad.

Jasmine waited for him to speak, hoping he'd give her an opening. She wanted to invite him into the bed, not for sex, but for his warmth. She wanted to feel his body next to hers like when he'd been shifted into tiger form. She wanted to feel protected. A tear slipped over her cheek. She wanted to be wanted.

"It's nothing," he said, his tone flat. "Anyone would have done the same."

Jasmine bit her lip. That wasn't true, and she had a feeling he knew it as well. Not many people would take on a stranger, protecting them from the Federation Military.

"Reid—"

"Go to sleep, Jasmine," he said, cutting off her words with his harsh tone. "I don't want to talk about it anymore."

"WE'RE STOPPING FOR FUEL," Jarek said as Reid came into the cockpit. They'd been traveling for four days, taking a long route back to Qurilixen. No one complained. It wasn't as if they were needed at the Var palace anytime soon.

"Where?" Reid asked. He shifted uncomfortably on his feet. He was tired. He'd been sleeping, or attempting to sleep, on his floor. Jasmine took the bed. After the first night, he merely informed her he'd be sleeping in shifted form. He had to. It was the only way he'd get any rest. Otherwise, his arousal was strained to the point of explosion. Aside from that, they'd hardly spoken.

She was allowed to do as she willed on the ship. Most of the time she was in the lounge with the others, quietly sitting in a corner watching them as they joked around or played cards. Not once did she join them, and when she spoke, it was always short, timid answers. Reid knew because he'd stood outside the door listening.

"There's an asteroid belt near here. Ziger Complex is right on the edge," Rick offered. He turned around and grinned. "Ever hear of the red light district?"

Reid shook his head in denial.

Jarek cleared his throat. "No, we'll stay clear of Ziger. Lady Jasmine is onboard."

"I don't see why Reid is the only one who gets a woman," Rick grumbled. "He's not even using his."

"Hey," Reid began, stiffening. "If you want—"

"Whoa, easy," Jarek said, his tone bordering on an order. "There is a small refueling station on Werten. Lady Jasmine can find transport from there. It's the only decent stop before we get back to Qurilixen."

Reid stiffened. "I don't know that we should leave her on a strange planet."

"Any planet is going to be strange to her," Rick said. "Unless we turn around and take her back."

"She won't have any protection there," Reid insisted.

"What do you care?" Rick frowned. "You just

said yesterday that you'd be glad for the day you could be rid of her."

It was true. He had said that. But, really it had been the constant aching in his loins that caused his ill temper.

Jarek crossed his arms and turned to face them. "Rick, leave us a moment."

Rick pushed a few buttons and left the cockpit. When they were alone, Reid said, "I'm not enamored."

"You're sure?"

Reid nodded. "I gave my word to protect her. That's what I'm doing. I will not dishonor myself by abandoning her on some refueling planet."

"She wanted a ride off Nozando. We've done that. If you drop her off safely at Werten, you've done your duty by her. You'll have kept your word." Jarek tilted his head. "Unless you wish to take her to Qurilixen."

"I haven't decided," Reid said quietly. He really didn't like that option either. Why would he take her home, knowing he couldn't touch her?

"She can mate to one of the soldiers. A Var warrior would treat her well. You cannot hope for a better fate than that for her, especially after what was done to her by her previous lover." Jarek reached overhead and absently pushed a few buttons before throwing a small switch. Reid watched, not sure what his brother was doing. He hardly knew anything about flying space crafts. Truth be told, he was ready to be on land, his feet firmly on the ground. Life in space wasn't for him.

"Husband," Reid said softly. "What was done to her was by her husband, not lover."

"What?"

"It was her mate. She's married," Reid said. He hadn't admitted the words out loud before now. They stung worse than he'd thought they would.

"You detected her marking?" Jarek's eyes widened in surprise. "I sensed no such thing."

"No," Reid said. "I kissed her and didn't sense it at all."

"Then?"

"She told me of it." Reid lifted his chin. "She abandoned her husband."

"Was she lying?"

"I don't believe so. Trust me, I would've detected the lie."

Jarek frowned. Turning, he looked at the large viewing screen. "She's human."

"Yes." Reid studied his brother's back, wondering what he was getting at.

"Was she married in the human custom?" Jarek asked.

"I don't know. Perhaps." Reid tilted his head to

the side, trying to get a better look at Jarek's face. "Why do you ask?"

"Many human customs are done with pieces of papers and words unless they are mating to a species like ours." Jarek sighed, rubbing the back of his neck. "If she was married by such a custom, there is no reason she couldn't marry a Var warrior if she wanted to. We do not recognize human or Federation law. If I remember correctly, often humans force their children into marriage to seal pacts."

Neither brother mentioned that King Kirill had made such a marriage pact with the Draig princes. If one of the dragon-shifters' princesses were to have a girl, that female would marry Kirill's oldest son. The child would have no choice because a pact was designed to ensure peace. Reid knew Jarek didn't agree with the betrothal pact. However, it was more of a gesture. On a planet where only one in a million births was female, it was a long shot that the marriage would even have to be honored.

After a thoughtful pause, Jarek continued, "She would be free game because technically she is not claimed, and if she left this man, obviously he has no claim on her heart. With you as her guardian, Lady Jasmine would be sure to make a fine match. And once back on Qurilixen, anyone looking for her won't be able to find her unless we want them to. As your ward, she'd have the unquestioned protection of the Var armies. You know as well as I that we could hide her far away from the palace, in places they'd never dream of looking."

Reid tensed. "I didn't say I was her guardian."

"Would you like me to claim her instead? If you find you have no wish to give her away in marriage, I will be glad to. It shouldn't be too hard. She's young and pretty. Someone will take her off my hands. If not a Var warrior, then I'm sure she will be allowed to participate in the Draig breeding festival next year."

"No. I'll be her guardian. It is my duty to protect her." Reid suddenly frowned. Why did he just claim Jasmine as his ward? The last thing he wanted was the woman living in his home, tempting him. Unless, what Jarek said was true, and the human marriage was meaningless. Reid frowned. He needed to speak to Quinn and perhaps his brothers' wives. Being human born, surely they would know something of this.

"Is it?" Jarek mused, chuckling.

"Yes. I said I'd watch out for her and I will."

"Great. Then it's decided. She'll come back to Qurilixen with us." Jarek grinned and clapped him on the shoulder. It was then that Reid realized his brother had manipulated the conversation for his own amusement. Jasmine's presence tortured him and Jarek knew that. Obviously Jarek thought it was funny to watch his twin brother squirm.

"I'll get you back for this," Reid said. Jarek's grin widened. There was no need to explain, his brother knew what he'd done.

Storming from the cockpit, he ignored Jarek's laughter. Rick was standing against the wall and smiled as he came by.

"All figured out then?" Rick asked, chuckling. He didn't even bother to hide his amusement.

Reid growled. He walked faster. Dev would surely be in the VR in training and Reid definitely needed to work off some frustration.

Was the whole ship amused by his torment? Viktor and Jackson were coming out of the lounge. They stopped, smirking at him. Reid's frown deepened and he walked faster. He had his answer.

18

JASMINE LOOKED around the lounge from her place in the corner, trying to get the nerve to say something to the crew. They'd given up on trying to start a conversation with her. She couldn't blame them. Each time they tried, she hardly gave them more than a two-word reply. Sometimes the men watched old Earth movies, other times they played cards. Jasmine desperately wanted to join in, but each time they invited her she found herself saying no.

For the most part, everyone treated her well. Reid ignored her, but she could hardly complain about that. She still wore the crimson shirt and tight pants she'd arrived in, forced by necessity to wash them every day in the decontaminator.

"I knew it," Rick announced walking in the

door. "We should've stayed at the Galaxy Play-mates' mansion. It's not like we have anything we need to be doing, and Jarek's insisting we fly around everything worth seeing. Oh, and Viktor, the porn monitor in my room is broken again, and I need you to take a look at..."

Instantly the men's faces paled, and they turned to look at her. Rick froze in mid-speech. Jasmine watched him as he slowly turned to her, his face stiff.

"*Oh,*" Rick said, drawing the sound out. "Crap."

Jasmine sat up. They were all still looking at her. "I'm going to leave."

Jasmine walked to the door, not meeting any of their eyes. She felt horrible. Obviously, she was a burden to them.

"Way to go," she heard Evan drawl as she left. The lounge exploded with low murmurs as she walked away.

"Okay, okay, don't get your panties in a twist. I don't know what the big deal is. Sam never cared," Rick said.

"Sam was different," Evan admonished.

Jasmine heard footsteps coming after her. She tensed. Rick called, "Hey, Jasmine, I mean, my lady."

Jasmine stopped. She looked at him, arching a brow. "I'm not a lady."

"Oh, the Var call all women lady and insist we do so as well, especially with you belonging to Prince Reid and all."

"I don't belong to him," Jasmine denied. Surely, Reid wouldn't like hearing Rick say that. It wasn't as if the Var prince actually still wanted her. He was gone every morning when she awoke, and he didn't talk to her when he saw her. In fact, she'd say that he definitely didn't want anything to do with her.

"Well, you know what I mean. With him claiming you as his and all." Rick smiled. "Anyway—"

"He did?" Jasmine gasped. "What are you talking about?"

"Yeah, Jarek said you were Reid's ward. Actually, I was eavesdropping and didn't hear everything they said." He gave her a sheepish grin. "But the gist of it is that you're under Reid's protection. I mean, have you seen those guys fight? Or shift and fight for that matter? Yeah, they'd rip my balls off and shove them down my throat if I were to even think about…"

Rick paused, looking pained by his own crass phrasing. Despite his rather obvious flaws, Jasmine liked Rick. He never took anything seriously, always was quick with a joke and winked audaciously at her almost every time she saw him as if he couldn't help himself. Oh, and he seemed to have an affinity for ancient Old Earth culture. Panties in a twist? That was one of many sayings she'd heard from the man. It didn't take a genius to figure out what it meant.

Rick continued as she stared blankly at him. "Ah, yeah, anyway, I did hear that Reid's going to marry you off to one of the Var soldiers or something. You're very lucky. I mean congratulations and all that. I know a lot of women like to do the marriage thing."

Jasmine felt the color draining from her face. Reid wanted to marry her off? Surely Rick was mistaken. Even if he weren't, she'd just refuse.

"My lady? You all right?" Rick asked. "Are you waiting for me to apologize for having a big mouth? I'm sorry if I offended you in there with the talk of porn. I didn't know you were so delicate."

"I'm not delicate. Apology accepted, though not needed." Jasmine nodded once. "Good day."

She turned to go. Rick sighed heavily behind her. "You want to go get drunk or something?"

Jasmine felt her lips twitch despite herself. Trying not to laugh, she kept her back to him as she said, "I don't drink, but thank you for the offer just the same."

"Well, why the hell not?" Rick had stepped closer.

The man was trying, she'd give him that. Somehow, Jasmine got the impression Rick didn't know how to talk to women unless he was coming onto them. It was adorable to watch him try to be nice to her. She much preferred him treating her like one of the guys than coming on to her anyway.

Jasmine turned to him. Her smile faltered as she laid her hand on her chest. "Heart condition."

"Ah, that sucks." Rick looked sorry for her. "Want to come watch us get drunk, then? You shouldn't be spending so much time alone. I guarantee we can get the rest of the crew to make asses out of themselves. All but Dev. He's a wet blanket. Though, he's easy to rile and turns even redder when he's mad. It's damned funny."

A wet what? Jasmine shook her head. "No, I—"

"Come on, it'll be fun." Rick winked, nodding emphatically.

Jasmine opened her mouth to answer. She didn't manage to get a word in before Rick continued talking.

"Did we ever tell you the story of how we met up with these Var princes?" Rick asked. He slung his arm around her shoulders, pulling her alongside him as he spoke. Jasmine's mouth stayed open, but he kept talking, ignoring her feeble protest as she tried to pull away from him. He clearly wasn't taking no for an answer. His arm tightened on her, not inappropriately, just keeping her in step with him. The weight of it pressed into her and the easy contact was so strange that she finally just went with it. "You see, there was this scavenger hunt for the giant market on Torgan. You ever hear of it? Bunch of ships go around collecting things and then sell them on the market while hoping to win a prize for finding the best stuff."

Jasmine nodded. Rick failed to mention that Torgan was mostly known as being a black market planet, filled with space pirates and those running from the law.

"Captain Sam, ah that would be *Samantha*, Lucien, Viktor, Evan, Dev and I were a crew. We all got drunk one night, well, not Dev, like I said, wet blanket that one. Anyway, Sam, Evan and Lucien decided that they were going to get a wild beast for the scavenger hunt." Rick led her back into the lounge grinning. "They were toe up drunk and kidnapped Prince Falke in his shifted form."

"Oh, you're not telling her about that," Lucien protested.

"And why not, rocket boy?" Viktor demanded of his brother. Then, turning to Jasmine, he asked, "Rick tell you that they stole my Torganian Rum?"

"Torganian Rum?" Jasmine repeated. "You

mean rum as in *roome-a*? It's not even liquor. It's a psychotropic given by Torganian shaman to enlighten their minds. I wouldn't recommend humanoids drinking it."

The men looked at her as if she'd sprouted a new head. Evan smiled. Lucien's jaw actually dropped. Viktor slowly nodded and held out his hands as if to say, '*thank you!*'

"We know that now," Lucien mumbled, giving his brother a grumpy look.

"So you actually kidnapped a prince?" Jasmine asked, intrigued by their story. "How are you not in jail?"

"Falke fell in love with Sam," Evan said, smiling wider. "They're married, even expecting a baby."

"They're going to name the baby Rick," Rick said.

"You wish, fly boy," Lucien contradicted. "Sam already told me it's going to be baby Lucien."

"She did not," Evan laughed. "Stop telling lies."

"Good thing she did marry him or else we'd really be in a sling." Rick finally let her go but stood between her and the doorway so she couldn't easily escape. He grinned at her, his eyes sparkling as if he knew exactly what he was doing in making her socialize with them.

"So how many Var princes are there?" Jasmine

asked. She noticed Lochlann in the back corner, sitting by Jackson. The man shifted uncomfortably in his chair but said nothing.

"The oldest is Kirill. He's just become king and married the woman who tried to have him arrested for some biological weaponry the HIA found on their planet," Lucien said.

"Ah, then there is Falke, Commander of the Var armies," Evan added.

"You not only kidnapped a prince, but a commander prince?" Jasmine asked. Curious, she sat down, taking a chair closer to the men. They grinned at her. Rick left his post by the door and went to a cabinet, pulling out a bottle of liquor and some large glasses.

"Yeah, wait until you see him too," Rick added, setting the glasses down on the card table. He twisted off the bottle's cap and began to pour generous amounts. "He's huge."

"Anyway," Lucien interrupted. "Next are the twins, Reid and Jarek."

"Jarek is the runaway, out here with us scamps," Jackson said. Coming forward, he took a glass, lifted it up to Rick in salute and began to sip.

"And Reid is the Commander of the Outlands," Evan said. He glanced at his hand-held and Jasmine could see that part of him wanted to get back to his book. "But you probably know all that."

Jasmine didn't say a word. Essentially, she didn't know anything about Reid. How could she? He didn't talk to her. Her heart did little flops in her chest. Reid was a commander? A warrior? It explained his size and his very toned physique, but knowing he was a warrior made her a little nervous. Strangely, though, she wasn't scared of him per say, just apprehensive of his vigor and prowess.

"Then there is Quinn, the true Var ambassador, married to an ESC scientist who came to rid the planet of the biological weaponry the HIA found." Rick smiled, before tipping his glass back and swallowing the dark brown liquor in two large gulps. Sighing, he set his glass down and refilled it. "That's all of them."

"Wow, five princes," Jasmine said when the men looked at her. "So who are the Draig?"

The men shifted their eyes to Lochlann. He raised his hand, giving her a slow smile. "We'd be the enemy to the Var."

Jasmine stared at him. He was a traitor?

"*Were*, I suppose is the better word," he amended as if seeing her thoughts on her face.

"And are you a prince as well?" Jasmine asked.

"No, the Draig have four princes—Ualan,

Zoran, Yusef, and Olek," Lochlann said. "I am not one of them."

Jasmine got the feeling he didn't want to speak of it, so she changed the subject back to the Var. She wanted to know more about the Var, about Reid. "You said the oldest Var prince is the king now? I take it their parents are deceased?"

"Falke's mother is alive," Rick said.

"Oh, I see," Jasmine said. "The king was married more than once."

Rick smirked, as he poured shots. "You could say that."

"What?" Jasmine sat forward to get a better look at his face. "He was married many times?"

"You could say that," Rick repeated.

"How many wives did he have?" Jasmine asked. Viktor mumbled something. "I'm sorry, I couldn't hear."

"He said," Rick grinned, winking at her, "King Attor had over a hundred and fifty wives at one time."

"Oh," Jasmine gasped. Why was she suddenly thinking of Reid? And why was she suddenly jealous to think he might have just as many wives? If he was married, then why in the world did he get upset because she was? "That is...extremely excessive."

Remembering what Rick had said about Reid

wanting to marry her off, she tensed. She didn't like the idea of marrying again, but she liked less the idea that Reid would try to give her away. It's not as if she wanted to be one of Reid's hundred and fifty wives, or any man's for that matter. She already tried the marriage thing and it was a mistake she wouldn't be repeating.

"Obviously," Jasmine said, when the men continued to look at her. She saw the glass in Rick's hand and stared at it. She'd only had a few sips of liquor in her life. Why was she suddenly tempted to try more? "It's a…ah, many such cultures have those types of practices."

Rick lifted the glass to her, offering it up. Jasmine met his eyes. Slowly, she stood and nodded. She took his glass, glanced around and then drank it as Rick had, taking it down in two big gulps. The liquor burned, choking her. Coughing, she nearly gagged at the horrible taste. Rick laughed, patting her on the back.

"Rick," Evan scolded. "What did you give her?"

"Just a little whiskey," Rick protested. "Nothing the medical booth can't take out of her."

"Damn it," Evan said. "She's allergic to the medical booth."

"Oh," Rick looked guilty. He patted Jasmine's

shoulder. "Maybe you should take it easy, then. Didn't you say your heart—?"

"Another," Jasmine said, liking the combination of fire and numbness in her blood. "My heart will be just fine."

"I don't think—" Rick began.

"Another," Jasmine insisted. She managed a smile for him and sat down at the card table. "So, gents, what's the game?"

"Kiss My Comet," Lucien said, laughing.

"The children's game?" Jasmine asked in surprise.

"It's all we can remember how to play when we're drunk," Lucien admitted. "Rules are, for each wrong guess, you have to take a drink. So if you ask me for an eight, and I don't have it, you drink. If I do have it, I drink."

"Sounds simple enough," Jasmine said. She looked expectantly at Rick for her own glass.

Rick glanced around. Then, shrugging, he said, "I'm going to need another bottle. I'll be right back."

19

REID STRETCHED his arms over his head as he left the VR room. He was tired from fighting the Grogs with Dev and wanted to go to sleep, but he knew he couldn't go back to his room yet. He didn't want to face Jasmine. Instead, he went to the lounge, knowing the guys were probably gathered there—drinking and playing cards. Hearing laughter, he smiled slightly. But, as he heard Jasmine's voice joining theirs, he tensed.

"So you're saying," she said, her voice abnormally loud, "that you think you could please that many women?"

"I know I could," Rick boasted.

"You'd try," Lucien teased.

Reid stayed behind the corner, listening. It took him a moment to get over the shock of hearing

Jasmine laugh. Then, knowing he'd never accomplished so much as making her smile, he felt his gut tighten.

"I should think King Attor's wives would be very lonely," Jasmine said, laughing harder. Reid's tension only intensified as he heard her speak of his father. What did she know of it? Of the Var way? "I mean, it's complete arrogance to think that they would all be satisfied by one man. I highly doubt the old king could make three women happy, let alone hundreds. If they were happy, they found pleasure in the arms of another to be sure."

More laughter sounded. Reid was sure he heard Lochlann's voice with the others. Stepping around the corner, he quickly assessed the room. Jasmine sat at the card table, laughing as she took a drink. They were all drunk, and no one even noticed that the cat-shifter prince was watching them. Rick, Lucien, and Viktor joined Jasmine at cards, laughing as hard as she. Jackson and Evan watched the game, their backs to him. Lochlann's eyes were the first to meet his. He sat alone in a corner. His smile faded, and he leaned back, not moving. Reid ignored him.

"My father pleased his women just fine," Reid stated coldly. He stared at Jasmine. What was she doing laughing and smiling? She never smiled at him. Anger rolled in him until he resented her.

How dare she laugh at his family? How dare she question his father's honor? Attor was dead, unable to defend himself to her. Jasmine's smile faded when she looked at him. Her eyes flickered down to the glass in front of her before boldly lifting back up to meet his.

"Sure, he did," Jasmine said, returning his hard stare. Was she angry with him? She dared to glare at him? "I'm betting he was a real…" She glanced at Rick. "What was that word you used? Stud."

"Reid," Rick began, standing on wobbling feet as he shook his head. "We weren't disrespecting your father at all. We were just talking about wanting to own a harem. We're jealous of him, truly."

"I thought you didn't drink," Reid said to Jasmine, not taking his eyes off her as he ignored Rick. She frowned and lifted her glass, defiantly tossing back the liquor.

Evan stood, coming to Reid's side. Quietly, he said, "She only had one real glass. Rick's been pouring her watered down whiskey the entire night."

Reid glanced at Jasmine's glass, noticing the liquid in it was indeed lighter than the men's. He nodded once at Evan to signify he heard him, but that was all he could manage. Just one look at Jasmine's flushed cheeks, and swaying body told him she was drunk regardless of what they had given her.

"I'm not your ward, your highness. I don't belong to you. I will never belong to you or any man ever again. I can do whatever I damned well please," Jasmine said. She pushed to her feet, wobbling violently at the sudden movement. Rick and Lucien were instantly by her side, holding her up by her elbows. She weakly tried to shrug them off. "You actually thought I would go to your barbaric planet and marry some stupid, primitive warrior? Dream on. You don't own me."

"You asked to be under my protection," Reid said, his tone warning her to back down. He made a move toward her. She flinched.

"I asked for safe passage. You don't own me, Reid. You can't decide to make me marry some stupid kitty cat-shifter thing. I don't want to be married at all."

Reid felt his face change subtly. The half shift was just as frightening as the full. The pupils in his eyes bent, becoming oblong as he scanned her body. Her pulse was quick. He heard it in his head. Her chest deepened with breaths and he smelled the liquor emanating from her pores. It was a subtle smell, but he had no problem detecting it. Breathing hard with the effort it took not to strike her, his voice became garbled by a roar, as he said, "Insult my people again and you'll pay."

"Truth hurt?" she snapped. "Please. I've seen what you're capable of. Don't tell me you can honestly claim that you could satisfy a hundred women." Her eyes slipped dispassionately over him, and she gave up trying to shake off Rick and Lucien's arms. "I doubt you could satisfy one."

Reid's rage slipped. She dared to call his manhood into question? She dared to insult him? The men gasped. Rick and Lucien looked at Jasmine in horror.

"Jasmine," Lucien began. He made a move to stand in front of her.

"You better run," Rick told her, trying to do the same.

"Reid," Evan said to his side. "She didn't mean it. She's drunk. She doesn't know what she says. She can't handle her liquor."

"She's human. She doesn't know the depth to which your kind takes insults," Lucien added.

"Yeah," said Rick. "It's not the same for humans. We joke about prowess all the time and don't mean anything by it."

"What would you know of it?" Reid asked Jasmine cruelly, not taking his shifted eyes from hers. He ignored the men's protests on her behalf.

"You can't even feel a man's touch. How did you put it? You're colder than an ice cap on Sintaz."

He was instantly sorry for his harsh words, but the rage still held him in its grip. Jasmine gasped, her face paling. Her eyes rounded, and she looked around at the men. They were staring at her, saying nothing.

"You're right," she whispered. "I know nothing about it."

Slowly, Jasmine nodded and wobbled around the table. The men let her go. The fight drained out of her. Stumbling, she made a wide arch around Reid while heading for the door. She didn't meet his eyes.

"Why did you say that?" Rick growled when she was gone. "I'm a jerk, and I know never to say that to a woman's face, no matter what she said about my manhood."

"Holy stars!" Evan swore. Hands on hips, he faced Reid. "I can only imagine the circumstances in which she would admit something like that to you. It has taken us four days and liquor to get her to stop flinching when we come near her. Do you think she'll even be able to face us now? Face you?"

Reid glared at Evan. It was taking all his concentration not to fully shift and run after her. If he were to catch up to her in his current state, he might actually attack her. Whether he attacked her with fists or with kisses remained to be seen.

"You have no reason to defend your manhood in front of us," Rick added, shaking his head. "We all saw the women you were more than able to satisfy."

"Listen closely," Evan hissed, "because this is the only time I will ever tell you what I've read in her thoughts."

Reid glared at him, doubting Evan could say anything that would ease his rage.

"She's married," Evan said.

"I know." Reid nodded. For some reason, he didn't move as he waited for the man to say more. Evan never spoke of what he saw. For him to do so now meant it was important that he listened. "I never touched her."

Lowering his voice so none of the others heard him, Evan continued, "Then did you know that her husband beat her senseless and then locked her in a closet for three days without food while they were on their honeymoon? All because of this problem of hers? Did you know that he's beaten her regularly ever since then for the last four years? Or that he's brought home prostitutes and had sex with them while she listened from the next room, telling the women how inadequate his wife was? That he made fun of her with them for not being a real woman? And she was forced to take it with a smile on her face or he'd beat her for daring to talk back to him? The flashes I see in her memories and the feelings inside her are things I won't soon forget. The man wouldn't give her a divorce, not the one she'd need according to human law. He'd have killed her first. As far as I'm concerned, she did the only thing she could."

Reid's head whipped to the door where she'd disappeared. "You should've told me this from the beginning."

"You should've been patient with her, and she would've told you about it herself. It wasn't my place," Evan shook his head in disgust, "it still isn't my place."

Evan crossed over to the table and grabbed a drink.

"I'll go after her," Rick said when no one moved to do so.

Reid looked up, shook his head in denial and turned to follow Jasmine. Once alone in the corridor, he took a deep breath. He was a fool. He'd seen the marks on her body, knew that she'd been ill-treated. Never mind that he'd done everything he could to stay away from her, he should never have said those words in front of the crew. He shouldn't have said them at all.

Sniffing the air, he caught her scent. The sweet

fragrance of her mingled with the more potent force of whiskey. He jogged after her, forcing the half shift from his face. She hadn't made it too far by the time he found her. Jasmine stumbled down the hall, her arm dragging along the metal wall for support as she moved.

"Jasmine," Reid said, his tone harder than he meant it to be. His voice was gruff because of the days burdened with unfulfilled passions, because of the rage inside him. Var were passionate, no matter the circumstance.

"No. Stay away from me!" She stiffened and instantly started to run. Her legs tripped over themselves, and she fell forward onto her hands and knees. The fall didn't stop her. She began to crawl from him.

Reid caught up to her and reached for her arms to help her up. "Jasmi—"

"Don't touch me!" she cried, jerking away. He had her half way up, and as she pulled from him, she fell down. "*Ahh!*"

Jasmine rolled onto her side and grabbed her wrist. Tears were in her eyes when she glanced up at him. Reid scooped her up into his arms, pleased when she didn't struggle.

"No medical booths. I can't. I'm allergic," Jasmine said. She closed her eyes, cradling her arm.

"You mentioned that before." Reid carried her

down the corridor. "I'm taking you back to my room."

When he arrived at the room, he laid her down on the bed. Jasmine glared up at him accusingly. "I thought you said you were busy men with lots of stuff to do."

"What?" Reid asked, confused. When he tried to examine her injured wrist, she swatted at him. He easily brushed her hand out of his way and lifted her arm. Jasmine winced.

"When you said you wouldn't give me a ride," she charged.

"It doesn't feel broken," he said, poking lightly at it.

"What would you know," she growled, still angry. He pressed harder, and she gasped.

"I've helped train armies, and I've been to war. I'd say I've learned a few things about sprains and broken bones. Now hold still while I try to find something with which to wrap it."

"Quit ordering me about, your royal-ish-ness," Jasmine slurred. "I can take care of myself. Just as soon as we land on Werten, I'm gone."

"You're in no condition to be making any type of decision tonight," Reid admonished, doing his best not to smile at her contrary tone. Sacred cats, but she was an infuriating woman!

"You're nothing but a rogue," Jasmine accused. "Taking hundreds of women—"

"That was my father," Reid said, pressing his lips together as he stood. He grabbed a black shirt from the dresser and began to tear it into strips.

"I've heard about you too, your highness," Jasmine said, closing her eyes.

"Have you now, *fea?*" If he could keep her talking, maybe she'd be distracted from the pain as he wrapped her wrist. Besides, he was curious as to what she'd heard. Was that jealousy in her bitter tone?

"I know you were at the Galaxy Playmates' mansion," she shot.

Reid looked her over, suddenly not liking where this was going. "Who told you that?"

"I added a few of my own rules to the game," Jasmine said. "A little truth or dare."

"Truth or what?" he frowned, not understanding.

"The men had to answer my questions if I won," she said, wincing as he moved her arm. "I know all about you and those three women you were sleeping with when they came to get you to leave the mansion."

"Jealous?" he asked, smirking at the look on her face. He was going to have someone's head. Who in the galaxy told her that one? Reid already knew.

Rick. The man had been most impressed by the feat.

"Not hardly." Jasmine tried to sit up. He gently pressed her shoulder, keeping her down. Her dark eyes widened as she stared at him. "You probably cry out your own name during sex."

"Would you like to find out?" Reid studied her, hoping to see a spark of something in her expression. If she wanted him, showed him some sign that what he felt for her was worth pursuing, that being with her would be worth the potential blow to his honor, he would have proceeded. His shaft was painfully full, always on the verge of an erection since that first moment he'd seen her. He'd been fantasizing about her more than he'd like to admit.

"No," she shot. "I don't care how handsome you are."

"You think I'm handsome?" Reid again lifted her arm and made quick work of binding it. Already it was turning purple with a bruise and was starting to swell. She didn't seem to notice.

"You're a rogue," she said. "That's what I think."

"You tell yourself whatever you need to, *fea*." He answered, enjoying the verbal battle between them. Anything was better than her silence, her emotionless eyes looking at him. His voice dipped naturally as he continued to hold her wrist. "Done."

"Huh?" she asked. Her chest rose and fell rapidly. She was breathing fast. Her eyes drifted to his mouth, and he saw the subtle purse of them as if she wanted him to kiss her. She didn't move.

"Your wrist," he said quietly, closing some of the distance between their mouths. His recent anger and his unfulfilled desires made it damn near impossible to concentrate. "I'm done."

It went against his very nature to go slow, but he had to. At that moment, he didn't care if she was married. No man who treated a woman the way she'd been treated deserved her.

Her lashes fluttered over her eyes. "I can never tell if your eyes are black or brown."

Reid let his mouth come against hers, barely touching as he waited to see what she would do. Her smell was in his head, wrapping around him. Every nerve centered on her until he was poised on the brink of pain and pleasure. He needed her. His body needed her until it physically hurt. His hands shook to touch her, flexing and fisting in the effort it took to hold them back.

"Sleep with me tonight," she said. Her eyes closed. "I don't want to be alone."

Reid tensed. Was she asking for what he thought she was? Just as he was going to crush his mouth down on hers and obey, a soft snore escaped her mouth. Very slowly, he pushed back from her, trembling violently. Jasmine was asleep.

With a pained laugh, he sat back on his legs and studied her. He wasn't a beast. He wouldn't touch her, not when she was passed out. This had never happened to him before. He'd never been brought to the brink, only to deny himself. Actually, he'd never been so aroused before, which said a lot.

Crawling to the decontaminator, his groin so tight that he flinched each time he moved, he shut himself in. He stripped off his clothes, letting the lasers run over his body, cleaning the sweat of exercise from his flesh as he touched his hard shaft. Even before he relieved his body of the pressure, he knew it wouldn't help. Still, what could he do? When he released himself, it was a painful surge that made him bite his lip to keep from screaming.

"Computer," Reid said, breathless and panting in the aftermath. The immense pressure was gone, but the desire he felt wasn't. "Define the human word, rogue."

"Rogue," the computer's monotone repeated. "There are over five hundred reference listings in the computer. Definition one, a plant that has an—"

"Computer, in reference to the origins of the

Old Star Language pertaining to humanoid culture," Reid said.

"Rogue," the monotone repeated, starting over. "A ne'er-do-well, a scamp, scallywag, charlatan, rapscallion, con man, crook, vagrant, beggar, devil, reprobate. One who is playful, mischievous. A—"

"Computer, that's enough," Reid said. It wasn't exactly the 'irresistibly charming sex god' answer he'd been hoping for. He gave a weak laugh as he stepped out of the small room. Going to a dresser, he slipped on a pair of loose pants. He preferred to sleep nude, but he didn't want to chance Jasmine's body rubbing up against his. If it did, he'd be making love to her before he even woke up enough to know what he was doing.

He glanced at the bed. Her hair spilled over her shoulders, trailing seductively over the crimson shirt. For some reason, he found himself imagining what she would look like in the gowns of his people, dressed as a Var woman. This was a lady built with grace, elegance, and poise. Her very bearing did her proud.

What was he going to do with her? It was clear Jasmine wouldn't appreciate being one of his many wives because that's what he would someday have. And that was if she even chose to be a half mate. After what had been done to her, he could see why she would not wish to try marriage again.

Reid didn't see himself giving her to another cat-shifter. He wouldn't be able to stand seeing her, her stomach large with another man's child, her body mated to another, belonging to another. The Draig were absolutely out of the question. He'd been at war with the dragon-shifters for too many decades to allow that to happen, even if it would keep her from his sight. Maybe he should just let her go on Werten. She said that's what she wanted, didn't she?

Marrying one female wasn't an option he'd allow himself to consider. Reid understood his father's point when he'd taught his sons never to life mate with one woman. Reid's grandfather had suffered the folly of mating with one woman. She died when Attor was born, and his father never recovered enough to breed with more women and produce sons. Although he took women to his bed, he left Attor without any brothers to help lead the Var nation. So, when Attor took over the throne, he became reliant on a few noble houses. One of those house nobles had even tried to kill his sons, proving that it was wiser to have many children by half mates than risk having a single child by a full life mate.

Reid sighed, staring at Jasmine. Perhaps he'd been looking at their situation all wrong. Maybe there was no need for them to mate at all. He didn't have to take her as a half mate to be her lover. Why not teach her pleasure and get some for himself?

Perhaps this situation with Jasmine wasn't as complicated as he'd made it out to be. Tonight, for a brief instant, he'd seen that she wanted him as he wanted her. It was a flicker of longing, fear, and anticipation. Tonight, he smelled her desire for him, the fragrance of it. Even now it wafted from her, teasing his senses and driving him mad. There was hope in that pheromone. Maybe all she needed was the right man, a man with experience, a man who knew a woman's body, a man who knew how to touch. Maybe all she needed was a man like him.

Reid's mouth opened, and he was torn between a groan and a scream. Instead, he kept quiet, gently touching her face. Letting a single finger trail over her soft skin, he asked her, "What are you doing to me, Jasmine? Why did you have to get on this ship?"

Jasmine didn't move, and Reid never received his answers.

Jasmine didn't wake up the next morning though she did moan a lot throughout the long night. Reid laid by her side, her soft body curled into his harder one as he watched over her. He lay on his back, too afraid to turn to her, lest he start making love to her before he could stop himself. Already his desire for her towered from his hips, pushing at his pants until it looked like a tent had been erected.

He stared at the ceiling, to where the monitor would appear if he ordered Earth porn. If he were a cad, he'd do it. Unfortunately, he was finding he had more morals than he'd ever given himself credit for. Although, this self-denial crap was getting really old.

At first Reid thought she was just sleeping off the liquor, but as morning turned to afternoon and afternoon to evening, he knew he had to do something. Jasmine was sick. She wasn't waking up.

Jarek landed *The Conqueror* on Werten to refuel. The shift into the planet's atmosphere was a bumpy ride. Reid was curious to see other planets, but didn't leave his room. With Jasmine asleep, there wasn't much option as to whether or not they should leave her behind. Secretly, he was glad for it.

As the guys stretched their legs on the planet's surface inquiring after a doctor for Jasmine, Reid stayed by her side. According to Rick, all they'd found was a fueling station and a small settlement. The people of Werten hadn't seen a doctor for years.

They'd left as quickly as they'd landed. Take off was just as bumpy.

Rick apologized repeatedly for letting Jasmine drink. Reid wanted to be mad at him, but he was too worried. If he'd been paying more attention to her, she wouldn't have had the opportunity to partake of so much. She was his ward, he'd swore to protect her, and he'd been too self-involved with his own arousal to pay the proper attention to her.

The door to his room opened, and Reid looked up from where he sat by Jasmine on the bed. He'd dressed, wearing loose clothes to hide his obvious arousal from everyone.

"Well?" Reid demanded.

Evan nodded. "I think you're suspicions are correct. I don't think it's possible for her to be allergic to the medical booth. I think her husband must've told her that so she'd hide the bruises he gave her. It would look strange if she were seen getting fixed up every week. Medical booths log records of the uses in their database. I'm sure doctor's records are forwarded to the other alliance doctors when a ship lands. Our booths aren't set to do that because of privacy laws, but hers most likely would have been. Plus, it probably gave the guy greater pleasure to see her suffering for longer periods of time after the beatings."

"You're sure, then?" Reid frowned, looking at Jasmine, willing her to wake up. "I don't want to make her worse."

"Every book I've looked in says she'll be fine. Maybe we can try it on her wrist first?" Evan frowned. "The new booth allows for lying down, but I'm not sure we should use it until it's been checked out. It came from Nozando, and if she won it, there might be something wrong with it. The old one is an upright model. Perhaps, one of us can hold her up or something."

Reid reached over to his side and grabbed a large bottle of pills. "These were in her bag. I've seen her taking them a few times. Actually, more than a few times. She eats them two, maybe three times a day. I can tell because she gets a strange smell afterward, not bad, just different."

Evan arched a brow.

"She smells sterile," Reid said. "Like a medical ward."

"What are they?" Evan asked, taking the bottle and uncapping it. A bunch of small white pills slid into his hand.

"I don't know," Reid frowned. "Anyway, can we analyze them?"

"Not onboard the ship," Evan said, weighing them in his palm before sniffing them. "Maybe Princess Tori could when we get back to Qurilixen."

Reid nodded. "Sit with Jasmine, would you? I need to go and talk to Jarek, and then we'll try the medical booth."

Evan sat down on the bed. Reid went in search of his brother, finding him in the cockpit with Rick and Lochlann. Reid eyed the dragon-shifter warily but said nothing. Lochlann nodded once. Jarek pretended not to sense the obvious tension between the two.

A small brown planet was slowly disappearing along the edge of the viewing screen. Jarek glanced at Reid before nodding at the planet. "Dust ball of a place, Werten. You didn't miss anything."

"How soon can we get back home?" Reid asked.

Jarek glanced at Rick. The man pushed a few buttons on the console in front of him and then answered, "Day if we give it all the ship has, and the course is clear."

Jarek looked back at Reid. "We need to do it?"

Reid nodded. "Jasmine's sick. She won't wake up. I want Tori to take a look at her."

Reid knew his brother needed no more explanation beyond that. Lochlann stood and whispered something to Jarek. Jarek nodded, and the Draig left the cockpit.

"Do it," Jarek said to Rick, as if he hadn't been interrupted.

"Give me twenty minutes to plot the course," Rick answered, turning back to the computer. His brows furrowed in concentration and all traces of the devil-may-care man were gone, replaced by a studious Rick they rarely saw, a Rick bent on doing his job.

Reid nodded to his brother and went to get Jasmine.

2 1

JASMINE YAWNED, opening her eyes. A thin thread of light shone from her feet, slicing through the darkness. The bed was soft and much bigger than Reid's bed on the ship. It took a moment for her to gain her bearings and even then she didn't know where she was.

Did Reid leave her behind? In a moment of panic, she sat up, scrambling to the end of the bed toward the ray of light. Her heart beat fast in her chest. Pushing aside long velvet curtains, she looked out into the room. She definitely wasn't on *The Conqueror* anymore.

The room was huge, bigger than any hotel she'd ever stayed at with Chad and twice as luxurious. The curtains hung all the way around the bed to block out the light. The deep purple color was brilliant in its jewel tone. By the soft, natural light, she construed that it was daytime.

On the wall opposite the bed, a long blue banner hung with a stylized wild cat on it. Was it possible she was at Reid's home? He was a prince, and this room was very palace-like. How long had she slept? Why had he brought her here?

Jasmine felt her head, waiting for a wave of nausea. Wouldn't she be sick after drinking so much? Then, eyeing her wrist, she frowned. She vaguely remembered spraining it when trying to get away from Reid. Though, to look at it now, you wouldn't know it. It was completely healed.

Jasmine closed her eyes, remembering. She'd said some nasty things to Reid and had been scared of what he might do if he caught up to her. If she'd ever spoken to Chad like that, he'd have beaten her within an inch of her life. Truthfully, she'd only said what she had about Reid's manhood because she was hurt that he would pawn her off on someone else. It was as if she was a burden to him. He'd made it clear from the beginning that he didn't want her on his ship.

Jasmine pulled her gaze away from her wrist and looked around the room once more, trying to figure out where she was. More velvet drapes hung over a raised platform. She couldn't see what was hidden behind them. There were long windows behind the curtained enclosure, showing off a blue-green sky. So, she was on a planet, not a starship.

Werten? Had Reid left her behind like she'd asked? She'd never been to that planet so had no idea what it looked like.

A barren, circular fireplace and couches made up the rest of the room. Swallowing nervously, she slid off the bed and stood on the tile floor. She wore a loose fitting gown of dark gray. Its shapeless form draped over her body and bulged oddly in the middle. Her feet were bare.

Gasping, she looked up toward the ceiling. A large chandelier hung beneath a dome of tinted glass. The crystal shards dangled like frozen rain-drops, lighting the large oval room. Staring at it as she walked, she slowly made her way across the floor. It would take five men, arms spread wide, just to make a ring around the stunning light fixture.

Jasmine found no joy in the luxury around her. Seeing a door, she automatically went to it. Wher-ever she was, it felt like a prison. The room reminded her of the gilded bars of her marriage. Pretty, sparkly things did not buy happiness. She'd rather live alone in a hovel than belong to a man in luxury, even if that man was Reid.

The door to the room was unlocked, and she didn't stop to think as she poked her head out. There was no guard, and the hall was empty. She didn't care where she was going, as long as she could go.

Running, Jasmine made her way through the maze of halls. She glanced up at the intricate carvings over the arched doorways, hoping they'd give her a hint as to where she was going. The floors were checkered with gray and white tiles, constructed from a stone much like Old Earth marble. There was also a definite medieval castle influence at play within the basic structure. The walls were decorated with symmetrical tiles inlaid into the walls. They were a brilliant display of colors—blue, red, orange, gold, green. Circular designs seemed to be a central theme in many of the halls. Jasmine didn't stop to admire them.

Rounding a corner, she almost ran over someone. She jumped back, her eyes rounding in horror. A large Var man was before her. He was half-shifted, his features not all cat and not quite human, and he wore a tunic. A light tiger striped fur covered his face and neck with orange and black, mimicked by the fur on his hands. His voice was a gravelly pitch as if garbled by the beginnings of a roar, as he asked, "My lady?"

Jasmine found she couldn't speak. Tears sprung into her eyes. She'd seen Reid shift, but somehow when he did it, she hadn't felt threatened. Now the fear was almost overwhelming. She stared at the tiger-man's teeth, slowly backing away from him.

"My lady?" he insisted, moving as if to touch her.

Jasmine squeaked in fear and ran from him, going full force down the hall. She heard footsteps behind her or thought she did. But when she braved a glance back, the man wasn't following her. The hall was empty. She stopped, shivering violently.

"Jasmine?"

Jasmine jolted in alarm, hearing Reid's voice.

"Jasmine?"

She watched him turn the corner, coming for her. Jasmine backed away, her whole body shaking as she looked him over. She felt shaky, weak, strange. She couldn't explain it, but she was frightened and nervous. However, she was also elated to hear Reid, to know he hadn't abandoned her.

"Jasmine, wait," Reid ordered, catching up to her. He pulled her arm. A strange shock went over her system at the touch. She screamed, jerking away. His face fell as he looked at her, and he didn't try to touch her again. "Jasmine?"

"Where are we?"

"Qurilixen," he said. "At the Var palace, my home. You were sleeping so we brought you here.

If I'd known you'd woken up, I'd have come for you sooner."

Jasmine was confused, overwhelmed with feelings and weak at the same time. She was at his home? The palace? She couldn't concentrate. Her heart was beating too fast. She was sick, getting worse by the second. Just how long had she slept? Days could've passed without taking her pill.

She didn't speak. As she stared at him, it was like seeing his muscular form for the first time. Jasmine had always appreciated his appearance, but now it was as if she was mesmerized by not only the look of him but the texture of him, the subtle nuances of his body as he moved. Why hadn't she seen it before? There was something slow, primitive, and seductive in the way he carried himself, like a hunter stalking his prey. It was as if the marble statue had come to life for her, and she wanted to touch the art instead of merely seeing its beauty.

Did he always look like this?

Dark stubble shadowed his chiseled jaw, giving him an animalistic appeal. Long, dark hair spilled down over his broad shoulders in waves. He always wore his hair down, but why hadn't she noticed the soft texture of it before, the inviting silkiness? She found herself staring at it, really staring at it.

Reid was perfectly built, not too broad and not

too thin. He wore an outfit much like the first one she'd seen him in on Nozando. Only this time black leather bands with threads of gold gripped tightly to his biceps and wrists, wrapping around both of his arms. Why hadn't she looked at it longer that first time? Surely his muscles had been just as exposed. Why hadn't she noticed?

Jasmine's eyes dipped over him. Her mouth was suddenly dry. His black tank shirt was held together by black and gold cross lacing beneath his arms, leaving his sides and waist exposed. Her heartbeat picked up, becoming even wilder in her chest as she looked over his lower half. A belt matched the armband, clinging around his narrow waist. His pants were of the same material as the shirt, soft, yet molding to his firm body. More cross lacing ran over the outside length of his thighs, revealing hard, tanned flesh all the way up his hip. No indention of firm muscle was left to the imagination.

Jasmine could barely breathe. There was something else that didn't require her imagination, the giant length of his arousal. It was full, large and pressing against the tight pants.

"Ah," she said, unable to tear her eyes away. Why hadn't she noticed the particular girth of that part of him before? What was happening? "Ah—*ah*."

A low growl sounded in the back of Reid's

throat. Her gaze whipped up to his. Too late, she realized she'd been staring senselessly at him. His pupils shifted as he took an aggressive step forward. She saw the beast he could become in his eyes, the untamed man with wild passions. The fire of his gaze burned brightly. Unlike before, she was terrified by it. Why had his shifting not bothered her before, only to terrify her now?

Jasmine's stomach hurt and suddenly her whole body throbbed and ached. Something was definitely wrong. Her heart was beating so fast she was sure it would explode.

The low growl sounded in his throat, cutting off her words before she could even think to protest. He took a bold step forward. "I don't know how you were hiding it from me, but I smell you now."

Smell what? What was wrong with him? Why was he looking at her like that? Like he was possessed by the devil?

Jasmine gasped, whimpering as he cornered her against the wall. The hall was empty, and she didn't have anyone she could call for help. He was breathing hard. He didn't touch her, and she was too frightened to push him away. For a long moment, he just stood close. His head tilted and he took deep breaths, obviously smelling her.

"Reid?" she whispered. He lifted his hands and

placed them on the wall on either side of her, trapping her further. "Prince?"

"Pheromones," he whispered, his tone low. His cat eyes stared at her as he leaned forward. The muscles on his arms bulged with the movement, showing just how much of a warrior he really was. His strength, his nearness, even his smell frightened her.

Then he kissed her. His tongue instantly parted her lips. There was no testing this time, no light probe. Reid just went for it, kissing her deep and longingly. His tongue thrust into her gasping mouth. His body leaned closer until his chest brushed over her nipples with their heat.

Jasmine couldn't breathe. Her heart was beating too fast. She felt faint, sick, and her body was beginning to leak. Terrified, by the onslaught of emotions, more emotions than she could ever remember feeling at once, she forced her lips from his, panting and wheezing for breath.

"Stop," Jasmine demanded, breathless. With each rise of her chest, her nipples skimmed his hard muscles. He didn't pull back and the ache she felt where he touched her only made her body all the more sensitive. "My heart is beating too fast."

"Good," Reid said, giving her a cockeyed grin. "It's about time you—"

"I need my pills," she interrupted. His smile only made her heartbeat worse.

"I don't think you should," Reid said.

"I need them," Jasmine said. She grabbed her chest, gasping. Reid's smile faded into one of concern. He pulled back, reaching to touch her arm. She jerked away from him. "Don't touch me. It's not helping. I need my pills."

"Jas—"

"Damn it, Reid," Jasmine cried. Tears streamed down her face. "Don't you see? I think I'm dying. My heart's going to explode. I have to take them."

Reid paled. He stiffly nodded. Without waiting to ask permission, he swept her up into his arms and ran down the hall. Jasmine closed her eyes. His touch wasn't helping at the moment. She concentrated on not feeling. It was no use. Her body felt like it was on fire. This was it. This was the end. She just knew it.

22

"YOU SAY you were married to a rich, successful doctor and yet you're still on a one-a-day pill regimen?" Princess Tori looked Jasmine over in disbelief, as she rubbed her very pregnant stomach.

Princess Vittoria 'Tori' of the Var was married to Prince Quinn, the royal ambassador. Their home was simple in design, colored with rich blues and creams. The wide tiled floor stretched before the front door, elegant and immaculately clean. Reid had deposited Jasmine on a low, wide couch that was on a slightly raised platform in front of a large fireplace. Long pillows were laid out on the floor at her feet, perfect for lounging. He would've still been with her, but for Tori shooing him out of the home. Jasmine was glad. Something about Reid's smell was making it harder to breathe.

Aside from the front, there were no doors in the home. Tall decorative arches in the wall led to a bedroom, a kitchen, and a large office that was being used as a laboratory for Tori. A wall of glass, so thick you couldn't see through it, guarded the bathroom. An inlet next to the fireplace, near the kitchen, led to a dining room. There were enough chairs in it to seat more than a dozen guests.

When Jasmine didn't answer, Tori merely hummed in thought. She sat down on the couch, studying her. The princess looked good pregnant. Her rounded stomach only added to her curves. She wore all black. The slacks were loose around her legs, and the tighter shirt clung to her belly. She had long dark hair and dark eyes.

"I'm not sure why Reid brought me here," Jasmine said, clutching her hand to her chest. Tori had given her some medicinal tea to drink along with one of her pills. It did help somewhat, but she would feel better when they let her have her bottle of medicine back in her hands. Tori informed her that she only had the one pill, as Reid had given it to her to analyze. Jasmine couldn't fathom why Reid would want her pills broken down unless he was worried that she was a drug addict. "I just needed my heart medication. I should be fine in a moment."

Tori opened her mouth to speak, but her front

door opened, stopping her words. Jasmine turned to the door, hoping it was Reid with her bag.

"Tori!" A woman with red-blonde hair that practically gleamed came into the home. Her stomach was also rounded in pregnancy, and her wide blue eyes were gorgeous. She was taller than Tori, statelier in appearance until she grinned like a naughty child and announced, "It's here. It came —*finally!*"

"Ulyssa," Tori scolded with a grin. "You scared me. I swear you've forgotten how to knock."

"What? Oh, sorry. No time for that. We're in a hurry." The dress Ulyssa wore was loose around her waist but was still very revealing for maternity wear. The style was like Reid's, only in dress form. Cross laces worked along the sides of the bodice, baring a subtle hint of her swollen belly.

Spinning to the door, Ulyssa turned and pulled a large cart into the entryway. A second woman pushed on the other side. This one was petite with short, choppy blonde hair. She wore pants and a tank shirt with cross laces. A blue tattoo wound around her upper arm. A streak of purple slashed through the bangs. The lock fell forward over her face, partially hiding her round violet eyes. Jasmine had never seen eyes that color before. She too was pregnant, though she appeared to be a few months behind the other two. Jasmine shivered, wondering if pregnancy was in the water.

"What do you have?" Tori asked, standing. A sheet covered the cart.

Ulyssa grinned and pulled the sheet back with a flourish, announcing, "Lithorian chocolate! I stole every last piece from the cargo ship. Now, we just have to hide it in your laboratory before Kirill finds out its gone. If we're lucky, everyone will just assume it never came."

"Again," the petite blonde added, grinning. Suddenly, her violet eyes found Jasmine on the couch. "What do we have here? Are you her?"

Jasmine looked helplessly at Tori as Ulyssa turned to look at her as well. Tori nodded her head, saying, "Yep, this is her. Jasmine St. Claire."

Ulyssa shook her head. She gave her a serious once over. "So, you're the infamous Jasmine St. Claire."

Jasmine stood, eyeing the woman. She was no longer smiling. In fact, she looked a little upset.

"And you are?" Jasmine asked, with nothing better to say.

"Jasmine," Tori said, not looking as concerned by Ulyssa's apparent displeasure. She crossed over to the cart and picked off a piece of the giant pile of chocolate. Popping it in her mouth, she moaned and said, "This is Queen Ulyssa of the Var, wife to

King Kirill and this," she pointed at the pixie blonde, "is Princess Samantha of the Var…"

"Sam," Samantha corrected, as she too reached for some chocolate on the cart.

Sam, the old captain to Jarek's crew. Jasmine looked at the woman. She didn't look like a captain.

"Wife to Prince Falke, Commander of the Guard," Tori finished as if she hadn't been interrupted. Then, picking another piece of chocolate, she said, "And this is Lithorian chocolate, the best pregnancy food in the world. We hoard it like gold and our husbands have to forgive us because we're pregnant."

"And because they let us have whatever we want," Sam added. "You'd figure big, bad warriors would be, you know…*tougher*. But, alas, no. All we have to do is sigh and pout our bottom lip, and they melt until they're putty in our hands."

"Quite right," Tori nodded in approval. "Though, don't get us wrong. They are tough."

"And not everything exactly melts," Sam winked. Jasmine didn't understand the jest but said nothing.

Tori sighed, a look of longing and pleasure on her face.

"Mm, yeah," Sam nodded in agreement. "Very strong. Very firm and muscular and—"

"Nice to meet—" Jasmine began.

"Sam. Tori," Ulyssa snapped. She looked at the two princesses. "Um, we're mad at this one, remember?"

"Oh, yeah," Sam nodded. She pushed the smile from her face. "Mad. Sorry, forgot. You know, chocolate on the brain."

"Right," Tori nodded in agreement. "Mad."

Jasmine backed away. What was the queen talking about? What had she done?

Ulyssa turned back to Jasmine. "I want to know what you've been doing to our Reid? Mind you, the poor man could stand to be taken down a peg or two, but certainly enough is enough. I mean, either you're in love with him or you're not, but to toy with the man's emotions like this…"

Ulyssa's voice trailed off as she shook her head in disapproval.

"Especially a Var man's emotions," Sam added over a mouthful.

Jasmine didn't move. What were they talking about?

"He used to smile and tell stories," Tori added.

"Now he just sits around and looks all depressed," Sam said. "You guys have been here for a week, and he hasn't laughed once."

"A week?" Jasmine asked.

"You've been asleep," Tori offered. She started

to smile, but quickly caught the look with a guilty glance at Ulyssa. Mumbling, she said, "Still no excuse."

"Jarek tells us you've been with Reid for several days on his ship and have been tormenting the poor man beyond belief, flirting with him and then denying him, sleeping with him and then not sleeping with him. Reid won't eat, doesn't sleep. We don't like it," Ulyssa said.

"It's not like him," Sam added.

"So, what did you do to him?" Tori asked, her voice the most pleasant of the three. "Or what did he do to deserve the punishment?"

Jasmine pressed her hand over her heart. "Nothing. I swear. Prince Jarek is mistaken. I haven't slept with him or flirted with him or any—"

"I knew it," Ulyssa said, suddenly smiling. She turned to the princesses. "I knew Jarek was just trying to make us feel sorry for Reid."

Jasmine contemplated running. She'd heard about mood swings during pregnancy, but these women had to be borderline psychopathic.

"Well, good for you!" Sam said. "It is about time someone said no to that man. I swear he gets more—"

"Ah, Sam," Tori broke in. She shook her head and glanced at Jasmine. "Not helping."

Sam guiltily blushed and didn't finish the

sentence. Jasmine didn't need her to. She'd already heard about Reid's great prowess from Jarek's crew.

"Your highnesses, please—" Jasmine began.

"Ugh, no, don't," Ulyssa held up her hand. "Ulyssa, please, and don't you dare curtsey or I'll behead you."

"She tells everyone the same thing, ignore her," Sam said, shaking her head. "She's just bitchy."

"Language," Tori scolded. Sam rolled her eyes. "Sorry, Jasmine, Reid mentioned that you were… ah…delicate."

"And proper," Sam added, nodding helpfully.

"We don't mean to offend you," Tori explained.

"I'm not," Jasmine said, smiling tentatively. She forgot all about her heart condition. The women might be a little strange, but she found herself liking them. "You haven't offended me."

"Blessed stars. That's a relief," Sam exclaimed. "I was so worried that you were going to be stuck up. It's hard enough for me to keep my mouth shut, but to stop swearing altogether?"

"Sorry to yell at you like that," Ulyssa said. She grabbed a hunk of chocolate and broke it in half as she moved toward Jasmine. "Here, take this. It's heavenly, and it will make you forgive me."

Jasmine reached for the half and nodded. She bit into the corner. The women were right. It was delicious. The smooth chocolate practically turned to cream in her mouth.

"It's just, well, we're very protective of our families, and when one of the brothers is upset, our husbands get edgy. Reid's been..." Ulyssa looked for help from the other two, before shrugging. "He hasn't been Reid since he got back. He's not once visited the harem since he's been here."

Ulyssa sat on the couch. Tori and Sam were right behind her. Tori sat on the chair, and Sam lay on the floor. When Jasmine offered to let her have the couch, she refused.

"And believe me, Reid used to live at the harem," Sam added. "That man has the sex drive of a true animal."

"Sam," Tori scolded, only to add under her breath, "Not helping."

"Or so I'm told," Sam said as a weak cover up. Tori rolled her eyes.

"It's all right," Jasmine assured them. She wondered why just hearing that Reid hadn't had sex with anyone would make her so fluttery inside. It's not like she should care.

"I'm glad to hear you're making Reid wait for you," Ulyssa said. "These Var men are hard-headed. I swear you have to be tough just to put up with them."

"But, don't get her wrong," Tori assured

Jasmine. "They're quite sweet, even if their intentions do get messed up in the act."

"What do you mean?" Jasmine asked.

"Show her the yorkin," Sam said, giggling.

"What is a yorkin?" Jasmine watched the private look they shared.

Tori stood, motioning for Jasmine to follow her. She went to the dining room. In a corner, which couldn't be seen from the front room, stood a horrific stuffed beast. It was twice as tall as Reid and had the course spine of an Earth porcupine along its thick back, looking as sharp as razor blades. His face was just as vicious with long, deadly fangs and eyes that looked eerie, even in its taxidermy state.

"That," Tori said, shivering, "is a yorkin. The thing of nightmares, isn't it?"

"What does that have to do with your husband meaning well?" Jasmine asked.

"There was this big misunderstanding about New Earth dating customs. He read up on them, but kind of messed them up. So, instead of a fierce teddy bear, he gave me a yorkin. The brothers assumed a teddy bear was a hunted offering used to prove Earth men's' prowess and ability to protect their women." Tori giggled. "You should've seen their faces when they brought it to me. It is a gift for the baby. They were so proud of themselves—Reid, Falke, Kirill and my Quinn. According to them, they took it down, just the four of them."

Jasmine smiled. "It's very sweet when you put it like that."

"See what I mean? Sweet men, with a messed up way of showing they care." Tori said, tearing slightly. She fanned her face. "Ah, look at me. All emotional."

"We still haven't convinced them that a teddy bear isn't a dangerous, poisonous, spry little shifter," Ulyssa said from her place on the couch. She laughed. "When they found out I was pregnant, they gave me weapons, sharpened swords and knives."

"Anyway, our point is that they're really stubborn and really hard to put up with at first, but if you stay strong, I'm sure you and Reid will work things out," Sam said.

"Oh, no, I think you have the wrong idea. Reid and I have nothing to work out. There's nothing between us." Jasmine tried to smile, but it was difficult. The women's faces fell. They looked saddened by her admission.

"You don't want him, then?" Ulyssa asked. "Is that what's going on? I mean, we'd never ask you to be with someone you didn't want or care about."

"No, it's not that, it, well, I can't," Jasmine

answered. She couldn't want anyone. "I'm...I'm still married."

"Jarek told us," Ulyssa said. "To an abusive doctor. He also said you'd divorced him."

"No, I left him." Jasmine saw the kindness in their eyes and almost started crying. It had been so long since she'd had other women to talk to. Chad didn't like her having friends. "He would never give me a divorce."

"Oh, sweetie, come sit down," Tori soothed. "Tell us everything. Maybe we can help. We are royalty after all and royalty does have its privileges."

"Why would you want me for Reid if you know I'm married?" Jasmine asked, helplessly following Tori's urgings back to the couch.

"Nothing is ever as it seems. We've learned to trust in fate," Tori said. "Besides, human law doesn't apply here. Technically, it could be argued that you're not married here unless you claim to be and want to be."

"So spill it," Sam demanded.

"Yes, tell us everything," Ulyssa added.

Jasmine found herself surrounded by three emotional, comforting women who started crying along with her as she told them her story. Ulyssa brought over a hunk of chocolate as they talked. Jasmine had no idea what made her tell them what had happened, but just seeing their faces, with nothing to lose or gain but her friendship, she just kept talking. She told them of the beatings, of the abuse, how she discovered on her wedding night that she was frigid, of her medical condition.

Finally when she was done, Tori said, "But, you're not allergic to medical booths. Reid and Evan had to use one on you after you drank too much on the ship. They were terrified that they'd hurt you, but you actually became better."

"They did?" Jasmine gasped. The women nodded.

"That's what we heard," Tori said. "Maybe you're heart isn't bad, maybe Chad lied to you about that as well."

"No," Jasmine said, shaking her head in denial. "When I was younger, I was sickly. I couldn't go to school, and my father hired tutors for me. Aside from a few older servants, Chad was the first man I'd ever seen. He's a good doctor, even if he is horrible as a husband. He was able to diagnose me. It's how we met. My father hired him to come and check me out. I thought I loved him, you know, he was the smart, traveled doctor who saved my life. It was all so glamorous and romantic."

The women continued to talk for hours, sharing stories, getting to know each other. Jasmine listened to how they met their husbands, of the hard time they had given them before they agreed to marry them. Ulyssa had been investigating the new king when she came to the planet. Jasmine already had been told about Sam kidnapping Falke, but it was funny to hear the story straight from the source. Tori had done her best to keep Quinn at bay, but he'd been persistent.

She also learned of the dreaded King Attor. Reid's father was not a very pleasant man, and Jasmine was secretly glad she would never meet him. King Kirill seemed like he'd be a much better ruler. Though, truth be told, she didn't want to meet him either. If Reid was grumpy, and the royal brothers blamed her for it, then they might not like having her around.

The women also swore their husbands would never marry anyone else, like Attor's harem of over a hundred women. Jasmine believed them. She could see the love on the women's faces and was jealous of it. She wondered which route Reid would take and concluded that he'd probably follow in his father's footsteps.

Jasmine had never been included in such a group before and wasn't sure what to think. The women were friendly and open, answering her questions about the Var culture. After several hours had passed, she felt as if she really knew them.

"So what happens if you don't take your pills?"

Sam asked, breaking the comfortable silence that had fallen over them.

"I get weak and fluttery. It's been getting worse. I think my condition is becoming more severe." Jasmine gave a weak shrug.

"How so?" Tori asked, looking very much like the scientist she was.

"It's embarrassing," Jasmine said.

"No, what's embarrassing is the size of my butt in this dress," Ulyssa said, snacking on the chocolate even as she spoke.

The woman laughed. Jasmine wiped her eyes. Ulyssa had looked so sincere as she said it.

"I hate being pregnant," Ulyssa grumped, still chuckling.

"I love it," Tori said. She tossed a piece of chocolate in her mouth. "We can eat whatever we want and get fat, and no one cares."

"I care," Ulyssa grumbled. "Kirill's baby keeps kicking me."

"You haven't thrown up," Sam said, rubbing her stomach.

"It can't be any worse than my problem," Ulyssa said. "Now, spill it, Jas. Tori's as good as a doctor, and maybe she can help you."

"All right. My heart beats incredibly fast," Jasmine said. The women nodded for her to continue. "That's nothing new, but it's been getting worse lately. And I feel fluttery and flushed, and my limbs go all weak on me until I can hardly stand up on my own. My stomach hurts, and I feel like I might throw up or something."

"Sounds like you're pregnant," Sam chuckled. "I'm with you so far."

"Not pregnant," Jasmine assured them. "I know that for a fact."

"What else?" Tori asked, her face serious.

"I've been, um, leaking," Jasmine said. "A lot."

"Leaking?" Sam asked, furrowing her brows in confusion.

"How do you mean?" Ulyssa leaned forward.

"You know, leaking," Jasmine motioned down to her thighs. "Not all the time, but randomly. It's… This is so humiliating." Jasmine hid her face in her hands and made a weak noise.

"Like your period?" Ulyssa asked.

Jasmine sat up. The three women were sharing a knowing look. "Same place, only different."

"Um, Jasmine…" Tori smirked, covering her mouth with her hand to keep from laughing. Jasmine's eyes widened. Why were they laughing at her? "Is Chad the only, *only* man you've been even slightly attracted to in the past?"

Jasmine nodded. "Like I said, he was essentially the only man I'd ever met that was from my own age group. I've met a few doctors and such over the last four years. Why do you ask?"

"And does this leaking seem to happen when Reid's around?" Tori persisted.

"Well, yes, it started the same day I met him, why?" Jasmine looked at them. If they hadn't been talking for hours, she might have started to cry at their reaction to her life-threatening illness. "Do you think I'm allergic to Reid? I have gotten a little woozy the few times he's tried to kiss me. And when he gets close, the symptoms become worse."

"Allergic?" Tori repeated. "No, sweetie, I don't think you're allergic."

"What, then?" Jasmine studied them carefully. "What? If you know what it is, please tell me."

"Happens to me all the time," Tori said. "Each time I see my husband walk into a room."

"Me too," Sam said, grinning.

"Me three," Ulyssa agreed, sighing heavily. "It happens when I just think of my husband."

"Is it a Var thing? What is it? Tell me." Jasmine's heart was beating fast again, and she was worried. "Please."

"Jasmine," Ulyssa said, leaning forward. "You're not sick though it does sound like you're in bad shape."

"What?" Jasmine persisted.

"You need to let Reid continue kissing you.

He's not my type, but it sounds like he's got your cure," Tori said, giggling. She shared another knowing look with the other two. "Trust me. Let him keep kissing you next time, no matter what happens. You'll feel a whole lot better afterward."

"But…?" Jasmine was still confused. What did Reid's kisses have to do with her heart?

"Oh, blessed stars," Sam exclaimed. Jasmine's eyes widened. Bluntly, the woman continued, "What we're saying is, you're not sick, Jas. You're just really horny. You need to get laid, and it sounds like Reid's the man to give it to you."

23

REID LIFTED HIS HEAD, looking at his brothers. It was good to have them all together. They'd come to the old council hall often as children, having made it their private fort. Now that they were older, they still convened there to relax and talk in private. There were no windows in the old section of the castle, not even a little slit. Deep-set, antique cushioned chairs were placed around a large, intricately carved fireplace. A fire burned brightly, giving the room light and warmth.

Quinn lounged on the long pillows that lined the red carpeted floor. Kirill sat near the fireplace, resting his chin on his fist as he stared absently at the flames. He smiled occasionally at some of Jarek's tales of space. Falke sat in a chair to the king's right. The commander's body was stiff with rigid discipline. After a half century of command, he'd become hard and unforgiving. And, only after a few months of knowing Sam, he'd become softer.

Reid noticed how all three of his married brothers seemed to have a contentment about them. They looked happy. Maybe it was because he'd been gone, but he saw a change in them. The men were in love. Reid wasn't sure if this disappointed him or made him jealous.

Thinking of Jasmine, he frowned. She'd preoccupied his thoughts since the moment he'd first met her. His frown deepened and he slouched in his chair. He'd kissed her, and she looked like she wanted to throw up on him. How could that be? He'd smelled her desire, hadn't he? His gut tightened, and he felt as if an unseen force was kicking him repeatedly. Maybe the smell hadn't been for him. Could it be that her arousal wasn't of his doing? Had she seen someone else? Met someone who did that to her? Made her feel? Reid bit his lip. That last kick went straight to his heart. Too bad it didn't finish him off.

"Ugh, Reid, stop brooding," Kirill grumbled. "You're making my head spin. Just go and tell her you like her already."

Reid frowned and automatically answered, "Who?"

At the word, his brothers shared a knowing

look. Reid knew damned well who. But if Jasmine didn't like him in such a way, he wasn't about to announce his interest in her to the world. Wouldn't his brothers get a kick out of that? The great lover turned down by the one woman he desired the most in all his years. Even Reid could grudgingly admit it was poetic justice.

"Oh, I'm sorry, I meant Jasmine," Kirill said. "I forget you have so many women. Though, if you're not taken with her, Navid did mention that he ran into her in the hall earlier. He has asked permission to court her if she's not already spoken for. I told him I'd ask you first since she is your ward."

Navid? Reid stiffened, his face tightening. Navid had seen Jasmine in the hall? Was that smell for Navid, then?

"Reid," Quinn asked, a small laugh in his voice, "is anything wrong?"

Reid bit the inside of his mouth, drawing blood. Stiffly, he said, "No. Everything's fine."

"Then shall I tell Navid to go ahead?" Kirill asked.

"No," Reid growled a little too quickly. The brothers looked at him, each trying not to smirk and failing miserably. Reid glanced at Jarek, willing his twin not to join in the conversation, as he said, "She's married."

His brothers already knew as much. For some

reason, Reid hadn't wanted them thinking the worst of her, so he'd explained about her bruises and how he wasn't sure if the marriage was still binding. Quinn was little to no help on the issue of human marriage rites. Reid sighed. Some ambassador Quinn was.

To Reid's aggravation, Jarek did speak. "We all know that human and federation law isn't recognized here. She's not mated to anyone. I don't see why Navid can't pursue her unless you don't want him to. In fact, maybe we can hold a contest and have the men fight for the honor to pursue her."

"Ah, now that is an idea," Falke said, nodding thoughtfully. "It's been a long while since we've held a tournament. Now that we're at peace the men would be up for the sport."

Sacred cats!

Reid growled, instantly standing. He stormed from the room. His brothers' laughter followed him out into the hall.

24

Jasmine agreed to a tour of the Var palace. Ulyssa didn't walk with them, claiming to feel a little fatigued. She was in the last trimester of her pregnancy and tired easily. Sam and Tori showed Jasmine around. The palace was beautiful.

"I have a theory that the Var somehow had contact with ancient Old Earth," Tori explained as she pointed out some of the Moroccan like features of the tiled artwork. "As soon as I finish up some of the ecological tests I'm running on the shadowed marshes, I'm going to look into it. Quinn claims he's never read anything about it one way or another in their old scrolls."

"Ugh, not again," Sam grumbled. "Jasmine, tell her you don't care."

"Well, I..." Jasmine stuttered, not wanting to be rude.

"She doesn't care," Sam said, grinning at Tori. Jasmine said nothing.

Tori rolled her eyes heavenward and led the way outside. The air was nice and cool. Before them was a long wide walkway made of smooth stone, adjoining the palace. Jasmine automatically looked up. The castle stood tall against the blue-green sky. Square turrets reached high into the heavens.

"It's outstanding," Jasmine whispered.

"Yeah, these barbarians have a few talents, don't they?" Sam grinned. She motioned for Jasmine to follow. "If you think the palace is neat, come check out the city."

They moved to stand along the stone rail. The large Var city surrounded the palace. It rolled down the countryside from the front gate. The homes were constructed of gray bricks, contrasting with the red earth. They were of beautiful workmanship, though simplistic in their rectangular design. People walked along the top of their houses, as well as on the bustling maze of earthen streets.

There were the three suns peeking from the clouded sky, two yellow, and one blue. Apparently, the planet only experienced darkness one night a year because of the suns. For that reason, many places within the palace didn't have lighting beyond the ceiling domes and fireplaces.

"You have a beautiful home," Jasmine said quietly. She really did like the two princesses and the queen. Taking a deep breath, she smelled the fresh air. What was she doing here? Where would she go next? Suddenly, she didn't want to leave. Qurilixen was tucked away in the Y quadrant. The Federation Military hadn't shown up again to look for her on Jarek's ship. The thoughts gave her hope. It was possible Chad would never think to look for her here. If she were lucky, he'd think she was in the Nozando wilderness. It would be easy to conclude she had starved to death or was attacked by wild animals with no part of her left behind to discover.

"What are you thinking?" Tori asked, searching her face.

Jasmine glanced at the women with their pregnant bellies. Those were a lot of what-ifs. Even if the possibility of Chad showing up here were remote, she couldn't risk it. She couldn't risk any of these people getting hurt because they'd been kind to her. Plus, with the Medical Mafia interested in hiring Chad, he might have more connections than she'd first thought. It hit Jasmine that she didn't know the man at all.

"I was just thinking of leaving," Jasmine said.

"Do you have a transport station anywhere on the planet? I have some jewels I can barter with."

"Leaving?" Tori asked, she leaned over and glanced at Sam.

"Ah," Sam said, quickly. She hesitated. "Um, don't you like it here?"

"Well, yes, it's lovely, but—" Jasmine said.

"But, what?" Tori interrupted. "You don't like lovely places?"

"No, no, I do, it's just—" Jasmine was again cut off.

"You're afraid you don't belong here?" Sam interrupted.

Jasmine looked helplessly at the two women. "Well, I don't belong—"

"Small matter," Tori said, hooking her arm.

"Yeah, easily fixed," Sam said.

"What do you mean?" Jasmine looked at both women. Maybe her first assumption had been correct. Maybe they were all crazy.

"I think Reid should explain that one," Sam said. "You just let him do that kissing thing we talked about."

"No, you don't understand," Jasmine tried to shake her head as she pulled her arms away. Both women watched her back away from them.

"Care to explain it to us then?" Sam asked, putting her hands on her hips.

Tori crossed her arms and tilted her head to the side. "Are you trying to say you don't like Reid?"

"No, he's been very kind," Jasmine's whole body shook. Were women friends usually this nosy? She'd just met them. Maybe she should've been more careful about what she told them. Her heart skipped a little strangely. "I think I need my medicine. I'm going in."

Sam stepped in her way. "What are you hiding?"

"N-nothing," Jasmine stuttered. She again tried to skirt past them.

"It's Chad, isn't it?" Tori said. "You think he'll come here for you. Reid won't let him take you."

"He won't?" Jasmine asked in surprise. "I mean…"

She couldn't even think of a good cover. There was no need. Tori and Sam were nodding their heads.

"No, he's claimed you. You're under his protection," Tori said.

"Reid never claims women. He cares for you," Sam added.

"He does?" Jasmine wondered why she cared and all the while knowing she really did. "I'm sure it's just an honor thing."

"I think it's a sex thing." Sam giggled.

Tori lightly hit the woman's arm and shook her

head. "Ignore her. Her pregnancy hormones are acting up again."

Jasmine was about to protest further when she caught a movement out of the corner of her eyes. Reid stood by the entryway, his arms crossed. She snapped her mouth shut and made a weak noise. The two women instantly turned to where she stared. Jasmine didn't pay attention to them. Her heartbeat picked up again, and the funny feeling in her stomach was back. Somehow, knowing she wasn't dying made her less nauseous, but the fear was still there. Being sick, she could deal with. Being attracted to an experienced man like Reid, was something she couldn't handle.

Jasmine swallowed nervously, taking in his lean form. He moved lazily toward them, walking like a man who knew he attracted women. He was confident, strong, and usually easygoing, though to see his stoic face now, one wouldn't know it. This was a man who would naturally expect a lover that could perform, at least on a basic level.

Jasmine grew worried. If she allowed him to kiss her, where did she put her hands? Did she make the first move? Did she let him? Did she have to tell him she wanted him to do more than kiss? And if she had to speak during all this, what exactly did she have to say?

The nausea came back but for a whole new

reason. Nerves bundled in her stomach and she suddenly felt like she couldn't breathe. She gasped, covering her mouth. Knowing she was going to get sick, she ran toward the palace. Reid stopped as she hurried by him, her hand covering her mouth. His eyes widened in surprise, and his mouth opened, but no words came out.

Jasmine didn't stop. How could she? Even if she didn't get sick, she'd just embarrassed herself. And, worst of all, if she got this nervous just by looking at Reid, how in the world would she ever make it past the kissing part?

25

REID BLINKED in surprise as Jasmine ran away from him. He watched her, on the verge of going after her to see what was wrong, when Tori grabbed his arm.

"Let her be," Sam said.

"We need to talk," Tori added.

"What did you say to her?" Reid demanded. He pulled his arm away, careful not to jerk his pregnant sister-by-marriage too roughly.

"Just let her go for now," Tori insisted. "I need to talk to you."

"But—"

"She's just having a little panic attack," Tori said. "She'll be fine. In fact, I think you might want to hear what I have to say."

Reid was still worried. Jasmine had appeared

pale. He wanted to chase her, already detecting which way she'd have gone by picking up her scent. "Tori, I appreciate——"

"Sacred cats. It's about Jasmine." Tori yelled, shaking her fist at him when he tried to storm away. Reid lifted a brow, giving her a strange look as she cussed like a true Var. Tori wrinkled her nose at him.

"Fine," he said gruffly. "What do we need to talk about?"

"I'm going to go see what the guys are up to," Sam said. Reid knew she meant her old crew. The last he'd seen them, they were in the banquet hall joking about visiting the harem. Reid thought about joining them. The women would gladly welcome one of their favorite princes back, and he'd already received invitations from them. Gods knew he could use the physical release, but for some reason, he found excuse after excuse as to why he couldn't go.

Looking at Tori's face, he frowned. Reid loved the closeness of his family, but sometimes he wanted to wring all of their meddling necks. Growling, he said, "You're just loving this, aren't you?"

She smirked, but said, "I don't know what you're talking about."

"Liar," he grumbled though he smiled slightly

to lighten the words. "I gave Quinn a hard time about the two of you when you were…doing whatever it is you two did."

"You did?" Tori asked in surprise. "Quinn never told me that."

"Oh, well, I'm fine with you now," Reid said, flashing an irresistible grin.

"Gee, thanks," Tori laughed. "How is it you are so smooth with the ladies?"

Reid's face fell. He glanced at where Jasmine had disappeared.

"I wanted to talk to you about Jasmine's pills," Tori said. "They're not what she thinks they are."

Reid tensed. Tori slowly walked toward the railing, urging Reid to follow her to where they could look over the city. "What are they?"

"It's hard to explain. You know nef, right," Tori said, "and how it makes a Var man feel when you take it."

"It calms us, or rather our sexual aggression and needs," Reid answered, nodding. "You're saying she's taking nef?"

"Not exactly." Tori took a deep breath. "This stuff is like nef times five hundred. Not only has she not been able to feel pleasure, she hasn't felt pure joy or even happiness. It's as if her emotions were purposefully kept in a catatonic state for the last four years."

"Why would…" Reid shook his head. Why would anyone give her that and then lie to her and tell her she was frigid?

"I don't know. But since she was asleep for so long, she hasn't been taking them. My guess is her emotions are waking up and are going to be pretty frazzled until she gets a handle on them. Think of it as an imprisoned child seeing the outside world for the first time. Whatever illness she had when she was little, she doesn't have now. It's been fixed long ago. That bastard kept her doped up. My guess, he's just plain sick in the head and liked having a wife he could control."

"You're sure?"

"I read the report from *The Conqueror's* medical booth six times. I'm sure. She's not sick, and she's not dying," Tori assured him. "Her reactions right now, especially every time you are near, are going to be difficult for her to process. In fact, she might think she's sick when she's just…"

Tori made a face, blushing. Reid frowned. "What?"

"You know, *aroused,*" Tori said.

"Oh?" Reid said, and then it dawned on him what Tori was telling him. Jasmine was aroused by him. A wide grin spread over his face as he said, more confidently, "*Ohhh.*"

Tori laughed. "Glad to see you're catching on."

"Thanks, Tori," Reid said, kissing her cheek. He grinned, feeling hopeful for the first time in a long time. Jasmine wanted him! "You've been a big help."

"Wait, there's more," Tori said. Reid tensed. She was toying with her bottom lip. That was never a good sign. "Those pills are most readily found through a connection to the Medical Alliance for Planetary Health."

"The Mafia?"

"Yes. The same."

"Like givres in the swamp, it seems as if those bastards just keep popping up." Reid cursed, shaking his head in irritation. "I liked it better when they avoided our part of the galaxy."

"Jasmine seems nervous and about ready to bolt off this planet the first chance she gets. We thought it best not to concern her about our fears, but Ulyssa and I both think it is possible Doctor St. Claire could come here for her. A narcissist like that is not going to take kindly to her running out on him."

Reid balled his hand into fists. "He can't have her."

"Take her to your home. She'll not be found there. Let Ulyssa contact her old mission director. If the Medical Mafia comes anywhere near here, they'll see them. Besides, I think it will be good for her to get away from all of the palace activity. If she can focus on you and how she feels, without prying eyes, she might adjust easier to being off the medicine."

Reid nodded. "We'll go this evening."

"We figured you might," Tori smiled. "Ulyssa is having clothes, soaps, everything a woman needs readied for her as we speak. She lied and told Jasmine she was going to take a nap, but we figured you might not know what to get for a woman's personal needs. Everything will be left outside your house for her."

"Thank you," Reid said. He made a move to go into the palace. "I owe you one, Tori."

"Actually," Tori laughed. "Our motives are purely selfish."

Reid tensed, feeling her coming closer to him.

"We all want to watch the mighty Reid fall," Tori said, lightly touching his arm as she walked past him. Reid didn't answer as he stared after the princess. Her laughter rang out as she strolled away.

26

Jasmine quirked a brow. Why was Reid looking at her like that? With that devilish smile on his face and the gleam in his dark, handsome eyes? If she didn't know better, she'd think he was taking her out into the forest to do away with her.

Narrow, uneven trails wound through the thicket of colossal trees. Many of their trunks were bigger around than most Earth homes. Jasmine felt really tiny walking beneath their wide branches. Strange yellow ferns grew over the red Qurilixen soil. The blue-green haze of the planet's atmosphere shone through the gigantic leaves of the trees.

They were walking to Reid's home in the forest. Tori informed her that she didn't have a choice. Her pills were lost somewhere. Jasmine never received a straight answer on it, and the only root that could mimic the effects of the drug was in the forest near Reid's home. Luckily, they'd left the palace so fast that she'd only been presented briefly to the male members of the royal Var family. The brothers were just as handsome as Reid and their faces just as stoic. They were definitely creatures she didn't want mad at her.

"So are the Draig out here?" Jasmine asked, glancing around. She'd heard that the Draig were dragon-shifters though she'd never seen Lochlann shift. Thinking of it, she unconsciously moved closer to Reid. He glanced down at her. His arm brushed over her shoulders. Jasmine tensed and pulled away. She wasn't sure which was more terrifying at the moment, the thought of shifting dragons or Reid touching her.

"What would you do if they were?" he asked, stopping to look at her. There was nothing around them but trees. Jasmine shivered. Why was he looking at her like that?

"I need my medicine," she said.

Reid turned his eyes from her. "I told you. No more medicine. It's all gone."

"I don't believe you—"

"Are you trying to start a fight with me?" He flashed her another mischievous look.

"Yes," she admitted, before biting her tongue.

Why did she just say that? What was happening to her brain? He grinned a sexy little grin and continued walking.

Reid's home was deep within the forest, north of the palace. There were no royal guards with them as they walked. When she'd asked about it, Reid had just laughed at her. And damn him! It was a great laugh that made her shiver from head to toe.

"We're close," he said, breaking the silence. His voice was low and a little husky. When she looked at him, he again smiled. It was a roguish look, one that left her even shakier than the sound of his laugh. "Just a few trees ahead."

"Trees?" Jasmine asked in surprise. "Are you saying you live on top of a tree?"

His smile widened. "Inside a tree, actually."

Jasmine laughed, sure he was joking. However, as he stopped by a particularly large trunk, her laughter died.

Reid's home was built above ground, inside one of the colossal trees of the forest. Pushing away a thick overhanging of branches near a large stone bolder, he revealed a narrow staircase carved into the side of the rock. The rock was pressed flat to the tree trunk.

Reid led the way up the steps and around the base, making it half way around until they came to a door carved into the trunk. A small window was fitted into the wood. A dark drape hung over it on the inside. Taking a key from his pocket, Reid unlocked the door and gave it a light nudge. It soundlessly swung open.

Jasmine had heard stories of how old redwoods on Old Earth could have a building carved into them, but she'd never imagined the stories to be factual. If she weren't witnessing it for herself, she would never have believed it.

Inside, the tree had been hollowed out, forming polished wood floors with gorgeous natural swirling designs, and walls carved to look like rustic planks. The ceiling, also carved from the wood, spiraled high revealing that the home had at least two levels. Without waiting for an invitation, she walked in and spun around in a slow circle before exploring.

Two stairs led up from the small opening of a front foyer to the main living area. Light filtered in from outside through little holes in the ceiling, reflecting off a small glass and mirror dome. In the center of the first floor was a comfortable living area, adorned with thick red couches and matching chairs, and throw rugs woven with the same designs that were popular in the palace.

The main level was circular, except along two flat sides where walls remained, and rooms were carved out behind them. An intricate door was carved into one of the flat walls, leading to a bath-room on one side. The other wall had an opening in it with a bar and barstools, revealing a large kitchen behind it.

"Impressed?" he asked from behind her.

Jasmine turned to him, nodding. "It's... Wow. I mean, it's so much cozier than the palace. I just assumed your house would be all..."

"All what?" Reid asked. She watched him grab a bag from outside the door and bring it in.

"Well, you know, less comfortable, more deca-dent." Jasmine shrugged. Was it suddenly hot in the room? She felt a little hot. And was Reid coming closer? It felt like he was coming closer. Jasmine grabbed the front of her shirt and began to fan herself.

"The bedroom is upstairs," Reid offered, walking with the bag to the staircase tucked in the corner of the room.

Jasmine tensed. The? As in one bedroom?

"Coming?" he asked, winking at her before going up.

Let him kiss you. Jasmine instantly told her brain to shut up. It didn't listen. *Let him keep kissing you. Follow him upstairs.*

Jasmine followed him up the enclosed staircase. It curved slightly before opening up into the floor of a spacious bedroom. She gasped, trying to instantly hide the reaction behind a weak cough, and waved her hand through the air as if the room was dusty.

Outside the bedroom, a long balcony was carved into the second level of the home. She could see it beyond a long, narrow window carved in the side. They were up high, near the branches of the trees. The soft light shone in over the bedroom from the window. A woodstove was along the other wall on a platform. There was a huge bed, big enough to fit five Reids. She wondered what a man did in a bed that big, and who he did it with. Jasmine was instantly jealous.

The bed was covered with a red coverlet. The wood theme of the room was accented with red and browns, very natural and earthy in design. A huge whirlpool tub was by a wall. She saw an open door leading to another bathroom with a stall shower. Fur rugs lined the floor near the wood stove. Reid threw the bag on the floor next to the bed. The only thing that didn't fit was the giant viewing screen.

"Like it?" Reid asked when he saw her looking at it. "I just had it installed."

"What for?" Jasmine asked, eyeing it. "Communicating with the palace?"

"No," Reid said. "For action."

Jasmine looked at him, confused. "Action?"

"Yes. Old Earth films," Reid said. Then grinning wickedly, he added, "And learning documentaries."

"Documentaries?" Jasmine repeated. "You mean you watch Earth movies on this thing?"

He nodded. She watched his face as he pointed out his speakers. The man was positively excited about it. "Sam introduced us to them. She even had the movies programmed in for us. Though, Viktor had to do the documentaries. I hadn't had a chance to play with it much before we had to leave for Nozando."

"You mean the Galaxy Playmates' mansion," Jasmine said, pressing her lips tightly together.

Why did she say that aloud? What was wrong with her mouth? She couldn't get it to shut up.

"Jealous?" he asked, stepping closer.

Jasmine wished he wouldn't look at her like that, all dreamy eyed and hot. Shivering, she took an involuntary step back. He looked primitive in that moment, stalking, wild. Her heartbeat picked up but for once she was too lost in his gaze to notice or care. So what if she died in this moment. What better way to go?

Say something clever, Jasmine.

"No, why would I be jealous?"

Not so clever, Jasmine. She felt like smacking herself upside the head.

"Then, you're not jealous?" he asked. Why was he still coming closer? Jasmine looked at his mouth, all too aware that they were alone in the room. She shivered. Would he kiss her now?

"Yes. No. I think I need some of that herb stuff. I'm feeling a little lightheaded."

Reid laughed. "I have a confession to make."

Jasmine didn't move. How could she? Reid came closer, reaching to cup her face in his hands. His touch was warm, gentle, caressing. She automatically leaned forward for his kiss, pursing her lips to him. "Yes?"

"I'm not going to give you any herbal stuff," Reid whispered. She blinked, barely processing his words. He smelled great, the way a man should smell. He looked good too, very sexy. His lips curled into the most provocative smile she'd ever seen. "In fact, there's nothing wrong with your heart. You're not sick. Those pills only dulled your reactions, your emotions. They did nothing for your heart. Everything you feel is normal and right."

Jasmine couldn't breathe. Looking into his eyes, as they steadily held her gaze, she knew he was telling the truth. Perhaps, she'd always known it. It was easy to believe she was sick, easier to take the numbness that came with her medicine. It had been easier than feeling, easier than knowing her husband hadn't wanted her, not really.

"Now that you know, ask me to kiss you," Reid insisted. His lips were close. It would be nothing to close the distance. "Tell me you want me."

Jasmine nodded weakly. Her voice was trapped in her throat. She did want him, wanted him so much that she'd lied to herself about it. Even so, she was scared of what she felt, of how it would be, frightened that she'd lose control or make an ass of herself.

She couldn't stop herself as she lifted up. Her eyes on his, she tentatively kissed him. He gasped, holding completely still as she rubbed her mouth along his. Drawn to taste him, she dipped her tongue along the seam of his lips. He tasted good. Really good.

Moaning, she gripped the sides of his face and pulled him closer. He finally moved, working his mouth passionately against hers. A low sound answered her needy call. He ran his hands down the side of her body, skimming her breasts as he lifted her off the ground. With her body pressing tightly to his, he cupped her butt, holding her firmly against his erection.

A jolt of electricity went through her system. Her body was on fire. Jasmine began tearing at her clothing, trying to part Reid from his at the same time. He gasped at her aggressiveness and dropped her back to the ground. Suddenly, his hands were helping her, practically ripping the shirt over his head as he broke the kiss long enough to strip. Jasmine pulled off her baggy gown, tossing it aside. She stood before him in her bra and panties.

Was it supposed to feel like this? Be like this? All hot and urgent? So frantic that she couldn't think, just react.

Reid saw her breasts and groaned. A wave of excitement crashed over her at the primal sound. His pants slid from his hips, leaving him naked. Her eyes instantly went down to his lower stomach. There, in a bed of dark hair, rose his desire for her. It strained, almost as if it had a life of its own.

"Sacred cats," he swore softly. "Don't stare at me like that, woman. My control is hard won as it is."

Jasmine made a weak noise by way of an answer, on the verge of covering herself up when he swept her off her feet. In several long steps, they were at the bed. Reid laid her on her back. His eyes were shifted, the pupils stretched, reminding her of just how wild he could become.

"Fire," he called. The stove lit up, casting a soft orange light over the bed.

Primitive noises came from his throat as he kissed her neck, grazing her delicate flesh with his teeth. His hands massaged her breasts, rubbing them through her lacy bra, pushing them up as his mouth moved lower to devour the hardened nipples. He sucked a breast deep into his hot mouth, kissing it passionately. Jasmine wiggled beneath him, her legs working between his naked thighs. His arousal pressed into her lace panties, searing her stomach with its fire. She was wet for him. Her whole being focused on his, the sounds he made, his smell, his warmth.

The urgency was too much. Jasmine pushed his shoulder, wanting to touch him, needing to feel him inside. His body had her pinned, and she couldn't move freely against him. At her shove, he made a sound of frustration and pulled away.

"No, please, Jasmine. Don't make me stop. Not again," he said, as he ceased his passionate kisses to her chest. He took several deep breaths, and she could feel him trying to pull away from her. His body was stiff, and he stopped moving. "All right, just give me…a…a minute."

"Take your minute." Jasmine wasn't sure what had gotten into her, but she was moving on pure instinct. Pushing Reid onto his back, she took him by surprise. "Let me know when you can catch up."

Straddling his waist, she ran her hands over his neck and chest, playing with his smaller nipples. His eyes rounded in shock at her words. The dark depths were streaked heavily with green. She liked the shifting of his eyes. They excited her. She liked the primitive, streamlined way his body moved. He was stalking, graceful, terribly sexy.

When she touched him, it was as if she'd never felt flesh before. It was firm, muscled, and wonderful. The texture of him burned into her hands. She couldn't feel him fast enough. In her urgency, her nails raked him. He arched, groaning loudly in pleasure. A claw grew from his fingertip, and he sliced through the front of her bra.

Jasmine gasped at the motion but was beyond thinking. The danger of him excited her. She liked knowing the beast ran beneath his surface, wild, barely controlled by the man. Reid urged her down to him, bringing a ripe breast to his mouth. He again sucked her deeply, running his tongue in torturous circles over the tip. Her nipple ached and with each pass she jerked violently, feeling it all the way to her toes. Moisture dampened her panties as she naturally rubbed herself along his toned stomach.

"Reid," she panted. Her hands braced the bed as she rubbed harder, feeling the sting of desire building inside her slick folds. Her slit glided over his rigid stomach. She worked faster. Her clit rubbed through the lace, a pleasurable combination of heat and rough. It felt so good, she couldn't stop.

Between that and his mouth, she felt the first wave hit her. Her limbs tensed and she shivered violently. Jasmine was so shocked she could only stiffen and let the pleasure overtake her, jerking her body from head to toe. Even her hair seemed to come to life. Breathing hard, she pulled back, her eyes wide.

"What…was that?" she asked, breathless.

Reid laughed, but when her face remained serious, his smile faded as he asked, "You're joking, right?"

Jasmine shook her head in denial. "Can you do it to me again?"

Reid groaned as she leaned back over him offering her breast to his mouth. She wiggled along his stomach, feeling the heat curl inside her once more. His hand slid over her hips, slicing through her panties. He tugged them from behind. Jasmine groaned. The feel of his flesh on hers was even better than the lace. She pushed up, liking the look of his dark body contrasting with the orange from the fire. The light from the balcony streamed in, but it was getting darker in the forest. His eyes bore up into her, still dangerously slit with the green of his cat form.

"I like your stomach," she said, sitting on it and moving back and forth in hopes of feeling the intense pleasure again. The smooth texture of him made her glide with more ease than before.

"I can tell," he answered, his voice hoarse. Then, taking her hips, he pushed her down. His erection pressed into her from behind, searing her cleft, parting her intimately. "But, why don't you try this instead."

Jasmine gave a small yelp of surprise as Reid tossed her onto her back. He devoured her body with his hands and mouth. His palms cupped her breast, lifting it to meet his lips so he could suck her nipple. Animalistic sounds of possession came from him, vibrating against her. He nipped her skin only to soothe the irritation with his long tongue. Jasmine could only hold onto the bed as he had his way with her, pleasuring her. Then, when his mouth worked lower to make its way between her thighs, she tensed. Reid growled, pushing her legs apart.

"Mine," he said, possessively. His beast was evident in that voice and so help her, she liked it.

Pleasure rolled over her at his words and in that moment she would've consented to anything. His tongue parted her wet folds as he lapped her cream. Fingers dug into her hips, holding her fast to his mouth. Then, as he sucked her clit, she felt the tremors start anew. Jasmine tossed her legs over his shoulders, arching up into him for more. He obliged, slipping a finger up inside her only to wiggle it back and forth. The pressure caused a torrent of cream to flood his hand. Jasmine came, crying out his name as the force of what he did overtook her. Then, when her body could tremble no more, he moved above her.

Jasmine reached weakly for his face. Reid didn't kiss her. Instead, he looked deep into her eyes, as if she were the only person in the whole universe. His hair fell over her shoulder like a dark curtain, making it all the more intimate as their harsh breath mingled in the little alcove. He watched her face, taking in every one of her reactions. She felt his shaft probing her, stretching her muscles to fit him. With so much control that it drove her mad, he pushed into her slick passage, filling her body by small, agonizing degrees. Her eyes rolled in her head as she waited for the moment he'd stake complete claim to her.

Stirring and rubbing along his entire frame as he held her trapped, Jasmine could feel the need in him to go fast and vigorously. But Reid restrained the beast inside him and took her gently. For all his jokes and wicked looks, he was a tender lover. Running her hands over his arms, she learned the slow rhythm he set forth and felt the tension building within her anew.

Reid couldn't take his eyes off Jasmine. She was so beautiful, her slender body, her rounded breasts, the dark nipples budded for his attention. It was sweet the way she kept staring at him as if the idea of hiding herself never once occurred to her.

At first, her aggressiveness surprised him, but as they progressed he saw the almost innocent quality in her, such as when she reached her orgasm. She'd been so shocked by it that he didn't know whether to laugh or cry for her. The sad thing was her climax had only been a tiny orgasm compared to what he could give her, *would* give her. So, he'd gone down on her, licking her addictive cream and making her come against his face.

Sacred cats, it had been sweet to watch, to taste.

Now, as he slowly eased his body into her, stretching her wider, he groaned. He kept his weight off her, bracing his hands on either side of her tiny form. Her passage was tight, almost virginal. It felt too damned good, but regardless of what he wanted, he found that for once he was focused on a woman's needs before his own. In the past, his partners had known what they wanted and greedily took it. With Jasmine, it was different. She didn't know what she wanted, and she gave as much as she took, maybe more.

Her wide eyes looked at him, watching him with such an open expression of shyness and awe, that he forgot himself completely. He liked the way her eyes roamed his flesh, lighting up in appreciation of his form. Reid had never felt so damned sexy in his life. A burning need to please her raged within him. He wanted to teach her how to enjoy her body and his. In that moment, he wanted to give her everything.

The depth of his emotions took him by surprise. Even as he tensed on the inside, he couldn't make his body stop moving. They'd come too far and he would help her to find her release again before finding his own. Her legs were spread to him and he worked his hips against her in small circles, thrusting until he was buried to the hilt. Even then he didn't stop as he continued the agonizing pace.

Sacred cats, he was close to coming. Reid tensed, forcing his orgasm aside, pulling the shivers back inside himself. He was well experienced in the ways of sex and used every ounce of his knowledge to thrust and push the sweet spot he'd discovered in her body. Lifting her leg, he placed it on his shoulder.

"Ah, that's it, *mmm*," he groaned, increasing the speed of his thrusts. Every urge inside him wanted to pound into her. "Ah, *fea*, come again for me."

"Oh, it's all right to talk?" Jasmine asked, smiling over her opened mouth panting.

If he hadn't been fully concentrated on holding back, he would've laughed. Instead, he ground out, "Of course. There are no rules."

"Oh, because I've been biting my tongue," Jasmine admitted.

Reid nodded, biting his. The sound of her voice was too much, low and breathy, so seductive it washed over him. He was almost relieved that she didn't start talking dirty to him. *That* he wouldn't have been able to handle, not at this point.

Sweat beaded his flesh. Jasmine began to moan, making soft purring noises that only grew louder with each thrust. He pushed faster, harder, deeper. Her body was like silk around his arousal, so soft and wet.

"Oh, oh," she cried, writhing and squirming. "Right there. Whatever you're doing don't stop!"

Reid pushed back, arching as he worked into her, keeping the thrusts shallow and deep. Her nails clawed his shoulders and then finally it happened. She tensed, her muscles clamping down so hard on him that he couldn't stop from coming. His seed unleashed itself from his body, spilling heavily inside her. The way she tightened was almost painful, but it was a glorious pain. Reid pumped a few more times, but they were jerking movements as he milked their bodies for all they had.

When they'd stopped shaking, Reid pulled out, gliding in the slickness of their combined climaxes. Weakly, he fell to her side, breathing hard. He'd never held back for so long, but in the end it had been worth it.

"I can't feel my bones," Jasmine giggled. "My whole body is numb."

Reid grinned. How could he not?

"Did you...?" she asked, peeking up at him through her lashes. "Was it...?"

How could she even ask that? Reid rolled over, unable to bear the look of insecurity on her face, but glad that she didn't hide her body from him. He got much pleasure from looking at her. Before he could stop the words, he found himself honestly answering, "It was the best sex I've ever had."

Jasmine blushed, even as she tried to protest. "You don't have to say that."

"But I do mean it," Reid answered. He stroked her face.

Jasmine smiled, placing a light kiss on his palm.

"Jasmine," he whispered, overwhelmed. "I lov...having sex with you."

She laughed, a light, breathless sound. "Does this mean we can do it again?"

233

Reid smiled and nodded. Leaning over, he nipped at her mouth. "Anytime you want."

"How's now sound?" she asked.

Despite his recent climax, Reid felt his body easily stirring for more. Being Var, he could naturally go several times in one night. He allowed her to push him over onto his back and begin exploring. He fondled her breasts, fascinated by how sensitive they seemed to be. With just one pluck of her nipple, he felt cream dampening his stomach where she rubbed against him.

"Can you…?" she hesitated.

"What?"

"Do that eye-shifty thing again?" Jasmine blushed. Reid grinned. Out of all the things she could've asked for, he didn't expect that. He let his eyes flash with green. Instantly she shivered and gave a little moan. Nodding as she leaned over to kiss him, she whispered, "That's really sexy."

Reid growled as their lips met. His body had been insatiable before, but he was sure he'd never get enough of this woman.

"WHAT IS the possible function of that outfit?" Jasmine asked, staring at the dress Reid had laid out for her. It had a very short, tight skirt with cross laces on the sides and a deep cleavage-baring bodice. She shivered, knowing she might be better off just wearing the blanket she had wrapped around her naked body. Almost mournfully, she thought of the ripped bra and panties that were now in the stove, along with the baggy ill-fitting dress she'd worn the day before. Shaking her head, she refused to pick his new outfit up.

"You'll look damned sexy in it, that's what," Reid said, his voice dipping. The morning sunlight streamed in behind him, lighting the room. He was handsomely tousled from their night of play.

"It's the most impractical thing I've ever seen," Jasmine said, affecting a haughty tone.

Reid's eyes glinted as she looked him over. Jasmine felt her body melting to him. Damn him! She should never have admitted to thinking his eye shifts were sexy. There was just something dangerous and powerful about the way his body could transform itself. Now, every time she looked at him, he did it. And every time she felt herself dampen between the thighs. By the very smug look on his face, he knew it too.

"Or," Reid's grin widened, "you could just wear nothing at all."

Jasmine gripped the blanket tighter to her chest. He'd pleasured her thoroughly the night before, and she had to admit she was a little sore, even though she'd enjoyed his attentions. After letting her ride his tight body, he'd shown her things she'd never even thought of. He put her on her hands and knees before him, taking her from behind like an animal. Jasmine wasn't sure if men usually took women like that, but there was definitely something quite primitive and fulfilling to the position.

Jasmine knew she was a little naive, but with each climax her confidence grew. Reid didn't seem to mind her ignorance and even appeared to enjoy instructing her. After, she sat on his lap in the bath. The warm water caressed them as he slowly lifted her up and down on top of him.

Not like Chad's 'just lay there' method, Jasmine thought bitterly. She had to look away, not wanting to think of Chad when she was with Reid. When she was alone, she'd have time to consider all of that. It wasn't as if she were cheating on Chad. All they had between them was a worthless ceremony. Theirs had stopped being a marriage seconds after they'd left for the honeymoon. She just hadn't realized it. Now that she could feel, she never wanted to be under someone else's control like that again.

"Jasmine?" Reid asked, his voice concerned.

She turned back to him, coming out of her trance. Seeing the look in his eyes, she quickly said, "Food. We need food." As if to punctuate her words, her stomach growled loudly.

Reid sighed but nodded. "I've been gone so there's not much in the kitchen, but you'll have to make do with what's there. I'll do some hunting later."

"*I'll* have to make do?" Jasmine asked, raising a brow. She didn't mind cooking, but there was something to the way he said it that made her bristle.

"Yes, you are the woman," Reid answered.

"I suppose you'd like me to clean as well?"

Jasmine asked, irritated. She'd been Chad's slave for four years. She'd be damned if she was going to be Reid's now. She was tired of cooking and cleaning and waiting on a man hand and foot. When was it her turn to be waited on? Jasmine lifted her chin but didn't say a thing. She was rational enough to know she needed to think things out before she wildly started accusing Reid of 'crimes' he hadn't committed.

"I do have a few women who come from town to clean, but if you like, you may clean as well, yes," Reid grinned, nodding as if he was bestowing a great gift on her.

"All right then," Jasmine didn't say another word on the subject. She turned to the bed, again eyeing the garment. He'd pulled it from the bag he'd gotten off the front step the evening before. Leaning over, she rummaged through the other contents of the bag, finding a pair of pants and a tank shirt with cross laces.

"But," Reid protested, watching her slip the pants on while remaining hidden by the blanket. "I've already found you a dress."

"That one is too revealing," Jasmine said, matter-of-factly.

"Ah, yeah, that's the point," Reid sighed. He glanced at the dress then back to where she was struggling to put the shirt on without dropping the blanket. Reid reached over and snatched the covers away, just as her breast got stuck in the tight cross laces. Her arms were trapped along her head as she gasped and tried to wiggle the shirt down. She managed to peek at him from just over the edge of the dark material.

"Reid," she protested as he pulled her hips closer to his body. Leaning over, he lightly licked her nipple where it poked through the laces. Instantly, she forgot her irritation with him. "*Ah-ah*, stop that!"

"Stop what?" he asked, pulling her nipple more firmly between his teeth. "Stop this?" He brushed his mouth lightly over the swollen bud. "Or this?" He nibbled her sensitive flesh just around it.

Jasmine's growl of protest turned into an instant moan of arousal, and she couldn't help thinking that maybe they could do it just one more time.

"Mm, or maybe you want me to stop doing this." He sucked her hard, letting his whole mouth pleasure her with its intense heat. She gasped, and he pulled back. As she stared at him, shocked that he hadn't finished what he'd started, Reid tugged her shirt down over her head and straightened it to cover her.

"I'm hungry," he said, turning and walking toward the stairs.

Jasmine's body stung with arousal as she watched his back. Then, gritting her teeth, she made a move to follow him. Oh, so he wanted to play games, did he? Well then, she'd play.

28

THERE WAS something freeing about having all her emotions back, and also something a little scary. When Jasmine felt, it was like she felt to the fullest extent of the emotion. She'd been dead inside for so long that now her feelings were rushing to catch up. The only time she felt completely centered was when she was having sex with Reid. And even then she was so driven with passion and so controlled by her need for him that nothing else mattered.

Reid didn't eat before leaving to hunt. He said the hunger would force him to work harder and faster. Jasmine didn't understand the logic but, as she watched her lover's beautiful body shift into a tiger, she didn't think to question it. There was something a little too arousing about the whole shifting thing. She'd watched him run off, his streamlined body gracefully moving through the trees.

After he left, Jasmine made herself something to eat. He was right. There wasn't much to choose from, and she ended up eating handfuls of nuts and dried berries.

Alone in Reid's home, she had a lot of time to sort things out. Chad slept with everything that walked. He hit her. He verbally abused her. He drugged her with unnecessary medication. He convinced her she had a weak heart and could never leave him. The medicine had even taken away her will to want to leave him. She'd been apathetic for the most part, in a walking coma. In fact, he'd given her that medicine when he'd been her doctor before he even mentioned marriage to her.

Did that mean he'd planned their sham of a marriage from the beginning? When she said 'I do' was it because she was manipulated into doing so? Had she been so emotionless, so uncaring about her future, that she had married Chad because he'd influenced her to?

The realization hit her like a blow to the head, and she gasped, her heart squeezing in her chest. Her wedding had always been a blur of a memory, but it was coming back to her now. She's always assumed the fuzziness was because all brides were supposed to be nervous. Now she knew it was because she didn't feel enough to be nervous. In fact, right after the wedding, is when Chad lowered her dosage, and she'd become a little more coherent.

At first, thinking of Chad and what he'd done, she became angry, so angry that she couldn't see straight and ended up punching Reid's bed until her body was so weak she couldn't move. Then, she felt sadness. How could Chad have done that to her? Why had he taken away everything that she was? He said he loved her but is that what love was? Control? Possession? Manipulation? Knowing that Chad didn't love her, probably never had, stung as well. She'd been nothing more than Doctor Chadwick St. Claire's trophy, a wife he could show off to other doctors, a wife he could control. She'd not even been a wife, but an unpaid, unwilling personal assistant. She'd cleaned for him, cooked for him, waited on him and his friends. She'd smiled and simpered and wrote his speeches for him. She filed his charts and scheduled his appointments.

"I love you, Jasmine," Chad said it every day. Every single, accursed day. *"I don't know what I'd do without you."*

"I know what you'd do," Jasmine hissed, punching the bed anew. "You'd have to iron your

243

own clothes and get your lazy ass up off the couch to the food simulator to make your own drinks. You'd have to laugh at your friends' stupid doctor jokes all by yourself."

At least Prince Reid was honest with her. Not once did he make promises, try to woo her with pretty compliments and flowery words. He didn't buy her expensive gifts, gifts that were no more than bribes. Reid said he loved having sex with her. At the time, the words had sounded odd, but the more she thought about it, the more she could appreciate the honesty of them.

Reid loved having sex with her.

Jasmine sighed. He didn't love her. He loved sex with her. It wasn't what most women wanted to hear, but she wasn't most women. She'd been told she was loved for years and where did that get her? Nowhere. If Jasmine never had to face a man's love again, it would be too soon. Right now, sex was enough. In fact, she loved having sex with Reid. She'd been suppressed for so long, it was time to live her life, and she planned to do just that. Reid wasn't the type of man who'd want to commit to one woman, and she'd already technically had a multiple-woman marriage. If she were ever to try the marriage thing again, which she highly doubted, it would be just one husband to one wife.

No. This arrangement with Reid was perfect.

She didn't want commitment, and neither did he. They both loved sex with each other. What more perfect arrangement could there be? And, the best part was, they didn't need to talk about it. It was what it was.

It was decided.

Then why did her heart skip around at the thought of Reid not caring for her beyond friendship? It wasn't as if she loved him. It wasn't as if she wanted a serious relationship. Did she?

"No," Jasmine said aloud. "I'm just confused. All these new emotions just have me confused."

Jasmine refused to think about it any longer. Chad was a rotten, no good bastard. There was no reason dwelling on what couldn't be changed. Reid was not the type of man to commit, and she wasn't in the position to be committed to. The less she thought about it, the better for her sanity. Reid was her lover. She was finally a free woman, who would not be doing Reid's cleaning and cooking for him.

It was decided. It was what it was. It was figured out.

Then why was she still thinking about it?

Groaning, Jasmine looked around Reid's room. It really was huge, taking up what had to be at least half of the downstairs. She wondered if there was more carved beyond the bedroom wall, or if they'd only made this one room on the second level. She didn't see a door, so assumed it was just the one room. Then, eyeing the giant viewing screen, she said, "Viewing screen on."

It didn't turn on. She frowned, looking around. There was a small remote on a table by the bed. Reaching forward, she pushed a button. The screen blipped, and a menu came up that said, "Action. Good movies. Women's films. Documentaries."

"Apparently women's films didn't make the good category." Jasmine laughed. Pushing the first option, she read the list she found under the title of action, "Large Explosions. Mass Fighting. Hand to Hand Combat. Funny Old Futuristic. Swordplay. Mild Explosions. Miscellaneous."

Jasmine laughed harder. Exploring some of the titles and movies, she discovered they were basically just Old Earth films classified into what kind of action they contained. The funny futuristics were full of space ships and zipping lasers. Some of the Old Earth people's ideas weren't too far from the truth. Others were so far away from it that she couldn't imagine how anyone would think it believable.

Good movies were just a list of different types of dramas and horror films. Some she'd seen. Most she hadn't. Earth films were making a comeback of sorts with many travelers. Spaceships were able to pick up some of the old, original transmission waves while in space. A lot of times, they were recorded illegally in New Earth's air space and then pirates would sell the copies on the black market. The direct broadcasts from New Earth were of better quality than the timeworn Old Earth transmission waves picked up by ships deep in space.

Women's films turned out to be romances and such. Picturing Reid watching a sappy girl movie was beyond hilarious. She doubted he even bothered with that section. Going to the last category, she expected to see Old Earth news programs. Instead, documentaries led her to nothing but old-fashioned porn. Jasmine gasped, sitting up. It was by far the biggest movie selection out of all the categories. Her mouth agape, she read the subcategory list, "Girl-Girl."

Jasmine grimaced. "Ugh, no thanks."

"Traditional. Multiples. Must Try. Awkward." Jasmine stopped reading though there were more. She scrolled down to the 'Must Try' option. Standing, she walked from the bed, stopping before the screen. As she pushed the button, a close-up of a woman's mouth flipped on screen. The woman was moaning and bobbing her head, as she sucked something in her mouth. Jasmine squinted, stepping closer to see what it was. Suddenly, the camera angle panned out. She gasped. The woman was kneeling and sucking on a man, using her hands to massage the extra length of his erection.

Jasmine started to turn away in disgust when she heard the man moan. Curiosity got the better of her, and before she knew it, she couldn't look away. Whatever the woman was doing, the man was enjoying it. Actually, by the look on his face, he was enjoying it quite a lot. She sucked his shaft, nibbling it with her teeth and twirling it with her tongue. Then, sucking a finger into her mouth, she wetted it, only to push it back into the man's cheeks, probing him as she went back to sucking his shaft. The man kept moaning and begging, "Please, baby. Take it all, baby. That's it, baby, suck it good. You're such a naughty girl. You like that don't you, baby? Ah, yeah, take it. Take it!"

"Must try," Jasmine whispered. Did that mean Reid wanted to try these? Did it mean these were things he hadn't done? She found it hard to believe that a man with as many obvious, undeniable conquests would have things he'd never done.

The sucking segment ended with the man making an amusing face, and another segment started. This time a man was tied to a bed as a woman slowly tortured him with her body. After that, a woman did a strip tease for the tied man, wiggling around as she danced seductively. Jasmine found herself swaying to the cheesy music, trying a few of the moves. Then, with the man still tied, the woman had her way with him by riding on top.

Jasmine kept watching the films, taking a seat on the couch before the screen. The music was most comical. The actors and actresses were over-dramatic and seemed to be forgetting some of their lines as they stuttered over their short speeches. Despite this, she squirmed in her seat, finding that she actually got a little aroused by the shows.

Next, the woman was in a swing of sorts as the man pulled her back and forth in front of him. Jasmine bit her lip. There was another strip tease, another woman sucking a man with him lying on a bed, another sucking scene where the man was in a chair. There was yet another sucking scene where the man was on top, pumping his hips down into the woman's mouth as he in turn had his face buried between her thighs. She wondered if the ongoing theme meant Reid wanted her to suck him into her mouth.

"Ride me, cowboy," Jasmine repeated softly, trying to remember some of the ideas presented in the 'documentaries' for later. All the women in these movies were extremely vocal. Some of them even said some pretty naughty things.

A slow smile crept to her face, and she just couldn't look away. "Must try, huh?"

29

REID WAS tired from his hunt. He'd been successful, but with his mind constantly on Jasmine and the memory of her sweet, naked flesh, he'd been a little distracted. It had taken him longer than normal to track, and even then two of his prey got away. Finally, he was able to bag a baldric and a prongin. As the baldric was a bird, it would only be good for a meal or two. The large prongin would give them meat for a long time.

He was still naked from the hunt but was well used to being out of doors in the nude. As a Var, he lost his clothes during a full shift.

After skinning the animals and preparing them for storage, he brought the meat inside. For some reason, he didn't think Jasmine would appreciate seeing the carcasses before they were prepared. She was a lady, through and through, proper, elegant, refined. He didn't want to insult her delicate sensibilities.

"Ah, ride me, stud!"

Reid froze to hear the womanly scream. It was instantly followed by a man's moan of pleasure. He tensed.

"What the…?" he began, swearing under his breath. Jealous rage swept through him as he dropped the meat on the floor. It landed with a heavy thud as he ran to the stairs. He felt his teeth elongate in his mouth as his body shifted half way. Fur prickled over his shoulders and chest, as a predatory growl sounded in the back of his throat.

He reached the top, taking several steps at a time. Jasmine stood in the middle of the bedroom, her hands behind her back and a guilty look on her face as she stared at him.

"Reid," she gasped, glancing around. He took a menacing step forward. "I didn't, ah, hear you come in."

"Obviously," he growled, taking in her flushed features. He easily caught the scent of her arousal in the room. Tension worked its way through his body. By the potency of her smell, he'd obviously interrupted something.

"Reid?" Jasmine asked, breathless. She backed

away from him. "What's wrong with you? Why are you all...*animal-ish*? Did something happen? Do you need some clothes?"

Even through this anger, he didn't want her to be afraid of him. Her eyes raked over his naked body. No, that wasn't just nervousness he detected. The beast in him excited her and she was trying hard to hide it. "Where is he?"

"Wh—?"

Reid pounced forward and gripped her arms. "I smell you."

"Bu—?"

"Where is he? I heard him," Reid demanded, shaking her slightly. Damn but she smelled good. If he weren't so jealous, he'd throw her on the bed and continue with a little game of stalker and prey. Something fell on the floor as he shook her, and suddenly a loud moan sounded behind him.

"Yes, baby, yes!"

Reid turned, surprised to see the Earth sex tutorials on the viewing screen. The screen was so new that he didn't even think she could be watching it. A slow grin crossed over his features as he turned back to her. He felt her tremble beneath his hands. Jasmine quickly pulled away and grabbed the remote, fumbling to turn the screen off. Finally the noise stopped.

Her wide eyes stared at him, so pretty and

open. She didn't play any coy games, didn't try to hide the fact that she wanted him. Licking his lips, he watched as her mouth puckered in invitation. Her gaze drifted down his body, and a light moan sounded.

"You should've waited for me," he said, his tone still gruff from his shifting. Drawing the fur back into himself, he let all but his eyes shift back to his human form. His shaft was hard, his body completely awakened by the intensity of his jealousy. He walked her back until they came against the wall.

A hesitant smile flashed across her features, fading just as fast as she looked up at him. She was breathing hard. Reid leaned closer. Jasmine gasped, tensing. Her mouth open, she leaned toward him, instantly kissing him in passion.

Reid groaned as she pressed her body tightly to his, rubbing along his taller frame as if she couldn't get close enough. Since he was already naked, there was only the thin material of her pants between them. He rocked his hips, feeling her wet heat pressing into him as her leg lifted along his outer thigh.

Jasmine drew her mouth away. "Do that growl again."

Reid growled, letting the beastly sound of his

cat form rumble his throat. Instantly, he was rewarded with an intense rush of hot moisture in between her thighs. He went for her neck, letting his sharper teeth come out to play. His voice hoarse, he said, "You like the beast, do you?"

"Yes, oh yes," she gasped, completely unashamed. She grabbed his hand and drew it to her hip. "Cut my clothes off me."

Jasmine was playing with fire, and she didn't even know it. The Var were sexual creatures, but to play with the beast, to encourage the very nature of the predator could lead to uncontrollable sex. He'd be mindless, unable to stop once he started. Reid knew he should pull away and get control, but one look at Jasmine's face, and he somehow knew that she didn't want him in control. There was no fear in her when it came to his shifted form. He extended a claw, letting her watch as he artfully sliced through the laces along her hip without hurting her. Her jaw dropped, and she tensed. The smell of her excitement thrilled him, spurring the beast on.

Reid ripped through her shirt, dragging a sharp claw between her breasts. She gasped, her back arching as if the aggressive act only made her all the more desperate in her arousal. He cupped the soft globe in his palm, growling over and over just to make her shiver with desire to hear his animalistic voice.

"Ah," she panted, standing before him in her tattered clothing. She pulled back, throwing her arms up against the wall. Her eyes begged him to take her. She bit her lip.

Reid growled, reaching to pin her wrists over her head with one clawed hand as he thrust the other along her slick folds. He retracted the sharpened claws, careful not to hurt her as he parted the sensitive, wet flesh. Arching forward, she licked at his fangs.

"You play a dangerous..." Reid took a deep breath, forcing the gruff words as his body shifted even more, "game. The beast within me is nothing to be trifled with."

"Don't pull it back this time," she whispered along his mouth. "I want to feel the animal in you. I want you to lose all control like I do."

Reid knew what she was asking. He would never take her in his completely shifted form, but she wanted the fangs and the claws. She wanted the wild, untamed beast he restrained. Her wide eyes begged him for it. Who was he to deny her? How could he even think to?

Roughly, he slid her up the smooth wall. Her legs were opened to him, and he took her, thrusting into her ready body. She was so wet, so hot, that he yelled in ecstasy to feel it. Unable to reign in the animal inside him, he laid claim to her, her soft cries driving him on. Her fingers dug into his shoulders, the nails biting his flesh.

Reid pumped his hips hard and fast, his butt tensing with each jerking movement. It felt too good. He couldn't slow, couldn't think beyond the driving need to release himself in her, to mark her as his woman so no man would ever dare to touch her. In that moment, he knew that she was who he wanted. The idea of any other man touching her made the passion inside him fiercer. Whether she realized it or not, she belonged to him, would always belong to him. He'd had his share of empty sex. Other women paled in comparison to her. When he'd released himself in Jasmine for the first time, he'd felt whole, complete. The burning, searching need in him went away.

His body worked into hers. Jasmine moaned and gasped, urging him on with every push of her body. Tremors racked her and she stiffened, arching back against the wall. Reid held her steady, keeping himself deep as the intense orgasm worked its way through her body. Only after he'd milked every bit of release from her, did he allow himself to come. His seed filled her. He kept her tight against him, giving it all to her.

It took a long moment before he could speak.

Swallowing, almost nervous, he pulled back. "I lov—"

When he'd started speaking, she'd already been leaning in for the kiss. She didn't stop, her lips cutting off his words. Reid put all the feeling and passion inside him into that kiss, giving himself over to her completely.

With a small giggle, Jasmine pulled back. Grinning, she said, "I know."

His heart raced. Pleasure tried to erupt inside him.

"I love having sex with you too," Jasmine said, giving him a shy smile. "I know what you're trying to tell me, and I agree. It's good that we don't have the pressure of anything more on us. We'll take our pleasure, have some fun and then when it's over, it's over. No regrets."

Reid let his head drop to hide the heart-wrenching expression that was surely crossing his features at her words. All she wanted from him was sex. He'd finally allowed himself to want more, to accept that there might actually be just one woman for one man out there. He finally realized what it was his brothers had found when they'd life mated to their wives. Only, unlike his brothers, the woman he'd found didn't want him back. Well, she wanted him, but just for his body. The fact left him cold on the inside.

He was still inside her, and he pulled out, slowly letting her slide down to the floor. Jasmine didn't seem to notice his turmoil. She giggled again, before admitting softly, "I like it when you get all wild on me."

Reid let loose a long breath and forced a light tone to his voice. "Mm, do you now, *fea*?"

He swallowed his heartache. Even in the wake of it, Reid was drawn to her. Letting a mask of playfulness come across his features, he licked the corner of her mouth before nipping at her bottom lip.

"So, mighty hunter," Jasmine said. "What are you cooking us for dinner?"

"Sorry, *fea*," Reid answered. "I hunt it. You cook it. Cooking and cleaning is woman's work."

Jasmine bit her lip. Pushing the center of his chest, she walked him back to the bed and gave a gentle shove. Reid fell on his back, automatically moving so that he lay completely on the bed. Jasmine shrugged out of the remains of her tattered shirt. His eyes devoured her. Sacred cats! She was beautiful.

Crawling over him, she rubbed her hands along his thighs, pushing his knees apart and up. When he was opened and exposed to her, she grinned and licked her finger. "You hunt. I cook. That's fair.

But, let's do a little negotiation on that cleaning part shall we?"

Reid tensed. He was about to answer when her mouth came down to kiss his shaft. As she sucked him between her lush lips, he moaned, closing his eyes.

I give in, fea. You can have whatever you want.

JASMINE COULDN'T BELIEVE she was cooking for Reid again. He didn't have a food simulator, which was odd though apparently he had at one point, and it broke.

So much for the 'I'm no man's slave' mentality. Besides, the one time she had tried to make Reid help it became apparent that he may be a mighty hunter, but he was a lousy chef.

Truthfully, she didn't mind preparing his food, had never minded cooking by hand. It had been Chad who insisted on the food simulator. And, not to sell herself short, she did successfully negotiate that a maid continued to do the cleaning while she was in his home. Actually, he'd caved really quickly.

Jasmine smiled, checking the brick oven. The turkey was almost done.

"Baldric," she corrected herself softly, biting her lip. The turkey thing was called a baldric.

There were a lot of things that were different about Qurilixen, but on the whole, it wasn't so bad. The people she'd met were nice, not that she'd met anyone while at Reid's house. They'd been at his home for five glorious, sex filled days. In fact, they'd spent so much time in his bed, on his floor, in the tub, in the shower, out on the balcony, on the couch, on the kitchen counter and the kitchen floor, and about every conceivable place in between, that time became one big blur of pleasure.

Things were good, better than they'd been her entire life. She was no fool to think it would last forever. Someday, she'd have to wake up from the dream they'd created. If she didn't do it on her own, Reid would surely do it for her. Jasmine saw his passionate appetites. Though she was able to match them easily, she knew that someday he would tire of her and want to move on.

"I know that's not your cooking, brother."

Jasmine tensed. That wasn't Reid's voice. She looked out of the kitchen, thankful she wasn't still wearing the skimpy little dress she'd done a strip tease in earlier. Reid's brothers stood in the entryway.

"Mm, yeah, it definitely smells too good to be something you'd make," Quinn said, laughing.

"What are you doing here?" Reid asked, smiling at them.

"Well, you left the palace in a hurry and we thought…" Kirill's words trailed off as he turned to look at Jasmine. He had the same dark eyes as Reid. She knew instantly what the men had thought. They'd decided to come and check her out. Prince Jarek was the only one not staring at her.

"Hey, Jas," Jarek said, breaking the silence. He grinned at her, crossing the distance to kiss her cheek. Whispering, he said, "Don't look so worried." Then, louder, he teased, "Does he actually make you cook?"

"Well, it turns out I'm a lousy hunter, so it works out in the end," Jasmine said, forcing a small smile. Jarek grinned and nodded. She tried to relax. "So, I take it you're all here to check me out?"

Kirill laughed. Quinn grinned. Falke nodded his stoic head though his eyes gleamed.

"Our wives wouldn't let us have any peace until we agreed to come and make sure Reid was treating you kindly," Falke answered. His eyes swept over her. "Are you well, my lady?"

Jasmine blushed, thinking of just how 'well' Reid had been treating her. She met Reid's piercing gaze and trembled. Slowly, she nodded.

"Ah, good," Kirill said. The brothers' eyes

turned to Reid. "There's something different about you, brother. Are you well?"

Reid nodded once. "Why wouldn't I be?"

Kirill and Quinn shared a quick look. Jasmine saw them smirk and wondered about it. Surely it was some sort of private, brotherly joke.

"If you'll excuse me I should go and check on the food," Jasmine said, backing toward the kitchen. "I've made plenty if you're staying."

"Thank you," Kirill and Falke said at the same time.

"Never pass up a meal," Jarek grinned, though he didn't look at her as he stared at Reid. Reid stared back at him, unmoving and apparently unamused by something that passed between him and his twin.

"Yes," Quinn added. "It smells delicious. Thank you, Lady Jasmine."

REID GLANCED at Jasmine as she disappeared into the kitchen. When she was out of the room, he said quietly, "What really goes on? Why are you here?"

"It is as we said," Kirill motioned to the couches, keeping his voice low. "Our wives have taken a liking to Lady Jasmine and wanted us to make sure you weren't forcing your unwanted attentions on her."

Reid frowned as he took a seat. He wasn't ready for reality to crash in on the little world he'd made with Jasmine. She never acted as if she felt anything for him beyond passion, but still he hoped that she might. He kept telling himself if he gave her enough physical pleasure, if he were patient, she'd come around.

"What's the real reason?" Reid asked. "The one you're not telling me?"

"Lyssa's director friend with the HIA has contacted us. There is a ship heading toward our quadrant. It's the Medical Alliance. We believe that Jasmine's, ah…" Kirill's words trailed off, and he looked at the ground.

Reid tensed. Jasmine and he had an unspoken bond not to speak of her husband. But, not saying it didn't make it less true. Still, it didn't matter. Jasmine was his. She belonged to him. Or at least she would if he had a say in the matter.

"You mean the man who claims to be my husband," Jasmine said softly. She'd been so quiet that no one had heard her enter the living room. The men turned to her. She sat a tray down on a low table in front of them. It was an array of nuts and berries. Reid glanced at it and then her. She wouldn't look at him.

"Claims?" Quinn asked.

"As a girl, I was sick, weak. Some doctors said I would grow out of it in a few years. Others said I'd die by the time I was five. They were all wrong. I didn't die, and I only gained moderate strength. That was until my father contacted Doctor Chadwick St. Claire. He cured me of my condition, but he also drugged me and married me when I was in such a state as to be unaware of my decisions. Even after the ceremony, I was kept drugged." Jasmine took a deep breath.

"You mean the pills Tori analyzed?" Quinn asked.

"Yes." Jasmine nodded. She glanced around the room before looking at her hands. "According to human law, you have to be legally of sound mind to make a binding contract. I wasn't of sound mind, haven't been of sound mind for several years. I'd say that pretty much voids any marriage contract I had with Chad."

Reid's whole body was tense as he watched her. Why hadn't she said any of this before? Why let him believe she was married? If there was nothing between them, then they…she… Then the realization dawned on him. She'd not told him because she wanted it between them.

"This is my problem," Jasmine said when

silence filled the room. She finally looked at him. Reid tried to read something on her face, any emotion that would tell him how she felt. She was blank, like when he'd first met her, like when she'd been on those damned pills. "You've all done so much for me, and I truly appreciate it and will never forget it. But, if Chad is coming here to get me, then I'll go without a fuss. He's my problem to deal with, and I think it's about time I faced it."

"Jasmine," Reid began. She looked away from him. He felt his brother's eyes on him. What could he say? Feeling helpless, he looked at Kirill, begging him to say something.

Kirill met his eyes, seeming to understand. "I would like to offer to let you stay at the palace. My wife is very fond of you, and I don't want her upset during the last of her pregnancy. Please, consider staying."

"You're too kind, but I hardly doubt Queen Ulyssa is so delicate that she needs me, a stranger, to stay on this planet," Jasmine said.

Kirill nodded, chuckling. "You're right. My Lyssa is no delicate woman. But it is still our wish that you stay and let us help you."

"I thank you, your majesty, but this is my fight. I'll deal with it. You don't need this hassle here. As you said, your wife is expecting. This is one less stress you need on your kingdom and your wife. I will go."

"My lady," Falke said. "We've dealt with the Medical Mafia before, and we'll not leave you to face them alone."

"You know?" Jasmine gasped. "You know about the Medical Alliance's connection to the Medical Mafia?"

"Wait," Reid stood, glaring angrily at her. "Are you saying you knew that Chad was part of the Medical Mafia, and you still intended to go back to him?"

"I wasn't going back to him. I was facing my problem," Jasmine argued, returning his heated glare.

"After what he's already done to you?" Reid growled, taking a menacing step forward. Instantly his brothers stood, blocking his path to Jasmine. It wasn't necessary. He could never hurt her. "What makes you think you can—?"

"Reid, now is not the time," Quinn said, resting a hand on his shoulder. "We're here to bring you back to the palace. If they do come for her, Jasmine will be safer there."

Reid nodded.

"Wait, don't I have a say?" Jasmine demanded. "It's not like the Mafia wants me, just Chad."

"No, my lady, I'm sorry. You don't have a say in this. I tried to give you one, but you wouldn't agree to it," Kirill said. "We have dealt with the Mafia before. Trust me, we are more than equipped to handle this."

31

Jasmine refused to talk to Reid the entire way back to the palace. They'd stayed at his home long enough to eat. It had been a tense meal, one that Jasmine could barely force down her throat. The Var men complimented her on her cooking and tried to make a few jokes to lighten her mood, all of them but Reid. It was pointless. She was upset with him, and hurt. After the meal, she hadn't been given a choice but to leave. With five very large Var warriors walking around her, she didn't stand a chance of escape.

A diffused light fell over the dense forest in a soft green haze. Reid and Jarek walked ahead of her. Kirill and Quinn stayed at her sides, and Falke brought up the rear.

Damn him! Jasmine thought, reminding herself

to be mad as she glared at his back. More often than not, she found herself staring at his tight butt and not concentrating on her anger.

How dare Reid let his family make decisions for her without even asking her opinion? It wasn't as if she was ungrateful for their offer, and on a very base level she was relieved that they wanted to take control over the situation, but out of principal she was outraged. She was living her life, not the royal cat-shifter family. Jasmine wanted to make her own decisions, whether good or bad. She was tired of being told what to do.

The sound of young boys playing echoed around them as they neared the city. Reid turned to her. Jasmine glared back, giving him her most evil look. He actually had the nerve to look surprised at her hostility.

They walked quietly through the city streets, winding along the maze-like roads. Beautiful woven rugs and blankets hung outside in the sun, drying on lines. Clay pots set outside doorsteps, some with flowers and other native plants. The walls were decorated with tiles, less intricate than the palace, but still lovely. The palace stood tall over the city, outlined by the blue-green sky. Jasmine stared at the square turrets, doing her best to pretend that she didn't see the curious eyes of the Var population on her.

They walked through the front gates of the palace. Quinn and the king took their leave to go and find their wives. Jasmine was almost jealous over the eager way they went to their women. Reid would never get so bent out of shape over her. Hearing laughter, the small traveling party turned toward a banquet hall. Jasmine didn't have much choice but to follow. With the giant Falke behind her, she didn't exactly think she could sneak away, and his size alone gave her reason enough not to try.

The banquet hall had a high domed ceiling of glass that let in the diffused light of the three suns. There were mosaic patterns on the walls and an exquisitely tiled floor. Long tables and bench seats were along the floor for group dining. At the front of the hall, on a raised platform, was the king's table. It was empty.

The laughter came from Princess Samantha and the members of Jarek's crew at one of the lower tables. Rick and Evan sat at her sides, grinning widely. Dev, Jackson, Lucien, and Viktor sat across from her. Lochlann was the only one missing. Remembering that he was a dragon-shifter and not Var, she wondered if Lochlann wasn't welcome at the palace. Jarek slid into a seat next to Jackson. Seeing how close Rick and Evan sat to Sam, Jasmine glanced back at Falke. He was smiling.

Sam saw her husband, and her whole face lit up with pleasure. She pushed on Evan's shoulder, using him to help her stand. Then, unashamed, she ran to Falke, jumping up to throw her arms around his neck. He kept walking as he hugged her, carrying her so that her feet dangled off the floor.

"Your son is making me tired," Sam said, giggling softly as she kissed Falke.

"That's just because his mother's lazy," Falke answered, his voice teasing.

Jasmine's jaw almost dropped. Did the big Commander Falke just make a joke? Sam's laughter rang out over them. Apparently, he had.

"I need to talk to you." Reid pulled on her elbow.

Jasmine turned, partially melted by the loving display of Falke and his wife. She looked up, seeing Reid's dark eyes. Then, as his words penetrated her brain, she jerked her arm from him. "Fine."

"Alone," he said under his breath, glancing around at the full table. Jasmine followed his gaze. They were being watched.

"Fine," she repeated, this time not so loud.

Reid turned and led the way from the hall. He glanced back several times as if making sure she followed him. Jasmine did, her body stiff. She plastered a determined look of anger on her face. Reid had to learn that he couldn't boss her around. So what if she appreciated the Var's help and didn't know how to handle the situation on her own. She didn't belong to him, no matter what intimacies had transpired between them.

They walked in silence through the maze-like halls. Then, stopping, Reid turned to a round mosaic pattern on the wall. He pressed a series of tiles on the circular pattern. The tiles didn't move as he touched them, but as he finished and pulled his hand away, the whole center circle pulled into the wall to reveal a screen. Jasmine gasped. It was a computer. She would never have guessed.

"Give me a strand of your hair," Reid said.

"What?" Jasmine looked at him, confused.

Reid reached for her, plucking a single strand from her head. It didn't hurt, but she protested anyway. "Hey, what do you think you're doing?"

Reid sighed and didn't answer as he pressed a button. A tray slid out, and he placed her hair strand inside. "Siren, please record DNA for Jasmine."

"Jasmine recorded, Prince Reid," a sultry voice answered.

"Who was that?" Jasmine needlessly glanced around. They were alone in the hall.

"That's Siren, the palace's mainframe computer."

"Pleasure to meet you, Jasmine," Siren said in a

tone that dripped honey and sounded like a pout. "My lord, what security clearance?"

Reid glanced at her.

"Hey, what are you doing?" Jasmine demanded.

"Eight, please, Siren," Reid said.

"Eight?" Jasmine asked, her tone hard.

"Very good, my lord, Jasmine stored," Siren said. Reid didn't take his eyes off her.

"What is eight?" Jasmine demanded. Reid opened his mouth to speak, but she asked instead, "Siren, what does eight security level mean?"

"Level eight is confinement to the palace, my lady, and limited privileges," Siren answered. Reid grimaced.

"What do you think you are doing?" Jasmine yelled, not caring if she was overheard. "Erase it at once."

"No," Reid said. "Don't think I couldn't see your mind plotting ways to defy the king's order. I saw you looking for a way to escape. Now you will be confined to the palace. If you leave, or if anyone tries to take you from the palace, Siren will sound the alarm. It's for your safety."

"This has nothing to do with the king's order," Jasmine yelled. "This has to do with you not giving me the right to make up my own mind. You have no right to keep me prisoner here."

"Haven't I?" Reid asked, his voice dipping. He

reached a hand to cup her cheek. Why was he looking at her like that? All soft and tender and sad? Jasmine jerked back, staying out of arm's reach. "When were you going to tell me you weren't married, Jasmine?"

"What does that have to do with anything? You didn't seem to care so much about it when you were sleeping with me." Jasmine backed away. How could he do this to her? How could he not trust her enough to make her own decisions? How could he make her a prisoner? Why did he have to look so handsome at this moment?

She tried to walk away from him, but he reached out and grabbed her arm. "I asked you a question, Jasmine."

"And I gave you the only answer I'm going to give you. I didn't tell you because my relationship with Chad is none of your business."

Reid drew back as if she'd hit him. Slowly, he nodded his head. His voice calm and his face suddenly very passionless, he asked, "Do you know the way back to your suite? Or do you need me to show you?"

"I'll find my way to my gilded prison just fine, thank you, your highness. I'm sure if I don't go there, your little slut of a computer will be happy to tell you," she spat. Turning on her heels, she stormed away from him.

Reid watched Jasmine go. Why did she have to be so stubborn? Didn't she understand that he logged her into the palace computer to protect her?

"Siren," he ordered.

"Yes, my prince?"

"Make sure she gets back to the purple guest suite," Reid said. "And monitor her life signs at all times. If she even appears to be in danger, I want to know about it."

"Yes, my prince."

Reid turned to go back to the banquet hall. He needed to talk to Falke and find out everything he knew about the Medical Mafia's ship. Since Jasmine had interrupted them earlier at his home, he knew he hadn't been told everything. His brothers looked at him as Jasmine's guardian and would let him decide how to best take care of her.

Stopping, he added, "Siren, please ignore her slut comment. She didn't mean it. She's mad at me, not you. Don't do anything to her, all right?"

Reid sighed. He'd called Siren a couple of names in his time. Damn Jarek for that. His brother had programmed the computer to be touchy to insults. Once, the damned thing had even locked him in the weapons chamber.

"As you wish, my lord, but I would rather log an apology from her," Siren pouted.

"She's my wife, Siren," he said softly, remembering how he'd marked her during sex. She'd been pinned up against the wall, and he'd never felt more complete. That was before Jasmine went on and on about how they were only lovers and their relationship meant nothing to her and that it was an affair of the bodies only. How could he tell her what he'd done after that? "Take her apology from me."

"Yes, my lord. Congratulations."

"Thank you, Siren."

32

Jasmine paced the guest suite for all of fifteen minutes before knocks sounded on her door. It was the same suite she'd woken up in. First came Queen Ulyssa and Princess Tori. They instantly hugged her, looked her over to ensure she was in one piece, and then hugged her again. Next was Princess Sam, her mouth pink and swollen as if she'd just been thoroughly kissed before stumbling through the door. She gave a guilty smile at Ulyssa's look and shrugged.

"I missed him," Sam said by way of excuse.

Tori went to a hidden food simulator by the giant Var banner and materialized drinks. Whatever it was, it was fizzy and made funny bubbling noises.

"Don't worry, it's not liquor," Ulyssa said, as

they all sat down around a table. "It's an old Earth drink. Soda. One of the Draig princesses gave it to us. They found the simulator programming codes in the Draig royal library."

Jasmine nodded, taking a sip. It was sugary, but not bad. "I was under the impression the cat-shifters and dragon-shifters didn't get along."

"Actually, we're trying to change that," Ulyssa said. "My husband has been working for peace for the last several months."

Jasmine nodded, very curious about the Draig. Reid never wanted to talk about it. Besides, it was nice to think about something that didn't directly concern her or her future. Her mind needed a break.

"We've signed a treaty and have made a betrothal agreement," Ulyssa's eyes fell.

"Betrothal agreement?" Jasmine asked. "As in an arranged marriage? Between who?"

"It's more of a formality," Tori said, patting Ulyssa's hand.

"If one of the Draig princes has a daughter, which is highly unlikely considering that the blue radiation makes female children all but impossible, she will marry the king's oldest son," Sam said. She too gave Ulyssa a sad smile. "It was a very grand gesture on Kirill's part, to join the future Var king to a Draig woman."

Jasmine glanced at the queen's belly.

"There are four of them, and they're all married with children due very soon," Ulyssa supplied. "We expect to get news any day that the princesses have delivered."

"And you're fine with this?" Jasmine asked, already suspecting the queen wasn't.

"The Var are my people now, and I love them," Ulyssa said. She placed her hand on her stomach. "But this is my baby. I wouldn't have him forced into a loveless marriage. What scares me is that he's his father's son and will undoubtedly be compelled by duty. My only comfort is that in time peace could be achieved another way and that this betrothal could become unnecessary. Besides, it's unlikely that the Draig princesses will give birth to a girl."

Jasmine opened her mouth. Ulyssa held up her hand.

"It's all right, really," the queen said. "I have great hopes that we will have peace before my son reaches marrying age."

"Yeah, we have, what? Eighty? Ninety years?" Sam laughed.

Jasmine giggled, thinking they were joking. Then, seeing their faces, she stopped. Her eyes rounded. "How old is Reid?"

Tori laughed. "Let's put it this way. Quinn's the baby, and he's fifty-six."

Jasmine's jaw dropped.

"Let's see," Ulyssa mused. "Kirill was about thirty-seven when the twins were born. He's ninety-eight now so that would make Reid...ah..."

"Sixty-one," Tori calculated. Jasmine gasped.

"Cat-shifters tend to live for hundreds of years, so technically, they're still young men," Ulyssa said.

"I had no idea." Jasmine was stunned. Before she could stop and think, she blurted, "And this doesn't bother you to know that your husband will outlive you by so long?"

"Outlive us?" Ulyssa repeated.

"Oh, no," Sam said, taking a sip. "We're Var now. They shared their lives with us. We've bonded. They call it life mating. It means we'll live for hundreds of years as well."

"So, you're not half mates?" Jasmine already knew the answer, but she said the words anyway, thinking of Reid. "Or do half mates live longer as well?"

"We're life mates," Ulyssa said, smiling. "I could never share Kirill, and he will never take another. That's how much he loves me. Half mates are more like the harem girls. They're bonded, but not as deeply and the bond can be broken if both parties will it. At least that's the way I understand it."

"Var men can only have one life mate. It's why they act the way they do toward their women," Tori said. "That and because women are so rare they feel they need to be protected."

"It used to aggravate me at first," Ulyssa admitted, absently rubbing her stomach. "Kirill would get so bossy and protective. He locked me in his quarters as punishment a few times until I learned to just listen to him. It sounds domineering, but they do know what they're doing, and they never act dishonorably toward us."

"Still," Jasmine frowned. "Doesn't it bother you that they just decide and don't ask your opinion?"

"They do ask our opinions," Ulyssa said, smiling. "Or at least they do now after we proved we could be reasonable. It took adjusting on all our parts, but it was worth it. Now, when Kirill asks me to do something with a certain serious look on his face, I know it's important, and I should listen. And he knows he can trust me and doesn't have to worry."

Jasmine still wasn't so sure.

"I know we're explaining this badly," Sam said. "You have to understand. Since they were born Var, these men can never take another life mate. Since we weren't, we could conceivably go on to

MICHELLE M. PILLOW

love again, but who would want to? It is said that many Vars have died of broken hearts because they lost their mates. It's one of the reasons our husbands' father, King Attor, taught his sons never to life mate. He'd seen what it could do. Lucky for us, they didn't listen to the old fool."

"Anyway," Tori said, giving Sam a stern look as she insulted the dead king. Sam looked properly chastised, and suddenly both women burst into laughter.

"Well, he was," Sam mumbled, grinning. Ulyssa and Tori instantly nodded in agreement. "Should something happen to us, they'd be alone for hundreds of years."

"That's why they tend to be overprotective," Ulyssa said. All three women studied Jasmine as if willing her to understand. "But once they know they can trust you, they ease up a little on the whole domineering thing. It takes them awhile to get over the fear that they might lose you."

"And with their father's teachings drummed into their heads, it's especially difficult." Tori leaned over and took Jasmine's hand.

Jasmine didn't move for a long time. Slowly, she drew her hand away and placed it in her lap. "You came here tonight with the sole purpose of telling me all this, didn't you?"

All three women gave her a guilty look.

"We wanted to see you, as well," Ulyssa assured her.

Jasmine nodded, her mouth tight. "You think by telling me this that Reid and I will magically get together?"

"Well, we thought…" Tori began, making a weak noise.

"Yeah, that pretty much sums it up," Sam broke in.

"We thought it might help you be more patient with Reid," Ulyssa explained.

"These Var men are a handful, but I promise their brains do eventually catch up to their hearts."

"It's aggravating, I know, believe me," Sam said.

"Believe *us*," Ulyssa amended.

"Do try to have patience," Tori said, her eyes shining with hope. "And just be blunt about how you feel. I swear, they can run a kingdom, but they can be so dense when it comes to their feelings."

"And, if that doesn't work, do what I told Tori to try when she was having trouble with Quinn. Hit him over the head until he sees reason or blacks out." Ulyssa grinned.

"Besides, if anything, slugging Reid a few times will definitely make you feel better." Tori giggled. "That one might be the most aggravating of the bunch. I know I've felt like smacking him upside the head a few times myself."

"He's tough. He can take it," Sam assured Jasmine, nodding. Jasmine laughed, despite herself.

"Don't get us wrong, Reid's a good man. He may joke around, but deep inside, he does have feelings. If you demand he tells you the truth, he'll tell it to you straight. It's a matter of honor with the Var. They don't lie unless it's a life or death situation, or if it can't be helped."

"They never lie to their women," Tori said.

"I don't doubt that all the princes are honorable." Tears came to Jasmine's eyes. The women were so sweet. Strangely, she felt close to them, closer than she'd ever felt to anyone, besides Reid. The problem with Reid was that she couldn't talk to him like this. "But I think you're misunderstanding what's going on with Reid and me. You're assuming I'm his woman. I'm not."

The women exchanged a look.

Tori's face fell in sympathy. "So you already asked him straight out then?"

"I didn't have to," Jasmine answered. "I already know."

The women exchanged another look. Slowly, they all nodded and said no more about it as they changed the subject.

33

KIRILL's royal office was much like the rest of the palace, with the same beautiful tile work on the walls and the same medieval castle feel to the structure. Opposite the king's desk, a large fireplace was dwarfed by the even larger sidewall. Long banners hung on either side of it. A large woven rug of red and blue lay on the floor. Its intricate pattern was perhaps the loveliest in the palace. Next to the rug were large chairs, so deep they'd nearly swallow a person whole.

Reid stood in the middle of the room, looking between Falke and Kirill, his brow arched in question. "Well?"

"The Mafia ship is in orbit. They've contacted the palace and wish to send someone down to negotiate the return of their property," Kirill said, standing from behind his desk.

Reid tensed. His whole body shook. "Jasmine is not their property."

"Knowing what we do about the Mafia, we will not send her back with them. Honor forbids it," Falke said.

Reid didn't care about his personal honor. He cared about Jasmine. Nothing else mattered.

"You know, I always thought that when you finally found out you had another half to your heart, we'd all have a good laugh," Kirill said. "But, I find nothing funny about your situation."

Reid looked at him.

"Do you remember what you told me, Reid? We do not live our father's life. It is up to us to make our own destiny," Kirill said. "King Attor was—"

"Do you think I'm being stubborn over some nonsense our father said?" Reid asked in disbelief. "I knew he was wrong the first moment I saw her. I didn't want to admit it, but I knew. She's been in my head with just one look at her. I've dreamed of her. She completes me somehow. I've been obsessed with her."

"Then?" Kirill asked.

"She's not obsessed with me," Reid answered

quietly. He turned his back, unable to meet his brothers' eyes.

"Have you asked her?" Kirill's voice was quiet, gauging.

"I didn't have to. She told me how she felt," Reid laughed, a low, sad sound that held no pleasure. "And, fool that I was, I mated her life to mine. I suppose it is some kind of poetic justice. The one who would never fall mates to a woman who would not have him."

"You didn't tell her?" Falke asked. "She doesn't know, does she?"

"What's to tell?" Reid lifted his chin. "There's no point in embarrassing myself further and making her uncomfortable in the process. If she wants me, she'll stay when the time comes to make that choice."

"Reid, no." Kirill shook his head. "Women are not like us. They need to be told. They're not Var. Don't make the mistake of—"

"What's the plan?" Reid interrupted, unable to discuss it further. He'd spent several glorious days with Jasmine, watching her every move for a sign that she cared for him more than a friend, more than just a lover. That sign never came.

"Quinn is talking with them now in the communications room," Kirill said. "He's stalling, waiting for our decision. Our wives are with Jasmine, keeping her occupied and safe. If she tries to leave, they will restrain her by any means necessary. Jarek took his crew back on his ship, and they are watching things from the sky."

"She's your wife, Reid," Falke said. "The decision is yours. Should you ask us, we will fight them."

Reid nodded his thanks, but he could not ask his brothers to fight. They had their own wives and children on the way. If there were another way, he'd find it. Fighting would be the last option. "Let their man come down. Maybe we can convince him that Jasmine's not here. Or, maybe we can negotiate with them for her. They're businessmen, seedy ones, but businessmen nonetheless."

"I'm sure we'd all like to get that Doctor St. Claire within punching distance," Kirill said.

Reid nodded. A fire burned in him. He would give anything to avenge Jasmine and give her peace.

"It is most likely they know she's here," Falke said. "Denying that will only create further distrust."

Reid nodded, forcing all emotion aside. "Very well. We'll say nothing, just let them make their proposal first. Tell Quinn to arrange it."

"I'll alert the soldiers," Falke added.

Kirill nodded. "We'll meet them outside on the landing dock. I don't want them in the palace. We'll have Siren on high alert."

Reid nodded. "Very well. Let's do it."

Jasmine looked around the table, eyeing the three suddenly very guilty looking women. They'd been chatting nonstop for nearly an hour. It became apparent that their minds were preoccupied elsewhere. But when Tori mumbled, "I hate this part," Jasmine knew for sure something was up.

"There's something going on, isn't there?" Jasmine demanded, standing up. The women instantly pushed up from the table. Jasmine made a move for the door.

"Siren," Ulyssa said. "Lock us in until I give the order."

"Yes, my queen," Siren answered.

Jasmine ran for the door, pulling at it. It was locked. "Siren, let me out."

The computer didn't answer.

"Siren," Jasmine ordered. "Do you hear me? I said let me out of here."

"I'm sorry, Princess Jasmine, but I'm just a slut and can't understand you," the computer answered.

"Did she just say she was a slut?" Jasmine demanded, facing the women who stood behind her. "And did she just call me a princess?"

"Oh, no," Ulyssa said, rubbing her belly. "You didn't happen to insult Siren, did you? She's really touchy."

"Siren," Tori warned. "Jasmine didn't mean anything she said. Don't zap her."

"Zap me?" Jasmine gasped, looking around the room. Nothing had changed.

"Apologize to her, quick," Tori said. "I made her mad, and she zapped my backside, making me pass out."

"I heard she locked Reid in the weapons chamber for calling her an overpriced piece of junk," Sam whispered.

"I thought he said she was ugly," Ulyssa said, furrowing her brow.

"It doesn't matter," Tori insisted in a rush. "Trust me. Apologize."

Feeling like an idiot, Jasmine apologized to the computer. "I'm sorry, Siren. I didn't mean it. I was just trying to make Reid mad and I…I apologize."

"Thank you, my lady," Siren said, the voice cheerful. "Apology logged."

"Will you please unlock the door, now?" Jasmine asked sweetly.

"I'm sorry, my lady, but access to such commands is denied to level eight security clearance."

Jasmine opened her mouth, about ready to call the computer a few other choice names when Tori rushed to her and covered her mouth. "Trust me on this one, Jasmine. Let it go."

"Oh," Ulyssa moaned. "I'm not feeling so well."

Jasmine frowned, thinking the queen was just trying to distract her from leaving.

"Oh, my…" Sam said.

"Ulyssa?" Tori asked.

There was a sound of water raining on stone. Ulyssa's gown was soaked from the waist down. She looked up from where a puddle gathered around her feet, her eyes wide. "I think I'm having a baby. I've been having cramps all day. I thought it was indigestion again from eating all that chocolate last night before bed."

"No," Sam said. "It's too early yet. You can't have this baby."

"I don't think that matters," Jasmine put forth. "Her water's broken. Go and get her husband."

"No, you can't," Ulyssa said. "He's with Reid, they're…"

The queen grabbed her stomach and moaned. Sam paled, reaching for her and then backing away.

"You were married to a doctor, Jasmine, is this…?" Ulyssa said, her eyes tearing in fright.

Jasmine shook her head, trying to clear it. Ulyssa misread the action and swayed on her feet. Instantly, Jasmine's mind took over with what had to be done. "Tori, tell Siren to monitor her life functions or whatever the command for this computer is. I'm assuming she can do that?"

Tori nodded and gave Siren the order.

"Do you have a medic?" Jasmine asked.

Sam nodded. "Yes, but he's making his rounds in the village today. The palace is on high alert until after…"

"You might as well tell me so we can get past it," Jasmine said.

"Argh!" Ulyssa screamed, her knees buckling as she grabbed her stomach. Near breathless, she said, "The guys have gone to meet with the Medical Mafia to see what they want. Aside from that, we don't know what's happening. We're just waiting to get word that it's all right to come out."

Jasmine tensed. "So you were sent to babysit me?"

"Yes," Ulyssa rushed. "Now, could you hate me for this later?"

"Get her on the bed." Jasmine shook, keeping focused. Tori and Sam helped the pregnant woman to lie down. "Tori, does Siren have any medical functions such as for injections or anything at all?"

Tori asked the computer. It wasn't fully operational as a medic, but it did have some uses. It monitored the contractions, and they were able to sanitize their hands in the bathroom. Sam rigged the food simulator to materialize something to help ease Ulyssa's pain. Ulyssa refused to drink it, worried it might hurt the baby. Jasmine knew it wouldn't, but she didn't press the issue.

Jasmine took a deep breath. Because Tori was a scientist, she was a big help. Between the two of them they managed to set forth a game plan. Sam held Ulyssa's hand, talking her through it and giving encouragement.

"Okay," Jasmine said, sitting on the end of the bed and taking a deep breath. Her fingers shook, but she tried not to let Ulyssa see her worry. "I think we're ready."

"*Ahhh!*" Ulyssa screamed. "That's good, cause ready or not, here he comes."

35

REID GLANCED AT KIRILL. His brother's face paled slightly. Quietly, he asked, "What is it?"

They stood on the walkway outside the palace. None of them liked the Mafia being so close to their home, but the Var guards were inside prepared for battle should anything happen. Besides, none of the brothers wanted to leave the palace or their women unattended while they met the men elsewhere.

"It's nothing," Kirill said, his jaw stiff. "I just felt Ulyssa for a second."

"If you need..." Reid began.

"No, I trust her. She can take care of herself. I'll feel it if she needs me to come to her," Kirill said.

Reid nodded as he looked toward the end of

the platform, wishing he could have such trust between him and Jasmine. The large ship had docked and three men in dark, form-fitting suit jackets that reached to their knees and buttoned all the way down the front, approached them. Their pants were loose around their legs. One of the men carried a small, square suitcase. Reid wasn't fooled. Even with their refined appearance, they were still criminals.

"Ambassador Reid," one of the men said, eyeing him. "Or are you Ambassador Jarek?"

"I'm Prince Reid," Reid said, lifting his chin. He didn't recognize the man who spoke but assumed he'd seen his speech at the medical conference on Nozando. The man with the suitcase stood a few paces behind the other two.

"I'm sorry, you highness. I didn't realize you were royalty." The man bowed, but he didn't look any more respectful.

Reid said nothing. The men eyed his brothers.

"I'm Doctor Ellington," the man who'd spoken said. Then, motioning to the man at his side, he introduced him. "This is Doc Francis. We've come to negotiate the return of our property."

Doc Francis was an older gentleman. He didn't speak, merely stared. Reid glanced behind him to the man with the suitcase. Was that Doctor St. Claire? He'd never seen the man so he couldn't be sure. The guy wasn't acting like a man who'd lost his wife.

"I wasn't aware we were in possession of your property," Reid said.

"Don't play games," Doctor Ellington snapped. "Your friend already talked."

Reid tensed. Friend? Did he mean Jarek or perhaps a member of Jarek's crew?

Doctor Ellington waved his hand. The man with the suitcase came forward and opened it. With a jerk, he dumped the contents on the ground. A severed head rolled toward Reid's feet. Reid took a deep, slow breath, forcing his nerves to be calm. Slowly, as if he hadn't a concern in the galaxy, he looked down. The head's face was pointed toward his feet. Whoever it had been, he'd had short black hair with graying temples. By the looks of the laceration on his face, he'd been tortured. His eyes were missing from his head. Reid didn't recognize him.

"Who's this?"

"You don't know him?" Doctor Ellington asked, surprised. "Perhaps you just don't recognize Doctor St. Claire. He has lost a little weight, hasn't he?"

Reid glanced down again. This was Doctor St. Claire? He took a deep breath, wondering how Jasmine would take the news if and when he told her. Reid couldn't say he was sorry for it.

"This is St. Claire?" Reid asked. "You've done me a favor. Now I can keep his wife."

The men exchanged looks. "This isn't a joke. I assure you, we're very serious."

"And I assure you," Kirill said. "We are as well."

"Then give us back our booth," Doctor Ellington said.

Reid tensed. Booth? They were here for a booth?

"I'm afraid I'm not following," Kirill said.

"And you are?" Doctor Ellington demanded.

"He is the king," Falke answered. The big cat-shifter took a step forward, towering over the men. The men's confidence faltered some, and they took a small step back.

"Your majesty," Doctor Ellington said, bowing respectfully while keeping an eye on Falke.

"What is this about a booth? You're not here for Jasmine St. Claire?" Reid asked.

"Who? Doctor St. Claire's wife?" Doctor Ellington laughed. "What would I want with that insipid woman? If you want her, keep her. We don't care. We just want our medical booth back. Jasmine won it in a drawing. Doctor St. Claire tells us it was put on your ship. He tried to swear he didn't know what was in it, but then he did trick you into stealing it, didn't he?"

Reid could barely breathe. These men didn't want Jasmine. They wanted the stupid medical booth on Jarek's ship.

"We want what's ours," Doctor Ellington said.

"Pick up your head," Reid answered, frowning in what he hoped looked like boredom and annoyance. Doctor Ellington motioned to the man with the suitcase. He placed the head inside and stepped back. "Go back to your ship. I don't know what St. Claire was up to, but he gave us that booth as a present. We did think it amusing at the time, especially when he said it was to pay us for taking his wife from him. But she's pretty and I desired a bed slave."

Reid didn't mean it, but it was the only thing he could think of. These men looked at the Var people as primitive, backward thinking barbarians. Why change their opinion? Let them think the Var were stupid fools.

"And the booth?" Doctor Ellington insisted.

"Let me keep the woman and agree to go away peacefully and I'll let you take the booth." Reid lifted his chin. "We haven't taken it out of the crate. You'll get it exactly as we did."

Doctor Ellington smirked. The look on his face was condescending as if he thought the Vars no more than a pack of fools. "Done."

Reid watched the men leave, standing quietly

until the ship took off. A warm gust of air blew around them. When it was far off the ground, Kirill asked, "What do you think they want with a booth?"

"I don't know. Have Ulyssa tell her HIA contacts. Make sure they stop the ship far away from here," Reid said. "If they thought it was worth killing people and traveling all the way to our quadrant, it can't be good."

"What about Jasmine?" Falke asked.

"Doctor St. Claire is dead," Reid said, torn between relief and sadness. "She's safe from him. The rest is up to her."

36

JASMINE LOOKED at the squirming baby in Ulyssa's arms. It was still a little purple in color, but Siren assured them the new life form's functions were healthy and strong. The child was swaddled in a cloth and the queen looked worn out, but very happy.

The door handled jiggled, causing them all to gasp in alarm. It was locked. A pounding started on the other side.

"Ulyssa?" Kirill's voice called, sounding worried. "Are you all right?"

"Siren," Ulyssa said softly. "Unlock the door."

"Yes, my queen," Siren said, seconds before the door burst open.

Kirill was the first through with Reid directly

behind him. Soon, Quinn and Falke joined them. All eyes turned to the bed where Ulyssa was lying.

"Come and meet your son," she said softly, looking at her husband. Kirill's eyes widened. Congratulations broke out as his brothers slapped his back. Jasmine watched Reid. His eyes met hers and his smile faded.

Kirill went to his wife and kissed her before taking the baby. "My son."

Jasmine pulled back as everyone crowded over the bed. This was a family moment, and she wasn't technically part of the family. The door was still open, and she slipped quietly out of it.

"Jasmine, wait," Reid called behind her. She turned in surprise, thinking he wouldn't notice her going. "I need to speak with you."

She nodded and glanced around the hall. "Here?"

"Ah," Reid too looked around as if thinking. "Let's go to Kirill's office."

He began to lead the way through the halls. Jasmine stayed a half pace behind him, eyeing his gorgeous body through the corner of her eyes to make sure he was unharmed. She'd been so scared when she learned he was going to meet with the Mafia. Her first impulse had been to run after him and protect him, which had been silly really. She knew instinctively that Reid would be able to take care of himself.

She was so relieved to see him safe, that she hardly cared about anything else. When they got to the office, he shut the door behind them so they could be alone. Jasmine faced him, keeping the distance between their bodies. She wanted him so much. Her body was starved for his touch. Searching his stoic features, she knew they needed to talk first. She pushed thoughts of sex from her mind.

"You met with the Medical Mafia," Jasmine said. It wasn't a question. Reid nodded, and she was glad he didn't lie to her. "What happened?"

"They wanted that medical booth you gave us. As far as we can tell, it must have some sort of information they need or maybe they're smuggling something with it. We've contacted Jarek, and he's going to make arrangements to give it back to them. Then, they're going to leave. Once they're out of our airspace, Ulyssa will contact HIA, and they'll intercept the ship once it's far from here. They didn't come here for you, Jasmine. They came for their booth."

"But, Chad, he—"

"Chad's dead."

Jasmine's eyes rounded. "You…?"

"No, them. I saw his head," Reid took a deep breath, studying her intently.

Jasmine gasped, her knees weakening with relief as she sank to the floor. Chad was dead? She was free? Reid was at her side in an instant, kneeling by her as he held her arms to keep her from falling.

Trembling, she asked, "You're sure it was him?"

"Did he have black hair, gray along here?" Reid asked pointing to his temple. Jasmine nodded. "Then, yes, it was definitely him. Doctor Ellington just assumed I'd know who he was."

"So it's done? It's over?" she asked. Chad was dead. Dead. She was free. "I'm free?"

"Yes, Jasmine, you are free." Reid let her go and slowly got to his feet. Jasmine pushed up from the floor. Without stopping to think, she went to him and wrapped her arms around his neck.

"Thank you," she said, kissing his lips lightly, "Thank you."

Jasmine kissed him again, this time letting her mouth linger a second longer. Pulling back, she looked at his lips, hesitated, and then leaned in to deepen her kisses. Her lips parted, and she moaned. Reid always tasted so good, so addicting. She felt his body lurch against her stomach, his shaft becoming full. Before she could gather her thoughts, she was passionately tugging on his waistband.

"I'm not wearing any panties," she said by way of invitation.

Reid growled, his eyes lightening to green, and she knew that he was as aroused as she was. His hands pulled at her skirt, lifting it up. In moments like this their bodies were so in tune. It was as if she could read what he wanted.

Jasmine untied his laces, loosening his pants. Her naked thighs brushed his. She glanced around. "Desk?"

Reid nodded in approval. Almost savagely, he twirled her around and leaned her over the desk. He came up behind her, holding her skirt out of the way as he grabbed her hips. Jasmine's breasts rubbed along the solid surface through the thinner material. The hard press only added to the urgency of their situation, heightening her desire. She gripped the sides, liking how the position gave him control. There was something very erotic to the game of being helpless before him, about to be conquered by the big, strong warrior prince.

Suddenly, Jasmine realized she trusted him completely when it came to her body. She knew he'd never hurt her. That is what made these games they played so much fun and exciting. So, if she could trust him like this, could she come to trust him with more than just her body? Could she trust him with her heart?

Jasmine felt his hard, hot tip pressing into her wet folds. Her body was aroused to such a fevered, needy pitch that she couldn't concentrate on her own questions. Tensing, she waited for that first thrust, for the feel of his thick mass stretching her wide. She needed to feel him inside her.

"Oh, yes, Reid," she urged, "take me."

Reid groaned, thrusting forward, filling her tight body to the brink. She gripped the desk and moaned. He pressed his hips against her in small, shallow strokes, hitting her in just the right spot. She squirmed before him. One of his palms laid flat at her side as his other hand came around her waist. He pressed a finger into her folds, finding the little bud hidden there. She instantly tensed as he stroked her with both his hand and his shaft.

Jasmine couldn't move, as he forced her to take the pleasure he gave her. Her toes curled. His hips continued to move in small circles as he picked up the pace. Her thighs hit upon the desk as his thrust became more urgent, deeper and harder. Animalistic grunts sounded over the room, attesting to his satisfaction. The two firm points of her nipples ground against the smooth surface, sending shockwaves of pleasure through her body. Reid pinched the wet bud between his fingers, rolling it back and forth.

The stimulation was too much. Jasmine tensed, crying out weakly as her orgasm hit. Her muscles clenched him, but he didn't stop. Riding her to a full release, Reid slowed his body. Only when she started to come down, did he stiffen, coming inside her.

He drew his hand away first, pressing it to the desk. Jasmine was glad she had the support underneath her. Her legs were shaking so badly she was sure she wouldn't have been able to stand without his support. After a long moment, he pulled back, brushing her skirt down over her backside. Jasmine groaned in protest as she stood up. Still breathing rapidly she leaned against the desk, her head down.

"Thank you," she said softly.

Reid chuckled. "You don't have to thank me for that."

"I meant, thank you for trying to protect me." Jasmine turned to him. He was lacing up his pants. "But, I want you to know I can take care of myself."

His smiled faded.

"I don't appreciate you taking decisions away from me. I don't appreciate having your sisters-by-marriage sent to distract me while you go out and fight my battles for me. Yes, it turned out well, but you should have talked to me first. You should've told me what was happening."

"So what if I fight battles for you? Is that so bad? I'm a man, a warrior. There is no shame in it." Reid practically shouted at her. "Just as there is no shame in you being a woman to be protected. We are what we are, Jasmine. You are the physically weaker sex. You can't take grown men in battle. I've spent most of my life at battle. Why not let me take care of it for you?"

"Reid," she said, taking a deep breath. Jasmine closed her eyes. "It's not the fact that you were trying to protect me that upsets me. It's the fact that you didn't explain what you were doing. If you had come to me—"

"You'd what? You'd have let me handle it?" Reid snorted in obvious disbelief.

Jasmine sighed. He was right.

"No," she answered honestly. "I probably wouldn't have. I don't like being under someone's control. I spent four years being told what to do, how to act, what to think and say."

"I am not him, Jasmine," Reid said. To look at him, no one would believe that they'd just been intimate. His whole body shook, and his face turned red. His fists clenched and unclenched at his sides. "I am not that man."

"I know," she answered, and then louder, she yelled, "I know!"

"Then why are you fighting me?" he demanded.

Tears came to her eyes. She couldn't look at him. "The computer called me princess."

Reid tensed. She didn't have to look at him to feel it.

"You made me your half mate, didn't you? That's why I feel so drawn to you, isn't it?" Jasmine shivered. "You didn't ask me first."

"Jasmine," Reid began. His words trailed off as she lifted up her hand to stop him.

"Please, don't say anything. I just need some time to think," Jasmine said, walking past him. "If you care for me at all, you'll just give me a little time."

"You look worse than I do, and I just gave birth four days ago," Ulyssa said.

Jasmine sat on the queen's couch. A soft light glowed from the fireplace over the living room. Arched entryways led to various parts of the house, and the walls were decorated with the long Var banners. It was a beautiful home, but Jasmine didn't look around as she stared at her hands. The king had left with his baby son, insistent on showing him how to get about the palace. Ulyssa had laughed. When they were alone, she'd confided that Kirill just wanted to show the baby off—*again*.

"It's nothing, I'm just tired," Jasmine answered.

"Reid been keeping you up late at night? You're one lucky woman. I've heard stories about that man," Ulyssa teased.

I wish, Jasmine thought. "No. I haven't seen him at all. Well, there was that one time Tori took me to the banquet hall to dine with everyone a couple of days ago. He was there, but he left without a word as soon as I came in."

"How odd," Ulyssa sat up. "When's the last time you talked to him?"

"Right after you had the baby, and we left," Jasmine said.

Ulyssa bit her lip. "Hmm, where did you go?"

"The royal office," Jasmine said. Suddenly, she blushed, remembering what they'd done over the king's desk. At the time, she hadn't even stopped to consider where they were.

"I guess by that look I won't have to ask what you did," Ulyssa chuckled.

Jasmine's blush deepened, and she needed to change the subject. Talking about Reid only made the ache inside her worse. "Tori mentioned that a Draig ambassador came by."

"Three boys and one girl born on the same day as my son," Ulyssa said. "What are the odds of that? Prince Zoran and his wife Pia had the girl. Politically, it's a good match. Zoran is like Falke, a true warrior and leader, and very respected amongst his people."

"It's so strange that they were all born on the same day," Jasmine said.

"Kirill calls it fate," Ulyssa chuckled, but the sound was a little sad. "He says it's a sign."

"What do you say?"

"What's done is done. If I've learned anything, the future is never written in the stars. They might point in a certain direction, but they never are set." Ulyssa smiled, eyeing Jasmine carefully. "Okay, let's figure out this situation between you and Reid. What did you talk about?"

Jasmine sensed the woman's need to change the subject. However, she couldn't help wishing Ulyssa had picked a different topic. But maybe talking it out would do some good. She was tired of crying herself to sleep at night, pining for Reid. "He told me what happened and that Chad was dead."

"Is that it?"

"Mostly."

"What's the rest of it? What's the last thing you said to him before you parted? Or what did he say to you?"

"We got in a small fight," she admitted, remembering the conversation clearly in her mind. "I told him I didn't like him protecting me about without talking to me first and telling me what was going on."

"Good for you," Ulyssa inserted, nodding.

"Then he got upset saying I wouldn't have let him take care of it if he had talked to me."

"Ah, I hate to say it, but he does have a point." Ulyssa shrugged. "Sorry, it's true."

"I know," Jasmine grumbled. "Honestly, I'm glad it's taken care of. Jarek got the medical booth back to them, and they're gone. Chad's dead and I'm free."

"Is that what you said to him?" Ulyssa asked.

"Not completely," Jasmine sighed. "I'm just thinking out loud."

"Get back to the fight." Ulyssa leaned forward, intently studying Jasmine's face. "What happened after he said you wouldn't have let him take care of the problem for you?"

"Ah, not much, I told him about Siren calling me a princess and that I knew about how he'd made me a half mate," Jasmine said.

"Did he deny it?"

"I didn't give him a chance. But why would the computer be programmed to say it if it wasn't true?" Jasmine leaned her head back and closed her eyes. She'd finally gotten what she wanted, freedom. Why wasn't she happy? Why did she feel so empty inside? "I saw the look on his face."

"I think you need to talk to him," Ulyssa said.

"I want to. He doesn't want to talk to me." Jasmine stood and began to pace. "He's avoiding me. I got mad at him for making me a half mate without asking first and told him to give me a little time to think, and he's just disappeared. It's like I suddenly have the spotted plague."

"You asked for time? What did you say exactly?" Ulyssa asked, moving to stand. She winced slightly and clearly thought better of it. Instead, she readjusted her body on the couch.

"I said that if he cared for me at all, he'd just give me a little time."

Ulyssa smiled.

"What's so funny?"

"Sweetie, he's not avoiding you. He's giving you time. He's showing you that he cares."

"Four days?" Jasmine said doubtfully.

"Think about it, Jas. He's a Var. His life span is for hundreds of years. What do you think he'd consider a little bit of time?"

Jasmine froze. Now that actually made sense.

"A year? Two years? Ten? What's all that compared to hundreds?"

"He's going to avoid me for ten years?" Jasmine gasped, appalled and hurt by the very idea of it. She couldn't go ten years without Reid. Then it hit her. She could barely survive half of a week without him. She needed him.

Jasmine sank into a chair. She loved him. She'd known it for a long time but had tried her hardest to pretend that if she didn't think the words they wouldn't be true. If she didn't think them, they couldn't hurt her. It didn't matter. Spoken or not. Her love for him was real, and it was there and it hurt deeply.

"Not if you go to him now," Ulyssa urged. "Find him before he decides the best way to give you what you want is by leaving. His honor will make him go. He'll go because he'll believe that's what you wanted him to do."

Jasmine didn't move. She didn't even know where to begin looking.

"Siren," Ulyssa called. "Find Reid for me."

"Yes, my queen," the computer answered in her syrupy voice. "Prince Reid is in the courtyard battling with Prince Falke. My sensors detect no weapons, my lady."

"Siren, where is the courtyard?" Jasmine demanded.

"I'm sorry, Princess Jasmine, but that information is restricted," Siren answered.

"Siren," Ulyssa ordered. "Change Jasmine's security level from an eight to a two, please."

"Yes, my queen. Lady Jasmine is now a two security clearance."

"Thank you, Siren." Ulyssa motioned to Jasmine.

"Siren, show me how to get to the courtyard," Jasmine said, adding a hasty, "*please.*"

Jasmine waved to Ulyssa as she hurried to

follow Siren's directions. She heard grunting before she saw Falke and Reid locked in battle on the practice field in the center courtyard of the palace. Four walls surrounded the grassy yard, blocking it in on all sides with a covered walkway of intricate patterns and detailed mosaics.

Jasmine's body tensed. A hot wave of longing washed over her. Reid's back was naked, his feet bare. His muscles strained as he sparred with his brother. Every nerve she had tingled with desire for him

Suddenly, Reid stopped to sniff at the air. Falke shook loose and punched him, sending him sprawling back. Jasmine gasped. Falke looked at her, obviously surprised by her intrusion.

"Ah, sacred cats, Falke! That one actually hurt." Reid grumbled from the ground, rubbing his jaw.

Falke grinned and offered him a hand. Reid waved him away, getting up on his own. Then, as if suddenly realizing what had distracted him, he turned to Jasmine. His hand fell to the side. She saw the bruise already forming on his jaw. Falke patted Reid's shoulder as he passed him, nodded once to her and left.

Reid looked at her for a long moment and then nodded. He stiffly moved to follow Falke.

"Reid, wait," Jasmine said. "Don't go."

He stopped.

"I want to talk to you," she said, willing him to turn to her. He didn't. If he'd just look at her and smile his crooked little mischievous smile, he'd make this so much easier on her. "Thank you for giving me time."

At that, he did turn. He nodded once. "You've thought about things? Already?"

Already? Jasmine wanted to laugh. Ulyssa had been right. What were four days to a man like Reid? Though, by looking at his face, he had suffered as she had. Jasmine could only hope.

"Yes." She stepped closer. "I like it here, Reid. I like Qurilixen. I like the palace, your family, your customs."

He didn't move.

"I even kind of like Siren," she said, trying to get him to laugh.

He didn't. "Is that all? You like it here?"

"I lo..." Jasmine took a step toward him. She was more frightened than she'd ever been in her life. *I love you, Reid.* "I like you, as well."

"You *like* me," he said, stepping closer.

Jasmine nodded. "I've missed you."

"And you've missed me." His mouth softened, just a subtle movement, not the great smile she'd been hoping for. "Is that all?"

"I know you made me your half mate, Reid," Jasmine took a deep breath. "I'm not happy about you doing it without telling me and, in fact, I'm not sure how you did it. But, if you promise never to do things like that again without telling me first, then…"

"Then?"

"I want to stay as your half mate," Jasmine said. It broke her heart to settle for less than what she wanted, but no Reid was worse than having a little of him. "I know you're not the type to settle down, so I won't make demands on you. I like it here, and I have nowhere else to go."

"So you're staying because you have nowhere else?" The slight smile fell.

Jasmine grimaced. "You're listening to me all wrong."

"Well, then you're talking all wrong." He placed his hands on his hips.

"I'm telling you that I'll be your half mate. That's what you wanted, right?"

"Did I ever say that, Jasmine?" he asked. His voice was low as he came toward her. She didn't move. When he stopped, he was so close she could feel the heat of his body radiating over her. Leaning his face closer to hers, he asked, "Did you once ask me what I wanted?"

"What do you want?"

"It sure as hell isn't a half wife," he growled softly. "I never made you my half mate."

"Oh." Jasmine's eyes teared. It took all her willpower not to start crying. "The computer...it called me and I thought...but you didn't...so that when...love..."

"Love?" he whispered.

Oh, sacred... *cats* or whatever it was they cursed! Did she just say that out loud?

Shut up, Jasmine, she thought. *You're going to make a fool of yourself. Play it cool.*

His dark eyes looked deeply into hers. Everything about him stirred her. She trembled and nodded. "I love you. That's why I want to stay here."

Reid grinned. "That's the excuse I wanted to hear."

"But—?"

Reid grabbed her about the waist and pulled her body close. Kissing her until her lungs burned, he pulled back. "Now, ask me what I want. Don't assume anything. Ask me."

"What do you want?" Jasmine bit her lip. It felt so good, so right in his arms. She shivered, her heart refusing to beat until he answered.

"I want you to be my wife. Not a half mate, not just a lover, but my life mate. I want you, Jasmine, all of you. I love you." Reid brushed his lips to hers. "Say you'll be mine, forever."

Jasmine gasped, nodding frantically because the

words wouldn't pass her tightened throat. Her lips worked, but no sound came out.

"Yes?"

"Yes," she whispered, hugging him close. "Yes, yes."

Reid took her about the waist, twirling her in circles. Her feet lifted off the ground. She'd never been so happy. Then, setting her down, he said, "I'm glad you said that."

"Mm, me too," Jasmine leaned up to kiss him. Something about the look on his face made her pull back. "What?"

Reid grinned. "I'm glad you said that because I already life mated us."

"You did?" Jasmine gasped. "When?"

"Back at my house when I had you pinned up against the wall after I went hunting." He leaned over and kissed her neck, letting his sharper teeth glide harmlessly over her skin. "Mm, you asked me to rip off your clothes, and I…" He nipped her ear, giving a wickedly delicious little laugh.

Jasmine blushed. Glancing around, she scolded, "Reid, shh! Someone might hear this."

His answer was a low, primal growl as his hands slid behind her back to cup her butt. He squeezed, lifting her up against his erection.

"Reid," she tried to look stern. "At least cart me off to your bedroom first."

"Do you remember afterward?" Reid continued, pretending as if he didn't hear her protests.

"When I said I loved having sex with you?" Jasmine asked, she giggled despite herself. "It's true, you know."

"No, not that. The part when you pushed me down on the bed and then began to lick your way—"

Jasmine gasped, instantly silencing him with her mouth. "No, that wasn't it, you licked my—"

Jasmine kissed him again, passionately. She thrust her tongue into his mouth to keep him quiet. Reid laughed and pulled back. Then, a wicked grin in his eyes, he said, "As you wish."

Throwing her over his shoulder, he carted her off to the nearest free bedroom.

TWO MONTHS LATER...

Jasmine sat on Reid's lap. They were in a chair in Tori's living room. She nestled into her husband's embrace. Reid kissed her neck, lightly nibbling her skin in a way that made her shiver. Two months and still her body couldn't get enough of him. She was insatiable. Good thing, because Reid's appetite for her was just as bad. It's a wonder they even left the bedroom long enough to remember to eat.

Tori was asleep in the bedroom, having just given birth. Ulyssa was checking on her. Kirill was in the communications room telling Jarek the news. Jarek had taken off on a space mission. It seemed that he was one prince who couldn't stay put on land for very long.

The baby's imminent birth was why Jasmine and Reid had come back to the palace. Tori had insisted Jasmine be there. The princess claimed she was a good luck charm since she'd helped Ulyssa during her labor.

Jasmine sighed and looked at the little bundle swaddled in his father's arms. Quinn had a wide smile on his face as he held his son for all to see. She didn't mind helping out when it brought such innocence and life into the world.

Sam rested in Falke's arms, her legs stretched over the couch as she slept. Her stomach had swelled since Jasmine first came to the palace, and the poor thing slept quite a bit. Jasmine worried about Sam, but Falke assured her that everything was normal. Sam's body didn't handle pregnancy like other women's and, because of this, she needed lots of rest.

"Let me tell them," Reid whispered. "Please. I've been good. You promised I could tell them if I was good."

"Not today," Jasmine said. "This is Tori's day."

"What is not on Tori's day?" Tori asked, coming out of the bedroom door directly behind them.

Ulyssa supported Tori by the arm to keep her steady. "She insisted on getting out of bed, Quinn. Don't look at me like that."

"I want more," Quinn said, proudly holding the

baby to look at his mother. "I want a dozen of them, hundreds of them."

Tori snarled at her husband. Jasmine swore Quinn looked like the proudest father she'd ever seen. He couldn't quit grinning. Though, Kirill had been much the same way. Apparently, it must have been a Var tradition to celebrate a birth by claiming to want more.

Quinn only laughed at Tori's look. "Isn't he just the fiercest little warrior you've ever seen?"

Falke and Reid instantly nodded.

"Very fierce," Reid said.

"He'll make his father proud," Falke agreed.

Jasmine giggled, wondering what Reid would be like as a father. Would he have that same silly look on his face as Quinn had, that Kirill still had? She felt Reid's hand press along her stomach and knew he was thinking about the same thing.

"Tell us what?" Tori insisted, looking at Jasmine. Then, seeing Reid's hand she grinned. "You're not?"

"Yes," Jasmine said.

"No," Reid said. "She is."

"What?" Jasmine turned, confused. "That's what I said. Yes."

"But, she said you're not, and you are," Reid insisted.

"No, she exclaimed, '*you're not?*' as in, are you?"

Tori frowned. "Huh? What did I say?"

"She isn't, is what?" Quinn asked. "I'm lost."

"Pregnant," Tori said. "We are talking about pregnant, right?"

Reid and Jasmine nodded.

"Wait, are you or aren't you?" Ulyssa demanded.

Reid and Jasmine looked at each other and grinned. In unison, they said, "We are."

The End

THE SERIES CONTINUES...

Need more *Lords of the Var*®?
The books continue!
The Pirate Prince

Want to read the Draig side of things?
Dragon Lords: Barbarian Prince

Dragon Lords and *Lords of the Var*® in
Modern Day Earth?
Captured by a Dragon-Shifter: Determined Prince

Read all the Dragon Lords and Var books?
Yay, you, keep going!
Space Lords 1: His Frost Maiden

ABOUT MICHELLE M. PILLOW

New York Times & *USA TODAY* Bestselling Author

Michelle loves to travel and try new things, whether it's a paranormal investigation of an old Vaudeville Theatre or climbing Mayan temples in Belize. She believes life is an adventure fueled by copious amounts of coffee.

Newly relocated to the American South, Michelle is involved in various film and documentary projects with her talented director husband. She is mom to a fantastic artist. And she's managed by a dog and cat who make sure she's meeting her deadlines.

For the most part she can be found wearing pajama pants and working in her office. There may or may not be dancing. It's all part of the creative process.

Come say hello! Michelle loves talking with readers on social media!

www.MichellePillow.com

facebook.com/AuthorMichellePillow

twitter.com/michellepillow

instagram.com/michellempillow

bookbub.com/authors/michelle-m-pillow

goodreads.com/Michelle_Pillow

amazon.com/author/michellepillow

youtube.com/michellepillow

pinterest.com/michellepillow

THE PIRATE PRINCE

THE SERIES CONTINUES

(*Lords of the Var® 2*)
by Michelle M. Pillow

Cat-shifter Prince Jarek sails the high sky doing what he pleases...that is until drug dealers kidnap one of his men. But the rescue mission goes wrong and instead of a crewman, he liberates a woman who he believes is desperately trying to escape her captors. He soon discovers he unwittingly kidnapped a princess.

Princess Mei has just learned her future from a seer, and it seems fate is giving her in marriage to a neighboring ruler. She will do her duty, but first she wants to experience an adventure. When the pirates come to steal, she knows exactly who she wants that adventure to be.

The Pirate Prince Excerpt

"What in the blazing star trails are we doing here, cap?" Evan Cormier grumbled, running his fingers through his short black hair. His eyes were focused on the great Lintianese palace before them. "What has that space cadet gotten us into now? I told him to leave that woman alone. I told him she was trouble, but can Rick ever see past his own lust? No! She batted her eyelashes at him and off he went like a little remloch mindlessly following a Grishelm floral dragon."

Jarek glanced at Evan and hid his smile. Evan was a good man to have on a crew, a hard worker and a hell of a smart guy. The man was part telepath, a fact he didn't share with too many, and it was those skills that Evan was referring to now. Rick was the pilot on their ship, *The Conqueror*, and every inch a playboy. Evan had warned him against going with the dark-haired enchantress who had flirted with him on Leinad's star port where they'd stopped for fuel, but Rick hadn't listened. The enchantress had kidnapped him, for some reason still unknown to them, and taken him with her to the far reaches of the planet of Lintian. Though, knowing Rick, he'd opened his big mouth and said something stupid to insult her. It wasn't likely she'd taken him with her because she couldn't live without him.

So, now they were on Lintian to save him. Jarek knew Evan was irritated by this detour. They were all irritated by the detour, but Rick was their friend, and they would never leave him behind—no matter how stupid he'd acted which resulted in getting kidnapped by an intergalactic drug trader.

"We're here because we're rescuing Dev's best friend," Lochlann teased, dryly. He was the only crew member aboard *The Conqueror* from Jarek's home planet of Qurilixen. Jarek was a Var, a cat-shifter. Lochlann was a Draig, a dragon-shifter. Usually, the Var and Draig were at war, but Jarek had never seen a reason for it. It was why he'd left his homeland and why his good friend, Lochlann, had come with him. In the wide open skies of space, things like race didn't matter. Everyone was different.

Dev snorted at Lochlann's comment but said nothing. The group of men tried to contain their laughter. Dev was half Belvon, a demonic looking race with red skin and a very stern temperament. Aside from the intense coloring, he appeared humanoid, only larger. He was the ship's muscle and a bit of a loner. Rick was the polar opposite of Dev. The Belvon was all about maintaining order.

Rick was all about breaking it. It often led to humorous fights. Sometimes when the crew was bored, they'd provoke them into an argument for the sake of entertainment. But, when it came down to it, if Rick was in trouble, Dev was there just like everyone else to bail him out. They were like a family.

A family of misfits, Jarek thought with a small chuckle. He wouldn't trade his life of freedom for anything in the world.

"I say we let Rick rot," Lucien mumbled, pouting. "Would serve him right for breaking my virtual girlfriend. Does he even realize how long it took me to get her breasts just right? And then he goes and melts all three of them off. Poor Fanessa!"

"Did you drink more Torganian Rum?" Viktor, Lucien's brother, demanded. The two constantly bickered but were actually quite close. If one said the sky was white, the other would swear it was black just for the sake of disagreeing. They were half human, half Dere, and had a milky white complexion that contrasted with the strangest red-brown and red-green of their eyes. Lucien was a communications genius, and Viktor was one hell of a mechanic. The man could rig anything. "We can't let him rot." Viktor paused. "He owes me space credits from that last card game."

"Yes," Jackson, a dark blond security officer, agreed. "And you owe me."

"Oh, right, yeah." Viktor cleared his throat. "I forgot about that. Well, how 'bout we cut out the middle man and just say Rick owes you?"

"Not likely," Jackson said. "He's not good for it and I'd rather not take your loss."

"Can we please concentrate on saving Rick? Then we can argue about who gets to kick his ass first," Jarek said, wondering briefly how he'd ever come to captain such a crew. Fate was funny that way.

They hid behind a long stone gate, looking up at the palace which was on top of a miniature mountain with a flat top. Long rows of stairs led up from the base, carved from the tan stone of the planet's earth. Their position was halfway up so they could easily see the front entrance. Platforms were carved intermittently along the stairs on the way to the top, decorated with black pots and golden statues inlaid with precious jewels. Jarek tensed. The Song Dynasty was a wealthy one. They must indeed have no fear of intruders if they put their treasure within plain view of the city below.

"One of us has to go in," Lucien said, eyeing Dev.

"Yes, I would make the obvious choice," Dev drawled, his tone heavy with sarcasm. With his giant red body, he was the farthest thing from the slender humanoid culture of Lintian.

Jarek tried not to laugh. Dev had been around Rick for too long and was beginning to pick up some sarcasm. Usually, the man was completely sober in nature.

"He's right, guys," Jarek said, "one of us needs to get in there and find out where the secret purple jade mines are located. My sources say that's where they've taken Rick."

All eyes turned back to the palace. The location of the mines wasn't known, no matter how much money he'd thrown down for the information. Most things about this planet were a mystery. Jarek could respect their desire for privacy. His home planet of Qurilixen was the same way. However, at the moment, it wasn't serving his purpose in finding Rick.

"Are you sure your sources are right? I hear tell that not even the greatest thieves can slip into this place," Lochlann said.

"Yeah, they guard their purple jade-like the Tog women protect their men," Viktor added. "Rick would have to get his ass dragged here."

Jarek frowned. He'd heard much of the same thing. Lintian was an isolated planet that many stayed clear of. The fact that its position was a long way off, combined with the rumored impossibility of breaching the security made it a daunting place, little worth a space traveler's time. Even if purple jade was valued quite highly, a pirate couldn't spend a fortune if he was dead. But they weren't here for jade. They were here for their friend.

"Why couldn't he have gotten kidnapped by Lord Maximus and taken to the Galaxy Playmates' mansion?" Lucien asked. "That way we could fight off half-naked playmates instead of these lethal warriors."

"Rick wouldn't want to be rescued from that," Lochlann said.

"Who would?" Jackson added under his breath. All of their eyes were still trained on the palace.

"I slipped through the city just fine earlier," Jarek said, hoping his men would take that to mean it was possible to get through. "Stealth is the key. This isn't the kind of place that you go in blasting. We'd never stand a chance against all those guards in a head-to-head fight. We're too outnumbered. Ideally, it's best if they don't know we're here."

The men nodded.

"Besides," Jarek continued, "no one has tried to breach these walls for centuries. Their guards have probably become lax. They won't be expecting us, especially not looking for a plain map. It should be a simple slip in and slip out type of job."

One long building made up the palace. It had

tiled roofs with wide eaves that tilted up at the ends toward the sky. A long open walkway supported by columns was across the front of the large structure. An entranceway opened up in the center, leading inside the building or down a long row of steps to the outside world. Guards stood along the columned walkway, their loose fitting clothing very reminiscent of the Draig casual wear. It looked comfortable, yet military at the same time. The building seemed to grow out at the side into an enclosed hall, slowly working its way from the very top of the mountain down the side until joining to a lower building that had its own columned entrance and guards.

"It doesn't look like walking up to the front door and slipping in is going to be an option," Jarek said, eyeing the dark skinned warriors. Their long hair was pulled back in a single braid, keeping it out of their faces. They were slight in stature compared to the Var warriors, but he wasn't fooled. He'd seen some of them practicing in a field as they had sneaked into the city. They moved with such graceful ease and deadly precision when they fought, that Jarek knew they would be formidable opponents.

"I'll do it," Jackson said. "I'm the best climber, and if the inside of the palace is constructed like the outside, I should be able to make my way across the ceiling without notice."

"No, it's too risky. All someone would have to do is look up," Jarek denied the offer. "There are too many guards. Besides, we have no way of knowing what the inside looks like. The ceilings could be smooth with nothing to grab on to."

"That doesn't leave us too many options. If we can't infiltrate, we'll have to fight," Dev said softly. He opened his mouth to continue, but Lucien's voice interrupted him.

"Oh, my..." Lucien let loose a soft whistle. "Would you look at that tempting piece of Lintianese culture?"

Jarek immediately saw what had caught Lucien's attention. A slight female shuffled out of the palace, meekly following a taller man whose hair was knotted on the top of his head. The topknot seemed to be a popular style amongst the people. Jarek could instantly tell the man was royalty, or at least a nobleman, by the way he carried himself and by the way the guards bowed in respect. However, the guards ignored the woman.

Jarek couldn't look away from her. His heart sped in his chest and his breathing deepened. She was lovely. Silken robes hugged close to her small frame. Her long, dark hair was plaited and pulled up on both sides of her head.

"That's what I'm talking about," Viktor added, his voice soft.

"Yeah, no wonder you two like her," Lochlann teased, eyeing Viktor and Lucien. "She even makes you look muscular."

"We don't have time for concubines right now," Jarek said. Even as the words left his mouth, he found himself still staring at her. His gut tightened with desire. How could it not? She was gorgeous. Her downcast gaze lifted slightly and Jarek let his eyes shift with the power of the cat as he narrowed in on her. Like her people, her eyes were brown, a soulful color that begged for a man's protection, and shaped in such an exotically alluring way that he couldn't take his eyes off her. She was so delicate, like a flower. The woman even looked like a flower, dressed in flimsy silk. Small, circular patterns were spread over the robe she wore, intertwined with floral designs. It was a simple motif, yet captivatingly beautiful. Truth be told, Jarek found the whole planet beautiful. The landscape outside the palace was lush and green, and inside the city was clean and designed to enhance the beauty around it. Beneath the palace, the streets of the city were clean, and the people were immaculately dressed.

A tightness developed between his thighs, as Jarek became aroused just looking at the slender woman. Too bad she was obviously this other man's whore.

Maybe you could liberate her, his libido seemed to tell him.

And do what? His inner reason argued. *It's not as if you want a woman on the ship with you. You're not like your brothers. You're not meant to settle down.*

It was true. Jarek had felt it since he was a young prince. Even then he would stare up at the stars, feeling their pull. He wasn't meant to be contained on one planet. He needed more than that. He needed adventure, change, a sense of danger. Women liked things such as stability and a home. Sure, he'd met a few who didn't, but they were no one with whom he'd like to spend his long years. And, usually, in the end, even those women settled in one place.

Jarek had four brothers, and they'd all found mates. Three had just had babies, and his twin brother's wife was expecting. It wasn't as if he *needed* to find a wife and have children. The family line didn't depend upon him. He was free to do as he willed.

"She's so tiny," Dev said, his voice not holding as much masculine appreciation as the others. "And delicate. She wouldn't last five seconds in the VR fighting a Huthin."

"I don't want her as a sparring partner in virtual reality, space cadet," said Viktor. Dev's black eyes narrowed in warning. Viktor quickly patted Dev's large shoulder in reassurance. "And by space cadet, I mean my very big, mean, tough warrior friend who would never think of crushing someone smaller than himself, like me."

Dev grunted. Jarek bit back a laugh but didn't look away from the beautiful woman for more than an instant. She was close. The Lintianese man's body blocked her partially from view and he leaned to the side to better see her. Soft laughter broke into his daydreaming about the woman. A hand on his arm pulled him back down.

"Uh, Jarek, you still with us, captain?" Lucien asked. "Or is your plan to get seen and captured? 'Cause if it is, please count us out."

Jarek motioned the men back, and they instantly crawled along the stone to stay hidden as the woman and her escort passed nearby, going down the overly long row of steps. Jarek watched from within an inlet in the wall as she moved away from them.

"I have an idea." Jarek grinned, still staring at the woman's backside. "I know just how one of you is going to get into that palace."

"How?" Viktor asked, leaning over to take his own peek at her.

Jarek's grin widened as he looked at Viktor and his brother. "Or should I say, the two of you."

For a complete, up-to-date booklist, visit
MichellePillow.com

COMPLIMENTARY EXCERPTS

LOVE POTIONS

BY MICHELLE M. PILLOW

Warlocks MacGregor Book 1

Contemporary Paranormal Scottish Warlocks

A little magickal mischief never hurt anyone...

Erik MacGregor, from a clan of ancient Scottish warlocks, isn't looking for love. After centuries, it's not even a consideration...until he moves in next door to Lydia Barratt. It's clear that the shy beauty wants nothing to do with him, but he's drawn to her nonetheless and determined to win her over.

Lydia Barratt just wants to be left alone to grow flowers and make lotions in her old Victorian house. The last thing she needs is a demanding Scottish man meddling in her private life. Just because he's gorgeous and totally rocks a kilt doesn't mean she's going to fall for his seductive manner.

But Erik won't give up and just as Lydia let's her guard down, his sister decides to get involved. Her little love potion prank goes terribly wrong, making Lydia the target of his sudden embarrassingly obsessive behavior. They'll have to find a way to pull Erik out of the spell fast when it becomes clear that Lydia has more than a lovesick warlock to worry about. Evil lurks within the shadows and it plans to use Lydia, alive or dead, to take out Erik and his clan for good.

Love Potions Excerpt

"Ly-di-ah! I sit beneath your window, laaaass, singing 'cause I loooove your a——"

"For the love of St. Francis of Assisi, someone call a vet. There is an injured animal screaming in pain outside," Charlotte interrupted the flow of music in ill-humor.

Lydia lifted her forehead from the kitchen table. Her windows and doors were all locked, and yet Erik's endlessly verbose singing penetrated the barrier of glass and wood with ease.

Charlotte held her head and blinked heavily.

Her red-rimmed eyes were filled with the all too poignant look of a hangover. She took a seat at the table and laid her head down. Her moan sounded something like, "I'm never moving again."

"You need fluids," Lydia prescribed, getting up to pour unsweetened herbal tea from the pitcher in the fridge. She'd mixed it especially for her friend. It was Gramma Annabelle's hangover recipe of willow bark, peppermint, carrot, and ginger. The old lady always had a fresh supply of it in the house while she was alive. Apparently, being a natural witch also meant in partaking in natural liquors. Annabelle had kept a steady supply of moonshine stashed in the basement. If the concert didn't stop soon she might try to find an old bottle.

"Ly-di-ah!"

"Omigod. Kill me," Charlotte moaned. "No. Kill him. Then kill me."

"Ly-di-ah!"

Erik had been singing for over an hour. At first, he'd tried to come inside. She'd not invited him and the barrier spell sent him sprawling back into the yard. He didn't seem to mind as he found a seat on some landscaping timbers and began his serenade. The last time she'd asked him to be quiet, he'd gotten louder and overly enthusiastic. In fact, she'd been too scared to pull back the curtains for a clearer look, but she was pretty sure he'd been dancing on her lawn, shaking his kilt.

"Omigod," Charlotte muttered, pushing up and angrily going to a window. Then grimacing, she said, "Is he wearing a tux jacket with his kilt?"

"Don't let him see you," Lydia cried out in a panic. It was too late. The song began with renewed force.

"He's…" Charlotte frowned. "I think it's dancing."

Since the damage was done, Lydia joined Charlotte at the window. Erik grinned. He lifted his arms to the side and kicked his legs, bouncing around the yard like a kid on too much sugar. "Maybe it's a traditional Scottish dance?"

Both women tilted their heads in unison as his kilt kicked up to show his perfectly formed ass.

"He's not wearing…" Charlotte began.

"I know. He doesn't," Lydia answered. Damn, the man had a fine body. Too bad Malina's trick had turned him insane.

To find out more about Michelle's books visit www.MichellePillow.com

PLEASE LEAVE A REVIEW

THANK YOU FOR READING!

Please take a moment to share your thoughts by reviewing this book.

Be sure to check out Michelle's other titles at www.MichellePillow.com